The *Iroshi*
Ca

"The action is nonstop and deadly, the details compelling, the story surefooted and satisfying."
—Rutledge Etheridge, author of
Agent of Destruction

"A blend of science fiction and martial arts with a strong element of fantasy . . . Entertaining."
—*Science Fiction Chronicle*

Iroshi
Laicy Campbell came to earth to learn the way of the sword, and became a ronin. But it is on the planet Rune that she discovers at last the task she was meant for.

The Glaive
The Iroshi returns—and when her mentor and friend is killed, she vows to seek the truth about his death. But the truth runs deep . . .

Persea
Martin Dukane's obsession with the Iroshi knows no bounds. And rather than see her powers wane with age, he will make her legend immortal. Even if he has to kill her to do it . . .

Ace Books by Cary Osborne

IROSHI
THE GLAIVE
PERSEA
DEATHWEAVE

DEATHWEAVE

CARY OSBORNE

ACE BOOKS, NEW YORK

If you purchased this book without a cover, you should be aware that this book is stolen property. It was reported as "unsold and destroyed" to the publisher, and neither the author nor the publisher has received any payment for this "stripped book."

This book is an Ace original edition,
and has never been previously published.

DEATHWEAVE

An Ace Book / published by arrangement with
the author

PRINTING HISTORY
Ace edition / January 1998

All rights reserved.
Copyright © 1998 by Cary Osborne.
Cover art by Royo.
This book may not be reproduced in whole or in part,
by mimeograph or any other means, without permission.
For information address: The Berkley Publishing Group,
a member of Penguin Putnam Inc.,
200 Madison Avenue, New York, NY 10016.

The Putnam Berkley World Wide Web site address is
http://www.berkley.com

Make sure to check out *PB Plug*,
the science fiction/fantasy newsletter, at
http://www.pbplug.com

ISBN: 0-441-00498-9

ACE®
Ace Books are published by The Berkley Publishing Group,
a member of Penguin Putnam Inc.,
200 Madison Avenue, New York, NY 10016.
ACE and the "A" design are trademarks
belonging to Charter Communications, Inc.

PRINTED IN THE UNITED STATES OF AMERICA

10 9 8 7 6 5 4 3 2 1

Acknowledgments

Many people have provided me with untold help in bringing this and previous novels into existence. I offer my thanks to the following:

Robert L. Hawkins, III, has critiqued this and other work, offering great suggestions and support. Thanks, Bob.

The Dorsal Fin Society: Cathy Ball, James Brazell, Ben Fenwick, Paul Marek, Marjorie Montague, Kim Pugh, and Ray Roberts. Thanks for your input and support.

Erin Girdler and Elizabeth Massie, for getting me started in the first place.

PROLOGUE

Arden Grenfell watched as her future went down ramp 5-B. Princess Jessa turned and waved goodbye before disappearing into the darkness at the end. The erstwhile bodyguard waited a moment in hopes that her heartbeat would slow. No such luck. Arden turned away, resolved not to stick around for the ship to take off. She maneuvered through the crowd, most of whom made way for her when they saw the sword slung across her back or the badge on the left breast of her tunic.

In the main terminal, she stopped again. One wall was covered with vidscreens listing departures, arrivals, and delays for starships traveling to a hundred other worlds or more; and for shuttles moving around her own world on imperial and civilian business. Jessa had urged her to take one of those ships, if not with her, then one going somewhere that the emperor's people could not find her, but Arden could not run away. She was a captain in the emperor's service—she fingered the embroidery of the badge—and that oath required her to take the punishment she no doubt deserved.

That was one thing being reared in a monastery had taught her: If you do something illegal or immoral, you had better be prepared to suffer the consequences.

Arden moved toward the exit and her car waiting at the curb under the no parking sign. A port officer saluted her then ducked under the roof extension. It had begun raining, tingeing the air with the wet-earth smell that she loved. Plenty of rain had fallen during spring and the flowers would be magnificent. Glory would live up to its name this year.

A ship lifted behind the terminal, the engines' roar momentarily drowning all other sound. The shining metal form rose above the building, and Arden stood beside her car and watched. She saluted, although she knew that it might not be Jessa's ship. Whether in that ship or another, the nineteen-year-old princess was headed for her own destiny. Alone for the first time in her life—surviving would take every bit of courage the girl had. However, the new life should be better than the one of benign neglect that was the best she could expect if she had stayed.

Carefully, Arden guided the car through traffic toward the palace. It would take half an hour to get there. She would wait another two hours for Jessa to make the transfer on Minerva, then find Don Vey. Tell him that Jessa had left Glory and of her own role in the escape. By nightfall she could very well be awaiting trial in one of the cells in the palace basement. Before that happened, she must hide the sword. If she ever got free, she would need it.

1

The cell door banged open. Arden jumped up from the bunk, hands balled into fists at her sides. Visitors always meant trouble. Two guards approached while a third stopped just inside. He watched while her hands were bound behind her.

"What this time, Prentiss?" she asked.

"You've been summoned," the sergeant answered.

"By whom?"

"You'll know when you get there."

They grabbed her arms and pushed her through the door. Prentiss drove the windowless van, the trip made quickly and silently. They disembarked in an underground garage she recognized as the one under the palace. The three men escorted her to a freight elevator and from there to a conference room on the third floor. Prentiss disappeared through a doorway at the far end of the room while Arden was pushed into a chair at the near end of the table. The two guards flanked the main door while they waited.

Utter silence descended, broken only by the rustling of her attempts to get comfortable. There was no way to sit comfortably with her arms bound behind her.

Suddenly, the inner door opened and Prentiss returned. He stood to one side, leaving the door open. A moment later, Don Vey entered. Prentiss snapped to attention, as did the two guards behind her. Out of well-ingrained habit, Arden jumped to her feet, trying her best to snap to.

Vey stopped at the other end of the table and looked at her a long moment. The prime minister signaled Prentiss, who pulled the chair out for him. Vey sat down, crossed his legs, and placed his hands flat on the tabletop.

"Sit down, Captain," he said, at last.

She did as he said, wondering why she had been brought to the palace to see Don Vey of all people. Her crime had been one of treason, not only because it had been committed against the imperial house, but also because her world was at war. All of the most highly placed people had attended the trial, even the prime minister. The only important people who had not attended were the emperor and his family. After being found guilty, she was locked up in prison to await execution.

For reasons unknown to her, that sentence had not been carried out for six years. The man sitting opposite her must have had something to do with the delay, about which she felt neither gratitude nor animosity toward him. However, she still disliked him as much as she ever had.

"We have a problem," he began. "The consequences of the princess's disappearance have become graver. It is imperative that we find her."

"As I said at the trial and after, I don't know where Jessa went," Arden said.

"Her mother is dying."

"Lyona?"

Vey nodded. "Her . . . addiction is the cause, of course. The emperor wants his daughter to come home before the seeress dies."

Arden said nothing, waiting for Vey to explain exactly why she was here. After all the persuasion they had used, before and after her trial, he knew that she did not know where Jessa had gone. She could not have resisted most of their methods, so she had made sure the princess never told her. If they had not found her after six years of searching, she knew Jessa must have chosen well.

"He believes it will help them both," Vey continued. "Jessa's place is beside her mother right now."

Arden shifted slightly to relieve the pressure on her wrists. Vey's right eyebrow rose.

"Take off the restraints," he told Prentiss.

"But, sir . . ."

"Just do it," he ordered impatiently.

The sergeant waved to one of the guards, who unlocked the bonds with a magnetic key. Arden massaged one wrist, then the other, and the feeling started returning. She sat back more comfortably in the chair.

"All right," she said. "I'll ask. What do you want me to do?"

Vey smiled slightly. "We want you to find Jessa and bring her back here. The sooner the better. Her mother won't last much longer. She's become blind, you know."

Arden winced. That was something she had not known. Was that another effect of so much lifeweave?

"Is she still weaving?" she asked.

"Oh, yes. The emperor could not get along without her foreseeing. Particularly in conducting the war. Her help is invaluable."

"And you hope her daughter can take her place at the loom."

"That is her place."

"That's the reason she left Glory. She has no taste for being chained to the loom."

"She has her duty to Glory and to her emperor, just as you do." He leaned forward and rested his forearms on the tabletop. "We know that your code allowed you to assist her in leaving Glory only because you had not been specifically ordered to keep her here. Your orders were to protect the princess with your life. In the two years you served as her bodyguard, you proved you were willing to risk yourself for her sake." Arden's fingertips touched the scar on her forearm through the sleeve. "However, by letting her leave, you did betray that trust. Once she was gone, you could no longer protect her."

That had been the one thing that had bothered Arden in all the agonizing hours she had spent deciding if she could do what Jessa requested. The princess had tried everything, including releasing her from her pledge, which technically had not been within her rights. Arden's orders had come from the prime minister through the commander of the imperial guard. However, part of the original orders had been that she was in service to the princess from that moment. A veritable tangle.

"The charges against you will be dropped if you find Jessa and bring her back," Vey continued. "Further, you will be taken back into the service."

"You would trust me to remain loyal? After everything that has happened?"

"You were never disloyal. You simply forgot to whom you owed your first loyalty."

That was an oversimplification at best, and an argument that was never used at her trial.

"If I don't agree to find her?"

"You will be returned to your cell and your execution will be scheduled for later this week. This should not be a difficult decision to make."

Not difficult? He was asking her to decide between life and death, but not only for herself. Being given a chance to redeem herself was the important part. She was pledged, after all, and that meant a great deal to a warrior of Glory.

"I'll find her for you. There are some things I'll need."

"Of course. Anything that will speed you on your way."

The road was as bumpy as she remembered, but the air coming in through the open windows was fresher. Flowers were in full bloom in every uncultivated field, and their fragrance was dizzying, especially for someone who had not been outside in six years.

She had concentrated on her surroundings during the drive, avoiding the larger question of Jessa and the arguments for and against bringing her back to Glory. What was there to consider, after all? She had been given an order and it was her duty to obey it.

She knew she was being followed, but it did not matter. Freedom was a heady thing, and they could do anything they wanted. Her orders were explicit and she would obey them explicitly, no matter how much Jessa might try to convince her otherwise. If she found her.

Meanwhile, there was work to do and plans to make. She had asked Don Vey for a month to prepare and he had agreed to two weeks. Not much time to undo the effects of such a long confinement, but it would have to do. The time she would probably spend traveling could be utilized for more training and practice.

Another condition had been that she be allowed to see Lyona, giving as a reason that Jessa might not believe her mother was dying if Arden had not seen for herself. It had been a disturbing sight.

Appolyona, the seeress, had been concubine to the emperor and was mother of Jessa, his first child. A daughter, though, would always be second in line to the closest male heir. In this case, Emperor Granid Parcq had a son by one of his wives. Prince Waran Parcq, heir apparent, had rarely been seen on Glory since his childhood.

Lyona, as she was called, was rumored to have been the most beautiful woman on Glory in her youth. The young prince was said to have lusted after her, but she was of low birth, and marrying her had not been possible. Although the royal family tried, he could not be convinced to give her up, and they had let him take her into the palace as his concubine.

There was little left of the beauty that had once driven Granid Parcq to defy his family. The woman in the darkened room, operating the immense loom and murmuring to herself, was difficult to look upon. Her once black hair had turned to silver grey, and still reached to her waist. The servants must make sure that she was clean and her hair was brushed, for she was clearly oblivious to these things.

"She is truly blind?" Arden had asked Prentiss in a whisper. He nodded, touching a finger to his lips for quiet.

Lyona stopped working.

"Who is here?" she cried. "Someone is here. Make them go away. Chase. Chase, where are you?"

A burly guard stepped up to the seeress from behind, put a hand on one of her thin shoulders, and bent to whisper in her ear.

"No! I don't want anyone in here. Make them go away."

The guard whom she had called Chase came around to confront Arden and Prentiss. His badge was not for the imperial house, and she guessed he must be pledged to Lyona's family.

"You must leave," he said. "Your presence is disturbing the seeress. Especially yours." He glared at Arden. "If it weren't for you, her daughter would be here to give her solace."

Arden did not remember him. Perhaps he had been at her trial, or maybe he knew what had happened just from the stories that had been circulated. Now he glared at her with hate in his eyes.

She nodded to Chase and turned with Prentiss to leave. Just before slipping through the doorway she turned back. Chase had returned to Lyona. Standing behind her, he brushed her long hair and made soothing noises. The gentleness of his hands belied their size.

He looked up just before she turned away. The look in his eyes held promise for the future, and she had felt chilled. Prentiss told her his full name was Colin Chase, when she asked.

She shuddered in remembrance now as the car bounced along in summer warmth. She would meet him again one day, and that meeting would not be to her liking.

At last, the road entered Lower Forest and those following her stopped, knowing her destiny was what it should be. Several miles into the forest lay the monastery that was her destination and the end of the road. Abbot Grayson was going to be very surprised to see her, and she now regretted not taking the time to call ahead. She had just been too eager to get there.

However, she had taken time for one other task before leaving the palace. She reached over and stroked the hilt of her sword. Originally a gift from the abbot, the katana meant more to her than anything else she possessed. It was an old sword, said to have been fashioned on Earth, what to her was the nearly legendary home of mankind. The abbot claimed to have been there once, but she was not sure that particular story could be believed.

Before turning herself in all those years earlier, she had hidden the sword, hoping one day to retrieve it. If not that, at least she could keep it from falling into someone else's hands. Finding it still in the niche behind the altar in the imperial chapel had not surprised her. The ancient altar was one of the holiest of relics—even the priests did not touch it casually, and it would seem that none of them had ever discovered the niche, hidden behind a spring door.

Curiosity, and a lack of awe for religious artifacts, had driven her to investigate the altar soon after she entered the imperial guard. Just another advantage of growing up in a monastery.

She rounded a sharp turn in the road and slammed on the brakes. A tree had fallen across the road, blocking its full width. She backed up a little, giving herself room for a quick retreat if it became necessary. Then she sat and watched, using the rear view and side view screens and the scene in front.

The only movement in any direction was that created among the trees by a soft breeze. Branches waved, leaves shivered, and low-growing bushes swayed slightly. Nothing overtly threatening, but an uneasiness held her.

When nothing happened after a long moment, she drew

the sword from its blue-lacquered scabbard, opened the door, and stepped out. The breeze ruffling her long, dark brown hair smelled of damp earth. She took a deep breath, wishing she could revel in the scent, but now was not the time. It took only a quick look to see that the tree had been deliberately cut down, and to spot footprints in the soft ground around it.

She took another quick look around. Someone must be watching if they went to the trouble to cut down a tree and stop her at this spot. Finding nothing, she turned to study the forest floor on either side of the road. There was not enough room on either side to get the car around, but if she went slowly, she might be able to drive through and over the branches on the top of the tree. They were small and supple so they should not hurt the undercarriage.

A soft noise spun her around. A warrior dressed in blue civilian clothes walked around the car. Another in brown approached from her left, emerging from the woods. Both carried swords, held ready for action. They wore no visible badges, but if they were pledged warriors, each had to have one somewhere. They could be mercenaries, unpledged, hired to kill her before Jessa could be found. However, speculation about who would go this far would have to wait.

At the moment, the important thing about them was that they were clearly after her.

Arden raised her own sword, moving into the road where she would have room to maneuver. The sword felt good in her hands, as if it was only yesterday when she had last used it. That was a false impression. For six years she had exercised without the sword. When the blue-clad man attacked, she realized with the first stroke that her timing was off and she was much slower.

He was large and strong but his movements were cumbersome. Arden could not hope to match his strength, but her grace should make up for what she lacked in size. They traded blows, testing each other's weaknesses while the second man drew nearer.

The second man, smaller and quicker, rushed in just as she stepped back from the first. With her sword raised just in time, their blades met. She spun under the locked blades and swung her own to catch the first attacker across his right side. He stumbled backward toward her car, leaned on it, clearly out of the fight for the moment.

The second man's sword cut her left arm and she cried out. She had gotten too sure of herself, lost her focus. He pressed the attack and she was barely able to defend herself.

Blood ran down the wounded arm. That and the pain were distracting. Her right arm absorbed most of the shock of the blows. It began aching, weakening. The man smiled.

Damned if he was going to win!

She continued backing up, trying to cast an occasional glance behind her. As he started to step forward to deliver another stunning blow, she saw her moment. With his sword upraised and only one foot solidly on the ground, he was off balance. She dropped to one knee. Her own blade was waist-high to him. She swung with all her remaining strength. The tip of the sword sliced across his abdomen.

His eyes widened and he gasped. He tried to bring the sword forward but could not, dropping it behind him instead. He stood another moment with arms raised over his head; then, very slowly, they dropped. His hands pressed against the gaping wound. Blood poured out, and Arden thought she could see entrails trying to poke through.

Quickly, she sought the second attacker. Still holding his side, blood oozing between his fingers, he pushed away from her car.

"Don't," Arden said. "Your friend is badly wounded and you're losing a lot of blood. If you hurry, you may save both your lives."

His companion dropped to his knees, then fell backward. The burly man looked from him to Arden. He hefted the sword in his left hand, then nodded.

"Can you make it to your vehicle?" she asked.

"I think so."

"Good. To whom are you pledged?"

He grinned and shook his head. "Maybe no one. Maybe someone."

"Do I have to search your friend for a badge?"

"You won't find one."

That should mean that they were mercenaries, but she did not feel so sure in this case.

"Tell the person who sent you that I am now forewarned. He would be wise not to try again."

"We'll see."

She dismissed him with a wave of her sword. "Get to your vehicle before your friend dies."

He nodded again and started back into the woods, using his sword as a cane. Arden knelt beside the other man and pulled his sleeve well above his wrist to reveal a lilac tattoo, symbol of the Assassins' League. She grabbed the hem of his jacket and wiped the still wet blood off her sword. It was part of the tradition of warriors of Glory to do so as a final symbol of victory in a fight. Some of the blood had already dried; she would have to clean the blade thoroughly once she reached the monastery.

She returned to her car, climbed in, and placed the sword beside the scabbard on the passenger's seat. The wound in her arm still bled, and pain rippled through her body. The engine started right up and she guided the vehicle slowly around the top of the tree. Branches scratched and scraped against the side and underneath. Several broke under its wheels. In a few moments, she was back on the road and moving away. Just before the scene of the fight disappeared from the rear screen, another vehicle appeared and her erstwhile adversary climbed out. He stood watching her drive away until they disappeared from each other's view.

Those two she would not have to worry about again for some time. She had not only beaten them in a fight, she had given back their lives. They now owed her, although she doubted that the one man would survive long enough for her to collect.

Less than an hour later, the monastery loomed over the surrounding trees in a small valley. The slightly red stones from which it was built could both blend in with the surroundings or stand out, depending on whether or not the sun shone on the visible section. Today, the sun was full on the upper walls, even though the trees had grown.

2

She drove up to the main gate, parking slightly to one side. Except for a multitude of birds chattering in the trees, silence surrounded her as she stepped out. Holding the sword and scabbard separately, she found the bell rope beside the gate and pulled. The bell rang loudly, a sound so familiar that it almost took her breath away. She had missed that sound, among so many other familiar things.

A feeling of homecoming overwhelmed her. Within these walls she had always been safe. And now, she was thirsty and her arm ached and it would be good to bathe away the dirt, blood, and sweat from the fight.

With a metallic grinding noise, the gate opened slightly. A monk appeared. She did not recognize him.

"Who is it?" he asked.

"Arden Grenfell to see Abbot Grayson," she said.

"Is he expecting you?"

"You'll have to ask him that. He always knows before anyone else does."

"He's very busy at the moment..."

She shoved her shoulder against the gate, pushing it open more and unbalancing the monk slightly. She winced at the pain it caused in her arm.

"Believe me, he will see me. I also need to see your physician."

His eyes went to her sleeve caked with blood, and he nodded. Stepping back even farther, he invited her inside. He led her across the courtyard, in through the main door, and into the reception room. Stopping just inside the doorway, he motioned her toward an overstuffed chair.

"I will tell the abbot that you are here and find the physician."

Without another word, he slipped from the room, closing the door behind him. Careful not to get any blood on its arm, Arden sat in the chair, laying the sword and scabbard on the floor beside her. The room was cool and she shivered. More a reaction to the wound than the temperature. She thought about rolling up her sleeve or cutting it off for the physician, but it felt too good to just relax in a place where she had spent so many hours in the past.

The floor was laid with a grey stone, contrasting with the reddish stone of the walls. A heavy iron chandelier hung from the center of the ceiling. An immense grey stone fireplace bisected the far wall, and large and small chairs, sofas, and tables were scattered about, seemingly haphazardly.

This room, like most in the monastery, was very masculine. As far as she knew, she had been the only woman trained within its confines, although some members of the household staff had been women at various times. Good training that, for in the emperor's service, she had not only been the only woman pledged for a number of years, she had also been one of the few lotus-trained. Most of the men had attended one of the many military schools and felt they had double reason to look down on her and her religious training. Although never quite accepted by her peers, she had nevertheless earned their respect with her abilities as a warrior.

Until the princess vanished.

Everyone had abandoned her then. Except Abbot Grayson, but there was little help he could offer beyond moral support. Speaking of whom—she looked at her watch. Ten minutes, and still no sign of either the abbot or the physician.

Maybe he did not want to see her. After all, he had never visited her while she was imprisoned, but she had thought that due to her jailers allowing no visitors at all. It had never occurred to her that Grayson might turn his back on her.

Someone cleared his throat behind her and she leapt to her feet. A monk stood just inside the door, which had opened as silently as it had closed. Damn! She knew better than to sit with her back to a door.

"Sorry if I startled you," he said. "I wasn't sure if you were asleep or just resting."

"That's all right," she said. "You must be the physician."

"Yes, Brother Marion. I would have been here sooner, but there was an accident with a piece of equipment out in the barn. One of our number cut his leg."

She wondered what had happened to Brother Carter, the old physician. Well, he had been old and probably died while she was locked away. Brother Marion moved to stand beside her. "Now, let me have a look at this arm."

She moved to a sofa that backed up against a wall. Brother Marion sat beside her, took scissors from the bag he had carried in, and cut away the entire sleeve.

"Hmm," he said as he searched in his bag. "Looks worse than it is. But I imagine you know that."

He pulled out a bottle and swabs and proceeded to clean the wound. Finished with that, he sealed the edges of skin together with an application of nuskin and a moment of heat from a low-power lasergun. At that moment, the door opened again and a very large man entered the room.

"You should come by the dispensary later so that I can dose it with ultrasonic antibiotic to prevent infection," the physician said. She rubbed the wound gently and nodded.

He walked past the newcomer, who patted his shoulder as he exited. Abbot Grayson stood looking at Arden, who still sat on the sofa. He was six feet five and weighed nearly three hundred pounds. His hair, once red, was now grey, although still thick. The charcoal grey monk's robe that he habitually wore made him seem even larger and greyer. And he always appeared formidable.

Arden stood. "It's really me," she said. What did he want her to say? Why did he stand there, looking like thunder?

"Your hair is so long," he said in a voice only slightly smaller than his physical size. "I thought I would never see you again, alive or dead. My dear child, it is good to see you."

It was then that she noticed a tear glistening in his left eye. It shuddered a moment before spilling down his cheek. Her own eyes misted over and she ran to him, just as she had when she had needed comfort as a child.

"So you're not entirely free, then."

"No, not now, maybe not ever."

They were comfortably seated in the abbot's private study. As they moved from the reception room to the suite, Grayson had explained that he was at the far end of one of the fields when word came that she was there. He had not even gotten word that she had been released from prison.

"Events must have accelerated in the palace," he had said. "Otherwise, I would have known that your release was contemplated."

"I know," Arden said. "I'm very surprised you weren't expecting me."

They had laughed and both had relaxed at that moment, the tension gone in a flash. The unexpectedness of events in the past twenty-four hours had brought that tension, and their joy at seeing one another dispelled it.

Now they sat in overstuffed chairs, drinking one of the best and sweetest wines produced by the monastery. The crystal goblets were old and expensive. The warmth of the wine added to the warmth that still settled within her from the hug they had shared in the reception room.

"You've no idea who sent the two men who attacked you?" he asked.

"None. It's useless to guess; there are several factions that would probably want to see me dead right now."

"Not least of all the princess, if she believes you could track her down."

"She did not tell me where she was going."

"You have other ways of knowing. Does she know that?"

"No. I never showed her or told her."

Grayson thought a moment. "Are you going to track her down?"

"I don't have any choice. I'm pledged to the emperor and his house, and I've been given my orders."

"You can't, Arden. It's too dangerous for you." He leaned forward to emphasize his words. "The stuff is addictive and the more you use it, the greater your chances are of becoming addicted. Not to mention that someone obviously would prefer that you were dead."

"I haven't used lifeweave in six years, Abbot," she said, ignoring the other problem for the moment.

"Then, maybe you can't use it anymore. Maybe it won't work for you after such a long time."

"It will. It always has."

He sat back in the chair and looked into the depths of the dark red wine. His brow furrowed, wrinkles around his eyes and mouth seeming deeper than the last time she had seen him.

"So," he said, and sighed deeply. "You will stay here the next two weeks and get yourself back into shape."

"Yes. I exercised as much as I could in that cell—I didn't have much else to do—but I'm in pretty bad shape. I could tell that earlier today, in particular."

"We had better set up a schedule for you, then." Abbot

Grayson heaved himself out of the chair and set his goblet down on the table between them. "Right now, though, it's time for dinner. You remember the way to the dining hall, I expect." She nodded. "Good. Your old room has been prepared for you. Go wash up and I'll see you there."

She set her own goblet beside his and stood. She walked over to him and wrapped her arms as far around him as she could. For a moment he remained stiff; then he relaxed and returned her hug.

"It will be all right," she said, and smiled up at him.

"That's what you said once before," he replied, but smiled in return. "Now go. I'm hungry."

He turned her toward the door and gave her a gentle shove. In her old suite, she found clothes that Grayson must have gotten from her apartment in the city and saved somewhere all these years. Her sword was laid across the dresser top, already cleaned but lying beside the scabbard as if for inspection.

She touched the cord-wrapped hilt with her fingertips, tracing the white diamond shapes. She traced the other decorations with her eyes, impressing them once more on her memory. The scabbard was decorated with two narrow metal bands near each end, bearing the same dragon design as on the blade of the katana. Definitely not Glorian, definitely old. Grayson had told her it came from her father's family when he gave it to her, but she suspected it was the abbot's.

He did cling to old ways. The vineyards, the methods of wine making. All of the food eaten in the monastery. Everything was produced by ancient methods without any synthetic products. She had developed an appreciation for all of it. After all, she had lived at the monastery from the time she was nine.

Arden started undressing to stop that train of thought. No need in dwelling on her father's death or his strange friendship with the abbot.

Later that night, after dinner, with the monastery even quieter, she did remember with the old mixture of sadness, happiness, and gratitude. What it was like for a young girl to lose her father, the only parent she had ever known. Then, to find security and love from a second father.

Alongside those memories came that of lifeweave and the abbot's words: "The stuff is addictive and the more you use it, the greater your chances are of becoming addicted."

Arden made her way to the dojo. Younger monks looked at her curiously. Older ones waved and shouted greetings. She ran her fingers through her now short hair several times. The monastery's barber had been only too happy to cut off most of her glossy tresses. It felt good to get rid of that thick mane, get down to the lean and mean warrior. In more ways than one.

Because of the slender diet served her in prison, she had grown thinner and her own clothes did not quite fit. However, she had lost not only weight, but muscle too, from not practicing. She could work as hard as she wanted to, but two weeks would not restore all that she had lost.

It would be a beginning, though. The rest she would have to do on the trip to whatever world Jessa was hiding on.

At the entrance to the dojo, she paused to take off her grey slippers, leaving them beside the door with four other pair. Inside the fifteen-by-thirty-foot hall, the martial arts instructor sat on the floor on the far right side. With a surge of relief, she recognized Brother Bryan. Arden bowed to show respect to the house, moved to the left side and bowed to the instructor. He bowed in return.

She sat on the floor with her legs folded under her. A shinai and practice gauntlets had been laid there for her. She and Bryan put on gauntlets, bowed, picked up their shinai, and stood. They moved toward each other, approaching the center of the practice hall. They bowed again, touched the tips of their bamboo blades, and everything was still.

With a sudden cry, Bryan attacked. He was better than the two assassins from the day before. Much better. Arden was pushed backward, turned in circles, and forced to desperate means to defend herself. He never allowed her to mount an offense, turning every swing of her shinai against her. In moments, she was panting. Sweat drenched her blue tunic, running down into the waistband of her pants. It got into her eyes and she regretted not wearing a sweat band. The sueded hilt of the shinai turned cool with moisture.

With cry after cry, Bryan pressed and she knew that he was only testing. He could put her down at any moment, but he prolonged the combat, cataloguing her every weakness and mistake. When her arms felt like they could not lift the shinai one more time, he attacked with greater fury. She backed up rapidly, trying desperately to keep her own weapon between them and not stumble over her own feet at the same time.

At last, her back was flat against the wall; she had nowhere to go. No room to maneuver. All she could do was hold the shinai like a shield. Bryan pounded against it, and her arms ached with every blow. She wanted desperately to drop them by her sides but knew full well that he would not hesitate to clip the top of her head, her shoulder, wherever he felt would give her the fullest lesson.

He swung his blade against hers and, instead of swinging again, he pressed against her.

"Enough," he said, and backed away.

Slowly, she slid down the wall to sit on the floor. Even now, she knew better than to drop the shinai from her hands. Once she was seated, she laid the weapon beside her in the proper position. Bryan sat five feet in front of her, his eyes closed as his breathing slowed.

"We have a lot to do, Arden," he said. "Your reflexes are bad. You have no stamina. There's no power behind your swing." He shook his head. "Two weeks..."

"It is all I have," she said.

"Then it will have to be enough. Would you like some tea?"

"Yes, please."

They took off their gauntlets, lay them beside the shinai, stood, and bowed. He led the way to another room. Its spare furnishings included a table, six chairs, and a sideboard where the tea would be made. A young monk appeared with a kettle of hot water and began the preparation. Arden and Bryan sat at the table, silent for several minutes.

"Actually, you're a little stronger than I expected," he said. "Six years is a long time to go without practice."

"Yes, it is. I exercised almost constantly, though. That was about all they would allow me to do. That and meditate."

The young monk set two cups on the table. "Thank you, Michael," Bryan said. Michael left silently.

Alone, they discussed the practice and exercise regimen she was to follow while at the monastery: Practice first thing in the morning, followed by exercise, then meditation. After lunch, the same routine, ending with a full body massage to keep her muscles from cramping and relax her for sleep. Diet was not an issue—everyone ate the same healthful food at each meal.

"Do you have any idea yet where you'll be going?" he asked.

"Not yet. I'll wait until near the end of my stay to seek that information."

Bryan shook his head. As a teacher of martial arts and a follower of ancient philosophies, he disapproved strongly of using anything to enhance mental abilities. As did everyone in the monastery, for that matter. But he was more against it than most.

"Even Grayson has no other way to discover her whereabouts, Bryan. I have no choice."

"But lifeweave. I suppose you've heard about Lyona."

"Yes, that's the reason Vey is sending me to find Jessa."

"Using that stuff could be the reason you've never experienced the red haze," he pointed out.

She flinched. Although an excellent warrior, tested in both practice and in battle, she had never experienced the red haze that came with nearly total immersion into herself. Beyond that was the void that she feared could only be found in actual combat. Bryan had never before mentioned lifeweave as a reason for her failure.

They talked a while longer about her exercise. He mapped out exactly how she was to proceed and how long with each segment.

After a time, the tea was gone and everything had been planned. She stood.

"It's time for me to go exercise, then," she said.

They hugged at last and he sent her on her way. Arden found an isolated spot in the gardens and, after performing stretches, she began the slow movements of the exercises she had been taught as a child. It was an ancient form whose origins had been lost generations earlier. These were the same movements she had practiced in her cell every day of her imprisonment. But here, in sunlight with birds singing around her and the sweet smell of flowers in every breath, it was a celebration.

As she posed, then moved with slow deliberation, her mind went back to those days and nights in artificial light that disappeared for only a few hours during the sleep cycle. The feeling of despair that had plagued her waking hours returned, but melted away in the light of day. The ordeal was not entirely over, but at that very moment, it was only a memory.

Her mind went further back, to the days when she had lived in the monastery. Taught and pampered by the monks, but with her own work to do each day, she had loved every moment. There had been so many things to learn, things to do, yet eventually, she had wanted to leave, to find out what the rest of the world was like.

It had all proved to be very different from what she expected: some things good, some bad. The biggest surprise was to find how old-fashioned life in the monastery had been. And still was.

She came to the end of the movements and sat cross-legged in the grass to meditate. Voices roused her some time later, and she found that the sun stood straight overhead. She headed toward the dining hall, led by the voices calling to one another, talking seriously, all so familiar to one another. A sudden sadness descended over her. Everything was at once familiar and unfamiliar to her. After so many years away, that was not surprising, but the realization that this was no longer her home was disturbing. She wondered if anything could make it so again.

The days passed quickly, repetitiously, and even she could see the changes. She was becoming noticeably stronger and quicker as her work progressed, always under Grayson's watchful eye. Each night, sitting in his rooms, they discussed the improvements, often moving to discussion of things they remembered, as they sipped wine.

Three days before she was to leave, she was able to match Brother Bryan move for move, although not beat him as she had once done. He congratulated her, then sent her off to exercise and to perform the rest of her routine. He insisted, of course, that she follow the schedule through her last day.

However, the day before her departure, Arden put aside all other considerations. Abbot Grayson produced a skein of lifeweave yarn and her old hand loom on which she would weave an eight-inch-by-eight-inch square. They sat in his study in the overstuffed chairs opposite each other. He handed her the yarn and the loom.

"Are you sure?" he asked.

"Yes. There's no other way to find her."

"Very well. I'll be here the whole time."

She nodded as he picked up a glass of wine and took a drink. She carefully tied the yarn onto one side of the loom, and began threading around the pins. Her fingers moved awkwardly at first, then with greater skill, remembering the patterns. The colors danced in the sunlight from the window, changing from the warmth of her hands and her own body chemistry, yet keeping their own character. As she started the second direction, she left Grayson's world and entered another.

"Oh, it's you," a familiar voice said from out of the darkness. "What do you want this time?"

"I guess you haven't missed me," Arden said.

"Not much."

The surroundings lightened until she found herself in a glowing void. She stood, but on nothing. Light came from everywhere. And the voice seemed to be part of the light.

"Let me see you," she said.

"If you must."

A figure began to form in front of her and finally coalesced into a tall, thin man of about eighty years, who looked as irascible as he sounded. He wore full-cut trousers gathered at the ankles, sandals, and a shirt with very full sleeves. His auburn hair was pulled back in a ponytail, his grey eyes smoldered, and his long hands and fingers were held at his sides.

"Is that better?"

She nodded. Pac Terhn was her guide in this world created by the hallucinogenic properties of lifeweave. Why she had been saddled with someone who hated his role she had never been able to fathom. Working with him was a trial in itself, and she wondered for perhaps the hundredth time if this was her safety valve: the one thing that would keep the effects of lifeweave from becoming too pleasant.

"I need your help in finding the princess Jessa," she said.

"You always need my help."

"It's been a while. But, yes, I have often needed your help. Can you find her?"

"Of course I can. It's more a matter of whether I will or not."

"What will it cost me?"

Pac Terhn smoothed his neat hair back with one hand, thinking, as she stood dreading the answer. His price was always high.

"Your pledge," he said at last, "to stay by the princess's side for the remainder of her life."

"What of my pledge to the emperor?"

"There will be no conflict."

That seemed a price with hidden meanings. A little negotiation was in order.

"I will pay the price with one alteration," she said. "There must be one way in which to break the pledge."

"Only by her sending you away. How's that?"

"But..."

"That's the price. Take it or leave it."

So, negotiation was over. She knew him well enough to understand that. As events unfolded, she could study the deal and, perhaps with Grayson's help, make whatever changes were necessary or possible.

"All right," she said. "It's a deal."

Pac Terhn grinned. "Then, let's begin," he said.

He waved his hands before her and as he disappeared, her surroundings changed again.

Glowing red rivers of molten rock snaked over timeless paths while steam and acrid smoke rose into the air. Heat ate at her skin like the sun on a cloudless day on Glory. The smell of sulphur caught in her throat, and she coughed.

The artificial overlook on which she stood was like a peninsula poking its nose into the dangerous flow of lava. The land had been built up from a wide base, tapering toward the top, covered with a heat resistant layer, giving what she hoped would be enough distance from any and all red rivers. In several areas, lava spewed continuously, building peaks even as she watched, making them ever larger, giving promise of more spectacular shows someday.

She tried to ignore the smell and taste of sulphur, but she could not hold back the occasional cough. She closed her eyes, and colored lights danced on the backs of her eyelids. She let herself enjoy their unself-conscious sport.

The someone or something from this world that would guide her waited. She must let her mind seek. Only that way could she hope to find it. Turn inward before seeking outward, settle the demands of body into minimal amounts. All of this part was simple meditation that she had practiced many times; checking functions and comfort came automatically. Everything in tune, she was ready to search.

On wings of thought, she flew over the world, directed by Pac Terhn, gently probing people, things, and spirits, some long gone, some recently dead, and others living. No trace anywhere that sentient beings had ever called this world home before the invasion by man, the current residents.

Immediately, she brushed past volcano spirits, sensing them to be surprisingly gentle and contented in spite of the volatility of their physical shells. Even the rocks had spirits, heavy and withdrawn because they were so recently formed. No vegetation survived close to the lava flows. Miles went by before something as large as a bush thrust its way through the soil. Trees stood even farther away. Trees were always gentle spirits; she drew close, eager to feel their quiescence. One especially large tree attracted her. It roused as she approached.

"They await you," it said.

Startled, she came to an abrupt halt.

"Who?"

"Those who summoned you."

It settled back into spiritual slumber. "They," it had said. More than one contact. Never before had there been more than one at a time. Changes brought uneasiness, but there was no stopping now.

The way continued in the same direction. "They" now

drew her along; Pac Terhn had relinquished control. She went over rocky cliffs topped with lush vegetation. Soon, the pull grew stronger, only a little at first, then tighter as if she were gripped in a vortex, its gently circling streams wrapping around her tighter and tighter. She could almost hear the wind. Then directly ahead they appeared. Creatures, aliens, figures like nothing she had ever seen before. Their shapes wavered in and out of vision as if they were reflections or smoke from the volcanos.

When they spoke, it was with one voice, yet she knew it emanated from all of them.

"We are the one who summoned you," they said with the one voice. She counted seven shapes. "Come close and receive our message."

She hesitated, watching their mouths work but not in unison with the words. She took a grip on her fear and closed in.

One last look and clear the mind. They had information to give, directions to reveal. Energy flowed from them to her.

Slowly she opened her eyes to the real world.

Abbot Grayson sat watching her. She tried to smile at him, but she was too tired.

He handed her a glass of wine. Her hand shook as she took it.

"You moaned several times," he said with concern.

"Did I? It was a very strange world." She sighed and took a drink of the wine. Its warmth felt good going down. "I saw much of it, but nothing there would tell me its name."

"Describe it and we'll figure it out."

Details of the visions always came slowly, one leading to the next like stair steps. She told him of the active volcanos and lava flows. She described the artificial overlook but remembered that there had been no people anywhere. He smiled as she described the spirits of the volcanos and rocks, nodded at mention of the trees. He frowned at the description of the smoke creatures and admitted that he had never heard of anything like them.

When she finished, he sat thinking for several minutes. They examined the lifeweave square, but the pattern showed a picture of a man neither of them knew. His hair was dark and receding, his eyes very blue, a near smile turning up the corners of his mouth. She liked his face, but that did not help them at all.

"Well, it doesn't sound like any world I've ever heard of," Grayson said at last. "Let's see what the atlas can tell us."

He went to the floor-to-ceiling bookcases behind his desk and searched a while before finding the volume he wanted. Returning to his chair, he opened the immense book on his lap, flipped pages until he came to the index.

"Let's see," he repeated as he ran his finger down column after column. "Ah." He flipped more pages. "No, that's not it." Back to the index.

"Here!" he said on the third try. "This is it."

He turned the book around on his lap, then handed it to her. The world described on the facing pages was called Caldera. She ran through the description, nodding periodically.

"Yes, this is it," she said.

"How far?"

She checked the sector, then consulted a chart in the front of the book. "Three weeks," she told him.

"Vey isn't going to like that."

"No, he isn't. But this is one thing he can't do anything about."

"Jessa will be there when you arrive?"

"Or shortly after."

They sat in silence for several minutes, examining the depths of their wine goblets. Tomorrow would be her final day in the monastery. Arden looked forward to her departure with both trepidation and relief. Get this task completed, lift the sentence of death, the sooner the better, and go on with her life—that was all she wanted.

So far, she had been able to keep from thinking of Jessa and what coming back to Glory meant for her.

"You haven't been off-world in a long time," Grayson said. "Would you like someone to go with you?"

She laid her head back against the chair and considered his offer. He was not offering to go himself. He had not left Glory in over twenty years. There were several monks who traveled a good deal on business and at least two lay brothers who might be persuaded. However, her plan was to meet Jessa, tell her that her mother was dying, and talk her into returning. A trifle naive, perhaps—exactly what Grayson told her when she turned down his offer.

"You have no idea what you might run into on Caldera," he added. "Or anywhere else you might end up." He leaned toward her. "Jessa may not come back on her own. Have you thought of that?"

"Of course I've thought of that." She sat up straight.

"What will you do then? She may have friends who will keep you from taking her. She may be warrior-trained by now herself. Are you willing to fight to bring her back?"

"I will do whatever is necessary to accomplish this task." Arden felt uncomfortable with this topic. In spite of recognizing the possible difficulties, she had convinced herself that Jessa would want to return for her mother's sake.

"Why is your life more important than hers?" Grayson pressed.

"What do you mean?"

"You will do anything to get Jessa back here, even bring her against her will, to free yourself from the death sentence. But bringing her back may be a death sentence for *her*. A long, slow death exactly the same as Lyona's."

"Whose side are you on?"

"Ah," he said. "You admit there are sides, then. And you could live with your new freedom, knowing that she was chained to the loom in that chamber in the palace?

with me." Grayson frowned. "Just in case. You know I've never been that attached to it."

"Just be careful." She nodded. "Promise me!"

"I promise," she said. "I will be careful."

Arden got little sleep that night. Every time she closed her eyes she saw Abbot Grayson with his hands in front of his face to hide his tears. She loved him dearly. If things had been different, they might even have been lovers, in spite of their age difference. But their father/daughter relationship was too ingrained.

There had been several lovers in her life, but only one who had meant a lot to her. Davide Slohn. He was a warrior like her, but he had a difficult time dealing with that, even though it was the same thing that had drawn him to her.

Remembering him led her mind onto another track, then another, and she tossed and turned until the window next to her bed began to lighten. Sleep came for a few hours; then she was headed for the dojo for her last morning's practice.

Brother Bryan chided her for not concentrating, but she knew he understood that her mind would not stop considering what was to come. Afterward they sat over tea and he reiterated the areas in which she needed to concentrate during her trip to Caldera. She paid close attention to his instructions; they could very well save her life in the weeks ahead.

When he had said everything, he took a small package out of his pocket and handed it to her. "For luck," he said.

She untied the string and pulled back the cloth. Inside was a small figure of an animal she did not recognize, carved of a hard yellowed stone. A narrow black velvet ribbon was run through a hole drilled in one end.

"The animal is called a turtle," Bryan said. "It's carved of some sort of animal bone or horn. It's an ancient figure of a type called netsuke. It is generally considered to be an amulet to bring good luck."

"Thank you, Bryan," she said, her voice choked.

That she might never again see the light of day?"

"I have to," she said tightly, "I'm pledged to the emperor..."

"And his house," Grayson interjected.

"And I must do as ordered. That is where my allegiance lies."

"You and your allegiance. It binds you too tightly."

"It's what you taught me. The code of the warrior. Loyalty. Responsibility. Honor."

She glared at him, daring him to deny it. He pressed fingertips to his forehead, hiding his eyes behind his hands. When he lowered them, his eyes were filled with tears. She went to him, knelt in front of him, took those hands in her own.

"I'm sorry," she said. Her words came fast. "I know this won't be easy. It's a job I don't want. And I don't know if I can pull it off. I'm frightened of failing and just as frightened of succeeding."

Grayson nodded, and she raced on.

"A warrior is what I am, and if I can't live by that code then I have failed as a person. Failing to accomplish this task would be bad enough, but failing to try would be devastating. I cannot involve someone else in this. I could only bring him down with me."

He nodded again and freed his hands to wipe away the tears.

"It's all my fault, you know," he said with a weak smile. "You wanted to learn to be a warrior and I let you. You were the best student this monastery ever had. I *am* proud of you."

He opened his arms, and she leaned in to hug him. They held on to each other for the space of several heartbeats; then she sat back on her heels.

"Well," he said, and cleared his throat. "I'll get you a copy of the information on Caldera to take with you. Let me or Brother Bryan know what else you may need."

She nodded. "Oh, I will need some lifeweave to take

They hugged and she repeated her promises to him to be careful and come back soon. When she left him, she retrieved her sword and took it to the armorer for sharpening. She could do it herself, but nothing surpassed a professional job. While he worked on it, she wended her way into the gardens. Standing in the midst of trees, bushes, and flowers, Arden was suddenly overcome by the feeling that she might never see them again. She recognized it as fear rather than precognition. It was overwhelming nonetheless.

Nothing stirred in the predawn darkness. Her slippers whispered against the stone floor as she made her way down the hall from her room. With the very dim light from stars and the setting sliver of moon, her familiarity with the monastery, and her keen night vision, Arden made her way to the main door without bumping into anything.

The hinges of the door protested slightly at being disturbed from their sleep, and she bumped the scabbard against the door itself as she slipped out. No alarm sounded; no one shouted for her to identify herself.

She set one of her bags on the ground and used both hands to pull the door closed as quietly as possible. She made sure the sword was tied securely to the bag, then picked it up. Gravel crunched under her feet as she made her way down the path.

The front gate was louder than the door in its protest at being disturbed, and she paused and listened before slipping out. The car sat where she had left it, but she knew it had been refueled and checked over within the past day or two, just as she knew the downed tree had been cleared down the road. She tossed the two bags into the back seat, placed the sword on the passenger's seat beside her, and climbed into the driver's seat. The engine turned over on the first try, sounding very loud in the surrounding silence.

She backed it away from the gate, turned it around, and started for the city. Her flight was scheduled to lift at eleven. There would be a couple of hours to spare.

"Goodbye, old friends," she whispered as she turned on the headlights.

If only she could believe it was only a temporary parting.

A large figure stood in the darker shadows cast by the wall of the monastery. He watched as Arden made her way out of the building, then followed after she had passed him, toward the gate, keeping to the grass to muffle his footsteps. He stopped under a large tree as she slipped out and closed the gate.

Moments later, he heard the car start and move away. Then he saw the glow of its lights when they came on. He sighed and remained where he was, for the first time in his life unsure of what to do next. He was a man who traveled little, a lover of fine things and a good life. Now, he realized that there were things in the past he should have done differently. Too late, now, of course.

He stood under the tree until the sky began to lighten in the east. He pushed away from the supporting trunk and started back toward the building. Turning for a moment, he looked at the gate again.

"Fare thee well, daughter," Abbot Grayson said, then headed inside.

3

Rafe Semmes's gloved hand poised above the door handle. So far, all he'd seen on the wrecked ship were the bodies of four crew members—three men and one woman. Two of them lay twisted among debris as if the impact had killed them. The woman's face was badly discolored; she might have died from the sulphur fumes. The fourth—Rafe had no idea what killed him. Not one of them had managed to get a suit on.

"Captain, we've got company."

The warning came over his headphones, the voice of Goron Liel, his second in command.

"Who and how many?" he asked.

"Just one orbital scout ship. Glorian by the look of her."

"They haven't identified themselves?"

"Not a word."

Finding a Glorian cargo ship crashed here on Caldera was a strong indication that something important must be on board. Why else would a cargo ship be this far from home? Now, a scout ship appears. Glory might be winning their war—last he'd heard—but they certainly could not afford sending not just one, but two ships on a minor mission.

"Broadcast the salvage message and let me know if they move to land near the derelict."

"Aye, sir."

Damn. This could mean trouble if the Glorians thought something on board the wrecked ship was worth breaking salvage laws for. He'd just walked a treacherous route around magma flows and dead bodies, and he wasn't about to give up the wreck—at least not until he knew what was so important.

The door handle turned easily but the door resisted, and he pushed with his shoulder. As it gave inward, he stumbled. Sweat meandered down his spine. The temperature control strapped to his wrist showed heat was building every moment. His suit whined as it automatically cranked up the cooling to compensate. He stepped into the narrow corridor.

Five more closed doors. Four opened into crew's quarters on either side, surprisingly free from damage. He hesitated at the fifth, at the very end, sure that whatever treasure the ship carried lay behind it.

Hell, that was the whole reason for being here, wasn't it? So, stop messing around and get to it.

This door resisted, too. He swore softly. Heat from the magma runs and the steam outside the ship was wearing enough without having to fight every doorway.

When Rafe used his shoulder again, the door banged inward, pulling him with it. Regaining his balance, he studied the cabin's contents: several dozen old-fashioned aluminum crates still strapped to each wall. The outer bulkhead had a gaping hole where something had exploded, damaging not only the wall but the crates that had been stacked there, throwing them around the deck. The metal of the bulkhead was bent outward, indicating that the cause of the explosion had been inside, not only inside the ship but probably inside one of the crates.

He stooped and set one of the damaged crates upright. Using his laser knife, he cut the straps holding two of them together. The knife made quick work of the weakened straps; he popped the catches and lifted the lid.

Lifeweave!

Although he had never seen it before, he would know it anywhere. Four conical spools filled the box. Fiber was wrapped around each, glowing in colors seen and unseen. He touched a cone, wishing his hand was not covered with the glove.

God, how many times had he heard of the fiber and the fabric made from it? It was beautiful and magical and ruinously expensive. He'd also heard it could be addictive for some who wore it and wove it, demanding an additional price beyond money or credits for possessing it.

Were all these crates full of the stuff? If so, this was the greatest treasure he and his crew had ever salvaged.

"Captain." Liel's voice broke through Rafe's disjointed plans for lavish spending.

"Yes?" The word came out husky and, worst of all, his voice quavered a bit.

"You all right, Captain?"

Rafe cleared his throat and put as much authority into the next words as he could.

"Yes. I'm fine. What's going on?"

"Our visitors finally made contact. They want you to meet with their captain. I think they want that ship real bad."

"I'll bet they do. I assume they want to meet on their own ship."

"That's what they *suggested*. They know we have minimal firepower."

Unlike salvage vessels, which by law were allowed few weapons, Glorian scout ships carried a lot of light arms. For something like lifeweave, they *might* break the salvage laws.

"All right," he said after a moment. "Tell them I'll be there as soon as I can. For now, send down another lander with two of the crew. We've got some crates here. It'll take at least two to carry each one out of here and several trips to get them all offloaded. I want as many as possible on the *Starbourne* before I talk with the Glorians.''

"What did we get?"

Should he tell Liel now? Better wait. What if something else filled the other containers?

"You wouldn't believe me." Rafe caressed the top of a spool. "You can tell the crew that we've got something better than usual."

"You're the captain." Liel sounded disappointed.

Rafe nodded. *Yeah, I'm the captain, and wondering what the hell I should do now.*

He lifted a spool out of the crate. It felt light. Wearing lifeweave was supposed to be like wearing nothing at all.

What else did he know about it?

The fiber was grown on a distant planet—Weaver, he thought it wasn't called. One of the rare family-owned worlds. They had a lock on growing and spinning the fiber but did not weave it. Seemed like someone once smuggled out some seeds and seedlings but not one of them grew, even though they were planted on several worlds. Probably something about the differences in soil and light. Only spun thread or yarn could be legally exported, and governments and industries competed for the right to weave it into cloth, increasing its value tenfold.

But what made the Glorians want it badly enough to risk two ships? True, the value of this many spools—assuming all the crates contained lifeweave—would buy three or more battle cruisers. Actually, he had expected to find weapons. A treasure of another kind, of course, but nothing to compare in value to this.

This being a cargo ship, there had to be a levitator for moving the crates. While he waited for the second lander, he paced heavily around the cabin, stopping at a smaller door hidden between two stacks of crates. He found what he needed strapped to the side wall of a tool closet. After cutting the straps on another stack, he thumbed the rocker switch on the tool and lowered a crate to the floor in its projected field. Okay, it worked. Better to keep busy while he waited. He began making smaller stacks of the crates, opening every third one to confirm the contents, while a thought nagged at him: some memory of something having to do with the Glorians and lifeweave.

Of course, Glory was at war with three other worlds in its solar system. Not unusual anymore, since many small empires had formed within that sector over the past several generations, out of what had once been a larger empire. The original empire had become too widespread and collapsed under its own weight.

Earth, from which all of the known worlds were supposed to have been colonized, controlled only its nearest colonial worlds. None of the independent worlds in that system, of which his home was one, could afford war, which suited Rafe just fine. It freed him and his crew from military duties and made possible the life of roaming and salvaging that he loved. And, with Glory's war well into its second decade, other conflicts within systems, and a certain amount of piracy, derelict ships were easy to find.

The fact that the salvage laws survived also helped make his job easier. They were seldom broken for several reasons: salvage helped keep arms and resources in circulation without costing the warring parties as much as new weapons would; it provided work for people like him, keeping them out of wars personally, and their home worlds, generally; and, the strongest of all, the tradition was so old, its origins were lost to general knowledge. Scholars probably knew where it originated, working in their universities, where they wrote long, boring tomes on the subject meant only for the eyes of their peers.

The sound of retro jets pierced the air outside, finding its way inside the ship. Rafe resealed the last crate he had opened and made his way back to the main door to look out. It was the lander. Two figures climbed laboriously out and lumbered toward him: Jessa and Tahr by their gaits.

"Welcome aboard." He greeted the two.

Tahr grunted as he stepped inside. "Could've picked a better place to crash," he groused.

Rafe smiled. Tahr always groused and Jessa held her tongue.

"Not bad enough we got volcanic flows all over the place," Tahr continued. "We gotta have . . ."

"The crates are down here," Rafe interrupted.

He led the way aft. Jessa gasped when they passed the bodies. He hurried into the corridor and the storage cabin.

"I want to get this one on my lander—maybe a couple more. Then get as many as you can handle on your lander and follow me up."

"What's in them, anyway?" Tahr asked, always curious.

"What about the rest?" Jessa interrupted, relieving Rafe of the necessity of answering Tahr.

"You and the rest of the crew work at them while I'm talking to the Glorian captain. I would like a lot of crates moved before I return the call."

"Yeah. That scout ship makes me a little nervous," Tahr said. "They shouldn't even be here."

"They might just want the bodies," Rafe said, without believing it.

He picked up the levitator and motioned toward the one Tahr had brought with him.

"It'll take both of you to carry a single crate. They're not heavy, just awkward. Jessa, help me move this one out to my lander first. Tahr, start cutting others free. Be careful none of them falls on you."

In spite of the suit cooler, sweat quickly dampened the inside of his suit again as they carried the crate toward his lander. Jessa's visor fogged up, and he guessed she was sweating too.

Rafe wanted to rub his eyes. They burned from the glow of magma flows they had to skirt, and from sweat running down his forehead. Once inside the lander, they sat on the floor, backs against the crate, letting cool air do its work while they created no more heat with their exertions.

"That last stream was a new flow," Jessa commented. "Just since we got here."

"Yes," Rafe agreed. "Looks like they change their paths all the time. You'll have to keep an eye peeled, make sure you don't get cut off from the lander."

She leaned out the door, looking ahead of and behind the little ship.

"Are they safe where they are?" she asked, referring to both landers.

"For a while, I think. Ready for the next one?"

"Sure."

The first one hadn't been too difficult for her to handle in spite of its bulkiness. He led the way back, in a hurry to get loaded and then find out why the Glorians were here. Their captain might think lifeweave worth fighting for. If so, Rafe did not intend to lose a crew member over the stuff. Maybe he could just let the Glorians squirm, then make them pay through the nose. He liked that idea.

Rafe looked across the table at Borana Lan, the Glorian captain. The pleasantries were over and, as host, it was her place to state the purpose of the meeting; however, she sat silently for a long time.

"We were not expecting to find a salvager here so soon," she said at last. He found her accent pleasant, almost too sexy for an authority figure. "We thought to be here first."

He shrugged. "We just happened to be in the sector."

The corners of her mouth twitched, which might have been anger or a near smile. She knew, as well as he did, that this sector was one of the most unpopulated and desolate within the human sphere. Except now, and for the next few months, it would be the most convenient lane between two more populated sectors.

"We want the ship and its cargo," Lan said. "It was on a very special mission, important to our war effort."

Her head moved slightly with intensity, shaking the ends of her short black hair.

"By salvage law, it's ours."

"I understand that," she said sharply, showing some of the hardness that must have helped her rise in rank. "We are willing to pay you half what it is worth. That will save you and your crew the time and effort of unloading and loading the cargo. After all, Glory has already paid full price for it once."

"Do you know what the cargo is?"

Her eyes widened slightly. She was a warrior, and negotiating was not her long suit. She could use the experience of a few hands of poker, an ancient Earth game he liked too much when he could find other players. Playing it had taught him to keep expression from his face when gambling. Her face showed a stronger tinge of anger than before, not at him, he thought, but perhaps at her superiors who must have told her little concerning the mission.

"I was told only that it is vital to our war effort."

"As you've already said. What price are you willing to pay?"

"Three million credits."

The crates of fiber were worth ten, no, a hundred times that.

"You have that much with you?" Rafe asked, feigning interest.

"Of course not. We must come to an agreement on means of payment. However, it would not be long in coming to you."

"My experience with governments," he said, "has not been, shall we say, very encouraging up to now. If we struck a deal, I would insist on keeping the ship and its cargo in my possession until full payment was made."

"We *must* take the cargo now."

Her voice was controlled but her hand, resting on the tabletop, tightened into a fist. There was much more to this shipment than its obvious intrinsic value, but he couldn't even guess what it was. Perhaps the Glorian emperor was addicted or... Again, that nagging, near recollection. He had heard something about the Glorians and lifeweave.

"We could take the cargo," Lan said in a flat voice.

"But you won't. What would happen all over the galaxy if you ignored—or broke—the laws on salvage?"

Actually, he had no idea what would happen, except people like him and his crew might be in danger more often. World governments were not above committing small infractions. Local governments were more blatant, but the laws remained and, by and large, were observed.

Now that he thought about it, things could get very ugly if breaking the laws became wholesale. Captain Lan certainly looked to be taking it all seriously.

"How would you be willing to deal so that we could take the cargo with us?"

Ah, the die was cast. The choice of options was now his. He hesitated, to give the impression that he had not already decided.

"What we can do... How much did you say you had on board the ship?"

"Five thousand credits," she answered without a hint that she had been tricked into revealing the amount.

"Yes," he said slowly. "Well, what we could do is let you take one crate for that amount—although it is worth much more. Call it a gesture of good faith. We would later meet at a mutually agreed-upon world—or a satellite would do—where we could finalize a deal for the rest."

"How much for the first crate?"

"The whole five thousand you have on board, for the time being."

"And for the rest?"

"Oh, I think sixty million would do."

Her face turned red, then paled. Her mouth opened and closed three times but no words came out. Too bad; he'd found her attractive until then. In a way, he was sorry to be so difficult with her. It wasn't her government he wanted to give a hard time. Or any government, for that matter. Of course, it was good business to get the highest price possible.

"Sixty million?"

The two words nearly choked her. Rafe leaned across the table.

"You really don't know what's in the crates, do you?" he asked again.

"No."

"Spools and spools of lifeweave," he told her. "Worth a hundred million, I expect." He leaned back in the chair. "At sixty million, your government is getting off cheap."

"You turned down three million credits?" Liel shouted.

Rafe got up to shut the cabin door. After reporting that all the crates had been moved, the executive officer had asked how much money the Glorians offered. Without thinking, the captain told him straight out. He hoped none of the crew overheard the outburst.

"It's lifeweave, Liel. In this quantity, it's worth a hell of a lot more than three million. It's worth a hell of a lot more than sixty million."

"Lifeweave? Sixty million?"

Liel collapsed into a chair.

"Yeah. I wasn't even sure it was all lifeweave when I was talking with Lan. I went ahead and told her what we'd take for it. At some place closer to civilization. They've only got five thousand with them. I offered one crate for that amount. Lan wanted to confirm the cargo."

A short time earlier, Owen, the loadmaster, had sent a crate to the Glorian ship and the credits were already in the stasis vault on board the *Starbourne*.

Liel still looked shocked. However, he was always one to get his priorities straight.

"One crate would be worth about a million and a half," he muttered. Then, "How did they intend paying the rest?"

"Lan said they'd make sure we got it."

Liel snorted. "With such a promise, I can see why you turned them down." He became thoughtful. "Are we committed to selling to them?"

"Not really. I gave our terms for sixty million and another site but they haven't accepted. The longer they wait, the more time for us to change our minds."

"We could take the stuff to Miga and auction it there. We'd sure get a better price."

Liel declined a drink and Rafe poured some cheap brandy into a glass. He sipped a little as he thought over Liel's suggestion. Miga was not his favorite place, but it was where the best buyers went for salvaged goods.

"Selling to someone else actually appeals to me," Rafe said. "Not so much because of the higher price, though. This lifeweave is too important to the Glorians."

"It can buy them a lot of weapons," Liel said.

"No, not just that," Rafe argued. "We know they've already paid for the spools once, at the source. Their own ship was carrying it and the hole in the side sure indicates the explosion was inside. It just has to be more than credits."

"You just want to spoil their game."

Rafe could not help grinning because it was true. More than once he'd sold a cargo for less than it was worth in order to keep a rich man, a government, a cartel, or a corporation from something it wanted.

"Jessa might know," Liel said.

"Jessa?"

"She's a Glorian. She might know what's so important about this lifeweave. She must still have family there."

Of course, he should have thought of her. But was it wise to let one more person know what they had on board? The crew knew it was valuable, more so than anything they'd salvaged before. However, his mother had always told him the only way to keep a secret is to tell no one. Not even one. Already, two on board knew. A third, and soon everyone would know. Almost by osmosis, certainly without intent.

Oh, well, they'd all know sooner or later anyway.

"Okay, Liel, ask Jessa to come in. I need to know what's so important about this stuff."

Liel left for the bridge and the captain put his feet up on the bunk as he tried to recall everything he knew about Jessa. She had been with him nearly four years and was the newest member of the crew—he liked to keep good people working for him. She'd come to him from another ship and . . .

Except for her being a hard worker and almost abnormally quiet, that was all he knew. She was almost pretty, with long black hair and green eyes, but he'd never been attracted to her—unlike Captain Lan, whom he had found attractive momentarily, even though Lan was heavier than was stylish for women these days. Personally, he didn't care for skin and bones.

Jessa appeared at the door a few minutes later. Rafe invited her in and offered her the chair opposite. He told her about the lifeweave and the Glorians' strong desire to get their hands on it. She said nothing, just sat staring at his feet on the bunk. He thought he detected sadness but couldn't be sure.

"It's probably for Lyona," she said at last.

"Who?"

"Appolyona. Seeress, prophetess—whatever you want to call her—to Granid Parcq, Emperor of Glory, Leader of the Unvanquished Armies, and so on. Lyona uses lifeweave to enhance, uh, certain talents she possesses."

"Such as?"

"She weaves it into pictures, diagrams, plans, that show future battles. It gives the Glorians the edge."

"You mean, fortune-telling?" he asked.

"Yes, in a way. But more accurate."

Jessa became suddenly silent, then just as suddenly began talking freely. First she went back, told how Lyona had been the emperor's consort. He would have given her anything; what she wanted most was lifeweave. She wore it everywhere, slept in it, even wove a blanket for her bed, and her addiction grew. After a time, she could no longer function as a lover or even a showpiece at court. But she continued to weave, and someone noticed one day that the weaving was prophetic.

"The way lifeweave shines, you have to hold the piece at a certain angle to see the pattern," she continued. "I guess it's a wonder anyone ever noticed, really. Oh, but when they did . . ."

She shook her head.

"This isn't just rumor or gossip?" Rafe asked.

"No, Captain. It's true."

He didn't doubt her word exactly, but how did an experienced astronavigator know all this?

Jessa smiled suddenly.

"Everyone on Glory had some inkling about it," she said, as if having read his thoughts. "There was all that lifeweave coming in."

Well, that was what he'd been trying to remember both down on Caldera and on the Glorian scout ship. Somewhere, long ago, he'd heard about lifeweave and how it was supposed to enhance some people's mental powers. He hadn't believed it, even though such talents were once supposed to have been fairly common. But that was hundreds of years before the first colonists left Earth.

"There were rumors about the effects lifeweave could have over the long term," Jessa went on. "It's been known to destroy some people's lives."

He and his crew knew nothing about the addictive properties of lifeweave. Specifically, would the crates containing the spools also hold the fiber's addictive properties within, thus protecting him and his crew?

"It's touching the fiber that causes addiction," Jessa explained when he voiced his concern. "You can't breathe it in or anything like that."

A knock on the door silenced them.

"Captain?"

"Yes, Liel."

The first officer entered.

"It looks like Captain Lan may be planning to leave. Her ship is powering up."

"I'll be right there." He turned to Jessa. "Thanks."

He followed Liel to the bridge. When Owen tried to raise the Glorian ship, it didn't answer at first. After several hails, he faced Captain Lan's image on the view screen. Jessa appeared on the bridge and took her seat at the navigation console.

"Captain Semmes," Lan said before he could greet her. "I inspected the crate you sent over and have confirmed its contents. I reported that back to Glory. I have been ordered to take possession of the remaining crates and to inspect our transport ship for damages. If those damages appear suspicious, I am further ordered to place you and your crew under arrest for piracy and to confiscate your ship."

"Look here, Lan. You know damned well that I'm not carrying the firepower necessary to bring a ship like your transport down."

"Their weapon systems have been powered up, Cap'n," Owen informed him.

"Please land, Captain Semmes," Lan ordered. Her expression was hard. He keyed off the sound transmitter.

"Break out the small arms," he told Liel.

"Swords, too?"

"Everything. We'll have to do this on the ground. We can't hope to match that scout ship."

"We can't match them hand to hand, either," Liel pointed out. "They outnumber us and probably have enough guns to go around."

"Captain, your answer please!" Lan said.

He keyed the comm unit. "Give us a moment," he said. He switched it off, then turned back to Liel. "The only chance we have is surprise. If I pretty much convince her that we're giving up, it might work."

Tahr muttered something under his breath from the pilot's chair. Jessa stared at her controls. Owen relaxed at the comm console. Vida had left her galley and was leaning against the hatchway. Six of them altogether against ten Glorians.

"All right, Lan," he said. "We'll land, but under protest. You're interfering with our legal salvage rights."

"Sue us," she said.

"I will. You can count on it."

Liel motioned for Vida to follow and left the bridge for the arms locker near the galley. Rafe fluttered his index and middle fingers on his left hand, a habit he had picked up as a musician, and turned toward Tahr.

"Find a spot that might give us an advantage," he said. "Where they can't land real close to us, anything that might shield us from their ship's guns or..."

"How about a spot that would be shielded from them by rocks?" Tahr asked.

"Perfect."

"I think there's one right..."

The *Starbourne* descended toward the planet. "They're staying right with us," Owen reported.

"Got it!" Tahr exclaimed.

"Captain Semmes!" Lan called. "Please land in a more open space."

"We're committed now," he answered. "Besides, you wanted us close to the transport, didn't you?"

"Not that damned close!"

Static covered whatever else she said. Rafe looked over to Owen.

"Increased seismic activity," the comm officer said, and grinned. "In other words, the volcanoes are acting up."

"Cut the comm, then," Rafe ordered.

Just then, Liel returned with Vida, both of them carrying pistols and swords. They had four pistols, the only weapons usable when wearing suits, which in turn were necessary because of the heat and sulphur fumes outside. Rafe took a pistol and handed the other three to Jessa, Owen, and Tahr. They would suit up and wait outside. Vida and Liel each took one of the swords. They would stay inside as the last line of defense. Of course, if the other four were all killed or disabled, their chances were slim to none.

"They're landing east of us," Owen said. "Tahr got us into a depression surrounded by rocks. They can't see us from there, much less try to shoot at us."

The captain nodded. "Let's suit up and get outside and wait for them," he said.

Jessa was nearly suited, and the other three began getting into theirs. A rumble penetrated the hull. The ship lurched suddenly. Owen, with one foot in his suit, lost his balance and fell to the floor. The others braced themselves. Everyone's eyes had opened very wide.

"What was that?" Rafe called.

Liel staggered to Owen's console as the *Starbourne* lurched again. He touched controls, studied the results.

"Seismic activity increasing," he said. "It's centered nearer the Glorian ship."

A steady rumble grew, vibrating the ship and everything in it. Rafe stepped out of his suit, got into the captain's chair, and strapped himself in.

"Let's get the hell out of here," Rafe ordered.

"The scout ship!" Tahr reminded him.

"They can fend for themselves."

The other three got rid of their suits while the captain began overseeing their preparations for lifting off. He kept one eye on the surface of Caldera. Volcanic activity continued to pick up.

Liel concentrated on the actual checklist. He was one of the best first officers on any kind of ship, and Rafe let him do his job. The *Starbourne* bucked, which would have thrown him out of his chair if he hadn't been strapped in. The ship reverberated from an external impact; then she groaned in pain.

"Dammit!" he shouted.

He looked to Liel for an explanation. All eyes were on the forward screen. The surface of the planet glowed brighter than before. Lava plumes shot upward, sparks flying into blackness, stars unto themselves for a moment.

The ship groaned as it lifted from the surface. She was damaged, that was sure.

"Captain," Owen called from his communications console. "I'm not getting anything from the Glorian ship."

"What about their ident signal?"

"Owen listened closely for a moment as he checked several channels. "Nothing," he reported.

"Put us into a low orbit, Liel. We'll wait it out, then see if we can help them."

"We've got damage to the aft section," Liel reported. "We're maneuverable but we'll have to make repairs before we can make the jump to Miga."

Tahr struggled slightly with the attitude controls but got the ship higher. All the while, he mumbled and everyone ignored him as usual.

From a safe distance, they waited and watched, fascinated by titanic explosions on a Caldera that was quickly changing from the landscape they had landed on. Owen reported communications silent except for magnetic and electrical static, which continued even after the volcanic action calmed later in the evening.

Half a day later, Rafe ordered the ship as low as it could get so they could see more clearly. What had been ribbons of solid rock at his landing site now lay under a red, roiling sea. Steam and smoke wafted across the screen. Even so, something as large as the Glorian scout ship should be visible.

However, neither that ship nor the original derelict that had brought them to this replica of hell could be found.

Several miles away, they finally found the scout ship. It looked like it had been moved on a red tide that held onto its prize as it cooled. The comm remained silent. Rafe ordered one of the landers made ready to launch. As he flew over the changed landscape, he found nothing on which to land, nor could he detect any signs of life. Lava bubbled through a huge tear in one side of the Glorian ship. Everyone *must* be dead. If not, they soon would be if they couldn't let him know they were there.

He buzzed the site, even bumped the metal hull twice, with no result. The crew would look disapproving when he returned; he would have given any one of them hell for taking the same foolish chances. Somehow, being in charge gave one the right to stupidity while denying the same right to those he commanded.

After an hour, and constant berating from Liel over the comm, it was time to give up. In spite of the brightness on the surface, the night would be too dark to safely stay. Nothing had been heard, Owen said, when he was back on the bridge. Several sideways glances and raised eyebrows indicated they all knew what he had done and would remind him at some later date. For now, there were lost spacers to mourn and a limping ship to repair.

"Guess that crate of lifeweave is gone, too," Liel said, always the pragmatist.

Rafe nodded. Jessa, seated at her console, showed no reaction. She concentrated on the controls in front of her, working with Tahr to keep the ship in orbit. Time to get to the nearest port for repairs. That was at Vega City on the other side of Caldera.

A sudden thought hit him: He had assumed, during the preparations for a possible fight, that Jessa would have done her part as a member of the crew. But those were her people in the scout ship. Had he assumed too much?

4

Lyona wove fiber in and out, never pausing to check the pattern. Her fingers knew the way, and she had lost the need for her eyes long before losing the use of them. The picture was half finished and, even in her euphoric state, she knew it held important information.

She sat in this room at least twelve hours a day, on a four-legged stool, while her hands worked the shuttles without conscious thought. Heavy drapes were drawn across tall windows, blocking out the light of the sun, whose warmth could be distracting.

During those twelve hours, she reacted little to her surroundings. Occasionally she issued instructions to waiting servants, most relating to the need for more lifeweave, sometimes requesting a drink of water or food.

Her existence consisted of battles not yet fought, but which she saw and heard to the last detail, forming beneath her fingers, giving her world's forces every advantage over Glory's foes.

Countless years she had been seeress to the emperor. He was one of the few who could afford to pay for so much of the fiber; she had paid the cost with her sight.

The end of the thread passed between her fingers.

"Another spool," she commanded.

A waiting servant heard and went to fetch the fiber. The weaver fingered the end of the strand in her hand, unraveling the individual fibers. As seconds passed, her hands began to shake. Colin Chase, her personal bodyguard, stepped up behind her and began brushing her long, grey hair. Gently he pulled the bristles through, kneeling to reach the ends that touched the floor, smoothing with his free hand. The thick tresses shone in the light from wall sconces placed around the room.

Lyona sighed; her hands came to rest in her lap. The lifeweave of her dress shimmered with each small motion. Her hands began caressing the fabric, following the colors as if remembering them through the fingertips.

"Seeress," a voice said, barely audible. "There is no more lifeweave."

Lyona stiffened and a low groan escaped her. The bodyguard placed a hand on her shoulder, staying close.

"Are you sure?" Her voice cracked.

"Yes, seeress."

"How has this happened?" she moaned, her voice breaking on the last word.

Her hands tightened into fists, her body began to tremble. One hand lifted to her breast with clawlike fingers, and she collapsed into Chase's arms.

"Seeress!" he cried. "Mistress!"

He made a choking sound, then lifted her and carried the small, limp body through the door into her bedroom.

Granid Parcq arrived moments later, looking stricken. Whether his concern was for the welfare of the woman or for his world, no one could know. Dr. Branard, chief physician, soon followed. He examined the seeress, asked a few questions, then turned toward his emperor.

"It's the shock of learning there is no more lifeweave for her to weave," he pronounced.

"Obviously," Granid Parcq said furiously. "But she just learned of this. And there is certainly enough in this room for her to fondle."

The physician shook his head.

"It's the emotional shock more than the physical," he said. "It is loss of purpose. The addiction has become more than just to lifeweave itself. She now must weave it. Having something to do with her hands, absorbing its addictive properties through her fingertips . . ."

Lyona's ragged breathing was the only sound in the room for a moment.

"Your majesty, is there a chance of getting more lifeweave soon?" he asked.

"A shipment is on the way," the emperor answered. "It is on the way."

"Well, can these other things—the dresses, blankets, all of it—be taken apart and rewoven?" the physician asked.

"We tried that once, to save money," the emperor answered. "For whatever reason, lifeweave becomes brittle if you try to reweave it. We must wait. And hope."

Three days passed and Lyona remained unconscious. All of her life signs grew weaker by the hour. Hallucinations tormented her, made her call out and struggle against unseen enemies. She struck out at those trying to help her: doctors, nurses, friends, others who were paid to wait on her, even Colin Chase, who stayed with her night and day. The doctors shook their heads; members of her entourage, and of the emperor's, watched in fascination and horror. Silently, each pledged to never again wear or touch lifeweave.

"How long can she last?" the emperor asked Doctor Branard, who only shrugged.

Late on the third night, Granid Parcq, fifteenth of his line, sat in his favorite chair in his quarters. The chief physician stood before him with head bowed.

"She's slipping faster than we thought possible, your majesty. There is no antidote, no substitute to help her. Painkillers have no effect, even the strongest we know of."

"If lifeweave arrived tomorrow, maybe next week . . ."

"Tomorrow might be in time, sire. Next week . . ." He shrugged.

"Then it's academic," the emperor muttered. "It's too far."

He sat brooding. The expected shipment couldn't possibly arrive in time, even if the scout ship started back that moment. A young girl with possible precognitive powers had been found, someone who might be able to take Lyona's place, but it could take a year to be sure that she had talent. Another year, maybe two before she could actually predict anything. As regarded the girl, then, a day or two made no difference.

He hit the chair arm with his fist, saw the startled look on the doctor's face, and dismissed the man with a wave. Branard backed away as the door was opened by the all-seeing eye of the computer.

By damn, whoever was responsible for letting the life-weave supply run out would pay dearly. Unfortunately, they might all pay dearly if the war started going badly because of it.

Lyona lay perfectly still, eyes open without seeing, breathing so shallowly that Granid Parcq's hand laid on her breast could not detect its rise and fall.

After several minutes, the emperor left the room, shaking his head. The woman lying there was not the one he had loved. That woman disappeared under the weight of addiction decades ago and, had he realized the loss at the time, he would have mourned then. He would mourn now, except this second death brought problems of another kind, and the emperor could not afford the time.

How would his smaller forces continue to dominate the war without Lyona's prophecies? If only her daughter hadn't disappeared.

Not many would be willing to give themselves over to lifeweave, not if they knew all the possible effects. At the end, Lyona had lived in a dream world and in the pictures, diagrams, and charts she created with the fiber. She had not *seen* her creations in several years. In fact, it was difficult for him to remember back to when she was not blind.

Except those times, late at night, when he lay sleepless in his bed—the touch of her hand, the softness and sweet smell of her hair . . .

He sank into the lounge chair in his private quarters, wondering for a moment why he didn't remember coming into the room.

No time for that question, nor for old memories. Somehow, a solution must be found to waging war with a new kind of blindness. For an instant, the possibility of a peaceful conclusion came to mind. However, that would mean surrender, something totally out of the question. Glorian domination of the system could not be allowed to slip away. But he had to stay focused, not let his mind drift into remembrances and old desires.

They had been so different in those early days, just before he had become responsible for Glory's welfare: Lyona, the dark-haired, voluptuous beauty who loved laughter; the angular prince who felt the weight of an empire on his shoulders. Even the birth of children had not changed anything between them. Her daughter and his son, given life by the empress a few years later, had always seemed to be smaller versions of themselves.

Jessa should never have been allowed to leave Glory. For years, the agents sent out by Don Vey had been unable to find her. From the reports received, she had moved around constantly, working various jobs, not bothering to change her name, at least for as long as they could track her movements. Even so, she had managed to elude all of them, staying a few steps ahead of them at all times.

Getting her back was the greatest hope. She must have inherited some of her mother's abilities. Everyone prayed for that, and for Jessa's return, except Waran, son and heir, half brother to Jessa. His fears were unfounded, though, since a woman had never ruled the Glorian empire, and she would never usurp his right to inherit the throne.

There would be other objections, of course. Jessa was an heir in spite of the male tradition; if something happened to Waran she could be the sixteenth of the Parcq line, but there would be no empire for either of them to inherit if the war got out of hand. Peace was out of the question. However, he might be able to buy some time by proposing a peace conference.

The door chimed.

"Come in," Granid Parcq ordered.

The chief physician entered, fear in his eyes, sweat marking his tunic.

The funeral was quiet, attended only by the emperor and a few of his and Lyona's staff. Chase stood guard, this time over her ashes, his face more deeply lined than before. He was in full dress uniform, the red tunic and gold braid making him appear larger than usual.

In the royal sitting room afterward, Don Vey stood away from the fireplace. No matter how warm it got, the emperor always had a fire lit these days. It was clear that Granid Parcq fought to pay attention while the prime minister presented a plan of action that he had already set in motion.

"This Grenfell woman can find Jessa faster than any of our people?" the emperor asked distractedly when Vey had finished.

Vey pressed fingertips against his temples. War business had kept him in the palace for more than a month now, and he was tired. Babysitting the emperor, calming his fears, had also taken a toll.

"I believe so," Vey answered. "She has all the training of a warrior and the resources of the empire behind her. She is a bit naive, I suppose, but Jessa trusted her once. And she has great incentive to succeed."

"She will do everything in her power to accomplish this?"

"She has no choice, sire. I've seen to that."

"Should we send a backup—someone to keep an eye on her?"

"That's been taken care of also. We don't need to worry about Arden Grenfell not cooperating."

5

Heat ate at her skin just as it had in the vision. Unlike in the vision, Arden wore a face mask as protection from the sulphur fumes, but still they crept into her nostrils, left their taste on her tongue.

She rechecked the guidebook. This was one of two such observation decks where newcomers could confirm the reasons for the planet's name. Caldera lived up to that name and more. She had bought the book at the hotel earlier that morning, wanting to learn her way around as quickly as possible. One surprise had already been sprung on her; she wanted no more.

That surprise had occurred at the spaceport on disembarking from the *Jefferson*. When her bags went through, the gun was detected. With little fanfare it was confiscated, with a promise to return it when she left. All she had to do was contact the local constable and he would make the necessary arrangements.

When she asked why guns were confiscated but not swords, the customs officer gave her a flyer that explained: "Since guns are more dangerous to a larger number of people than are swords and knives, all such weapons are banned from Vega City. They will be confiscated upon entry and will be returned upon exit." It was signed by Constable Arnold Harris.

The woman who took the gun was already scanning another piece of luggage for another traveler. Arden picked her bag up and headed for the ground shuttle station. In less than half an hour she was in the Vega City Imperial Hotel, where a room had been reserved.

She had unpacked quickly, bought the guidebook at the front desk, and rented a rover just down the street. There was little traffic to contend with. Caldera was too far from the mainstream of interstellar travel and too little known for ships to detour just for tourists. Souvenir merchandise consisted of the types of things company men would take home to their families when their three-year tours of duty were over. Volcanic rocks with scenes and faces painted on them were favorites.

Set on the fringes of the so-called badlands, the overlook was identical to the one in her vision, even to lava flows on each side. According to the guidebook, this violence was mild compared with that in the center of the volcanic activity on the other side of the planet. Violent explosions frequently sent plumes of lava rising even into the airless vacuum, and seismic waves through to the settled side of the world. It would be a lot of years before mining operations, or any other commercial activity, were moved there; maybe never.

The overlook was empty of people. Arden took a seat on one of the benches and, after a glance at the rented rover to make sure it was still there and whole, she opened the bag she had been carrying. From inside she pulled the blue, six-inch hand loom and a small ball of lifeweave yarn. Time for Pac Terhn to give up more information on Jessa's location and time of arrival.

She began threading the loom deftly, as if the last time had only been yesterday. Although she had practiced her swordsmanship and exercised daily on the ship, the loom had stayed in the bag, unused, unseen. Using it to foretell had frightened her ever since she realized what was actually happening. That fear had grown since she had seen Lyona. The seeress, in her fifties, had looked at least twenty years older. That was bad enough, but the dead eyes were worse.

Arden shuddered. She could not concentrate with such thoughts running wild in her head.

She took a deep breath and concentrated on the loom. She worked deliberately at first, but as it filled with thread, her mind fell into the shimmering patterns. Soon she floated in darkness. This time, Pac Terhn greeted her immediately.

"I was not expecting you so soon," he said.

"Of course you were."

He chuckled. "You are right. I was. And now you want to know when Princess Jessa will arrive."

"And other details that will enable me to find her."

"Let me see," he said. "What will the price be this time?"

"Enough! This is all part of the same deal, and you know it."

"I have to try," he said.

He always did. To him it was a game, something he may have learned on the world from which he came. She had tried to ask him about his origins, but he would not talk about any of that.

"Can we just conduct our business and get it over with for once?" she said. "I'm tired and would like to get the information as soon as possible."

"I see. You are not happy with this particular task, are you?"

"That doesn't matter. I obey my orders."

"Not always. I refer to your letting Jessa leave Glory."

Pac Terhn was probing her weak spots, something he always did. She had never known if he intended to harm her one day or if he had some other purpose in mind. Given his irascible nature, she suspected that one day, when she was vulnerable, he would probably destroy her.

"Let's go," she said. This time, he did not argue.

Once more, she was flying over the Calderan landscape. In a moment she realized he was leading her over the uninhabitable side of the world and she demanded to be taken back the opposite way. All she was interested in was finding Jessa. However, Pac Terhn continued over lava flows and eruptions of various sizes. They moved quickly this time, and none of the spirits spoke to her. At last they came upon a scene that might have some meaning in her quest: two ships. One lifting off, the other seeming to be mired in lava. As the first one rose, it bucked and she saw that it was damaged.

Clearly one of them must be Jessa's ship. That was why she was here. One ship was Glorian by its markings. It had been caught by the lava flow and, after a moment, she was sure that it would never lift again. In her mind, she could hear the screams of its crew. She ordered Pac Terhn to take her away from there, but he did not answer. She shut her eyes tightly, willing herself to move away. This was her vision, after all.

"Is it?" Pac Terhn asked from nowhere.

"Yes. And I'll be damned if I'll let you have total control of it this time."

She could feel him smile, and as usual had no idea why. Maybe it was because she was actually following the departing ship.

"Is Jessa's ship coming to Vega City?" Arden asked.

"It's the only port on the planet with the capability of repairing ships of that size," he answered.

In spite of his smile, there was no merriment in his voice. Nor was there any derision, which was what she expected from him. He had obliquely confirmed that the princess was on board the safe ship. Well, not quite. However, he had not denied it, either.

The one thing about Pac Terhn that could always be relied on was that he never lied. Given that, the ship would dock in Vega City within the next few days and there was no need for her to continue following. She told her guide that she was returning to her own space and time. He looked at her strangely.

"You have changed," he said.

"Being in prison did that to me."

"Hmm. Oh, one more thing. Jessa has a lover."

The vision faded and she opened her eyes. The setting was as it had been. However, Pac Terhn was right; there was a difference. Inside her. She had been in control within the trance at least part of the time. She had noticed that, of course, but once she was fully conscious of herself and her surroundings, the realization hit home and hit hard. Pac Terhn had never before let her control any of the visits, not even for a moment. It seemed liberating that it happened now, on her second visit after a six-year absence. She liked the difference.

Arden glanced down at the square still impaled on the pins of the handloom and saw a man's face. Unlike the one in the square she wove in Grayson's study, this man had very blond hair. His handsome face appeared more angular, but he too had blue eyes. Could this be Jessa's lover?

She sat for a time, letting the hangover from the lifeweave recede; then, slowly, she reloaded everything back into the rover. Soon she was on her way back into the city. The road was two lanes and she met only one vehicle going in the opposite direction. For the first half hour, the landscape on either side was barren of vegetation. Wisps of smoke and steam rose in isolated spots, becoming rarer the nearer to town she got. Rock and lava gradually gave way to a softer landscape of patches of grass and occasional bushes and distorted trees. After a full hour, more trees and other vegetation began to appear. The effect was of a single continent adrift on a sea of magma. The mine shafts, dug through such young rock and dirt, must be virtual hellholes of heat and ash. She could only imagine how difficult it must be to shore up the tunnels against collapse.

Traffic appeared only at the outskirts of Vega City, but it was minimal. Within the city itself, there was little need for signals. Signs at each intersection ordered stops in one direction or another. The streets were narrow, which seemed to indicate a severe lack of foresight. When the mining really took off, large vehicles would be running up and down the roads.

Well, maybe not. So much of the planet would not be accessible for generations. The mining companies probably just planned on taking what came easily, then moving on to the next virgin world that would also give up its chastity to their rough seduction.

Bastards!

The spirits of this world did not deserve to be treated so roughly, but few humans even suspected their existence. Nor was she going to tell them. They would think she was crazy, or worse, in their eyes, a conservationist of some kind.

She smiled at that thought. It would be fun to mess up their plans a little bit. Just enough to put a chink in their smugness. She shook her head. Others had earned her distaste more, but even they were not worth her attention right now. She had a job to do and, by damn, she was going to get it done and get on with her life.

That could wait until Jessa's ship, the *Starbourne*, arrived in Vega City for repairs. Tonight, she could sample life in the city. So far, it had proved very different from what she was accustomed to on Glory, settled several hundred years now, seeming staid and complacent in comparison to the hubbub here. The night should be very interesting.

She reached the hotel and parked the rover in the underground garage. In moments, the elevator had taken her to the north wing and up six stories. Her room was cool and the bed inviting, but she opted for a shower and a change of clothes. The trip to the lava beds had left her tired and hungry, and she intended taking care of the latter first. She chose a plain green tunic over her grey leggings and a black belt. Hanging from the belt was the netsuke on its black ribbon that Brother Bryan had given her. With the sword in its scabbard slung over her back, she left the hotel.

Down the street to the right seemed as good a place to start as any. At first, the street maintained a respectable character. The shops and restaurants were well maintained and clean. Within three blocks, however, the character changed, became seedier and louder. More people were out on the streets, some drinking from bottles they hurriedly stuffed back into jacket pockets. Voices were loud, shouting to one another across the street, occasionally challenging. If she stayed in the area long enough, there would surely be at least one fight to witness.

By the fifth block, her stomach growled loudly and she picked out one of the cleaner dives. It was crowded. Loud music played somewhere, filling the room to the high ceiling. She selected a table in the far corner from where she could watch its occupants come and go and interact with each other.

Arden had visited only a few places like this on frontier worlds where life could be hard and people played hard. Usually, life was cheap—the number of people with knives and swords seemed to confirm that.

A woman came up to her table. "What'll you have?" she asked.

"A sandwich," Arden responded. "What kind do you have?"

The woman rattled off a list.

"What kind of vegetable base are your hamburgers made from?"

"No veggies. Real meat."

There was a surprise. So far from anywhere, and real meat. It was a sure thing that animals were not raised on Caldera for food.

"I'll have one of those and a beer."

She said the last word with a question in her tone. If they had real meat, they might also have real beer.

The woman merely said, "Okay," and went off to place the order. This was going to be a bigger treat than she had thought. Real meat. Maybe real beer. Foods she had not enjoyed since leaving Glory. Interstellar passenger ships could not carry such things, and fed their passengers mostly dehydrated replacement fare.

A shout near the front door brought her attention back to studying the crowd of people. A small group jostled each other, but settled down when a burly man with a no-nonsense air about him spoke to them. A few minutes later the woman delivered the sandwich and beer. Arden flinched when told the price, but handed over the scrip plus a sizable tip. Vey had been quite generous with expense money, so she could reciprocate.

She took a bite of the hamburger and washed it down with a sip of beer. Both tasted so very good, and she reveled in the luxury. As she took the second bite, she noticed two men walking toward her table through the milling crowd. They started past the table, but suddenly one of them sat down in the chair opposite her. He grinned amiably, while the second man stood behind him with his hand in his jacket pocket.

"I have a pistol aimed at your stomach under the table," the seated man said. He was missing a front tooth and the words were spoken with a slight lisp. She swallowed the half chewed mouthful. "First, I want you to put your hands flat on the table." She did so. "In a moment, get up and walk toward the back door." His head tilted in the desired direction. "When we get there, you will open the door and step out into the alley."

"I need a swallow of beer first," she said.

His smile turned to a look of incredulity, but he did not stop her when she lifted the mug and drank. She set it back on the table.

"Now?" she asked.

He nodded, the smile returning. They both rose to their feet and he slipped the pistol under the edge of his jacket. Then he stepped back slightly to allow her to pass in front of him while his partner led the way. No one paid any attention as they made their way toward the back door.

Carefully, she stepped through, not wanting to give him a reason to fire prematurely.

The alley was dark, the only light coming indirectly from the street. Noises from all sides were muffled by the buildings. A gunshot would probably be muffled in turn and no one would know the moment of her death. If she were to die.

Just the slightest misstep . . .

She heard the man behind her stumble slightly over some debris on the ground. She spun around, knocking the gun away with her left hand, drawing her sword with the right. He grunted as the gun skittered across the hard ground. Deftly, he stepped aside and drew his own sword from the scabbard hanging at his waist. It was a short blade, more suited for stabbing in the back in a crowd than for face-to-face combat. He was good, however, and parried her first two blows skillfully.

They faced each other, already breathing hard, sizing each other up. He appeared to be about five feet ten; Arden was only slightly shorter. Her reach was longer because of the longer sword. His partner stood back, watching.

He attacked, the blows from his sword harder than she had expected. However, she deflected the blows easily enough. One thing learned: he was stronger than he looked. He was also quick. But she was quicker.

Her turn to attack. The sound of sword striking sword filled the alley for more than a minute as she forced him backward a few steps. Then he held his ground, attacked in turn. They whirled and struck; sidestepped and defended. Neither gained an advantage until she feinted low and brought the blade around in an arc to strike from above. His blade met hers just in time, but he was off balance. She pushed him away, prepared to slice across his body.

"Hey!"

The shout came from behind her, but she did not falter. The blade cut the man's torso from his left shoulder to his right hip. The second man was behind her, probably with gun drawn, and she started to drop to the ground. Something hit her in the side. As the lights faded even more, she heard a second shot. Then her knees buckled.

Consciousness returned slowly. Arden opened her eyes but everything remained dark. Even though she lay perfectly still, her head hurt. She knew for certain that if she moved, it would hurt even worse. But that was all she knew.

The surface underneath felt soft. A bed, maybe. Over her, a light covering. The air was cool: air conditioning. Where these things were and how she came to be in this place, she had not the foggiest memory. She realized that she was naked under the covering when she moved an exploratory hand.

The sound of movement came from close by, and she froze. It sounded like a person rather than an animal or something mechanical. She held her breath, listening, thought she caught a faint exhale. Suddenly a light came on, dimly, but enough to blind her momentarily.

"You're awake," a man said. His voice sounded vaguely familiar.

Gradually the light brightened a bit and she saw that she was in what looked like her own room in the hotel. A man stepped into her field of vision on the left side of the bed. He looked very familiar.

"He hit you pretty hard," the man continued. "You dropped like a rock. If I hadn't distracted him, his aim might have been better."

Nothing he had said so far brought any memories to mind.

"Where . . ." she started, but her throat was too dry and nothing else would come out.

"Where are you? Or, where did it happen?"

"Both," she croaked.

He disappeared from sight as he talked. "Right now, you're in your room in the Vega City Imperial Hotel. Last night, we met in an alley behind the Hoboken Bar. A couple of assassins were intent on ending your visit to Caldera."

He reappeared and handed her a glass of water. When she tried to sit up to take it, dizziness overcame her and she fell back.

"Easy," he said. "You lost quite a bit of blood."

He sat down on the edge of the bed beside her and raised her up with an arm under her shoulders. She drank slowly, letting the water moisten her mouth before swallowing.

"We found your room key in your pocket and brought you back here."

She finished the water, and he let her lie back. She swiped at moisture on her lips with the back of her hand.

"We?"

This time, her voice sounded more normal.

"Oh, yes. My name is Jackson Turner. My partner and I followed you out of the bar last night."

He went on to tell her that they had been sitting in the bar and noticed her departure under what seemed abnormal circumstances. Turner went out the front door while his partner, whom he called Spohn, started to follow out the back. The press of people had blocked that route for more than a moment. Meanwhile, Turner, seeing events developing between Arden and her would-be assassins, stepped in.

"I got a shot off at the one who shot you," Turner said. "I don't think I hit him, though. I searched your pockets, found the key, and we brought you here."

"The other one?"

"The one you were fighting? You got him good. He died before help came. We got you out of the way before Constable Harris arrived. All we told him was that we'd heard a shot and found him dead in the alley. Harris pressed us pretty hard. Seems he wanted to know how the man happened to die from a sword wound and we heard a shot. I don't think he's through with us yet."

"Why did the two of you come to my rescue?" Arden asked.

He grinned and stood up to put the glass away. He returned to the bed and sat at the foot.

"I thought your first question was going to be who undressed you," he said, still grinning.

The question had occurred to her, but the motive behind this Good Samaritan action was of greater importance. When he saw she did not return his smile, he answered her question.

"First, it looked like you were outnumbered. Second, we were bored. Our job was done here and we had been waiting for three days for a ship to take us home."

"I didn't think you looked like a miner."

His white linen shirt and dark blue wool pants were in the latest style. So were the short leather boots that matched the color of the pants. None of the materials looked artificial, and that made them very expensive. His blond hair was arranged in a short military style that looked good on him. The hair color looked natural, but it was so hard to tell these days. Suddenly she remembered where she had seen him: in the last lifeweave square!

"Hardly," he said with a flash of that smile again. "I'm a private investigator and came here to do a job for one of the mining companies."

"Hmmm," she said, immediately feeling more suspicious. "Have you and your partner been here very long?"

"Almost a week. Just doing some security work. We can't get off this damned rock for another three days and she's going stir crazy."

"She? Did she undress me?"

"Oh, you're asking at last. Yes, Spohn undressed you. She insisted that would be more proper and would not let me take advantage of you."

"I'll tell her I'm grateful when I see her."

Her eyelids were becoming unmanageable, wanting to close no matter how hard she tried to keep them open. One question kept plaguing her and she had to ask it.

"Where is my sword?" she mumbled.

"It's here."

Jackson held it up where she could see it. That done, she let her eyelids have their way and drifted into sleep.

When next she woke, the curtains were open and full sunlight shone in. At first the bright light hurt her eyes, but as they adjusted, it became cheerful and warm. Lying there, soaking in the warmth, she remembered Jackson Turner and the alley. How long had she been out? Had the *Starbourne* docked yet? Lord, she had to get on her feet and find Jessa.

The sound of a key in the door stopped her as she struggled to sit up. The door opened, and she looked for her sword. It lay across the chair by the window. Too far.

A man stepped into the room. Turner. Arden lay back on the pillow and took a deep breath to still her heart.

"You're awake," he observed for the second time. He turned to take something from someone behind him. "We brought you some breakfast. Except that it's past eleven, so I suppose it should be called brunch."

As he approached the bed, a woman followed. She too had short blonde hair, but obviously dyed, and was tall and muscular. She smiled down while he set the tray on the bedside table and helped Arden sit up.

"I'm Spohn Bryce," the woman said. Her voice was deep but not unpleasant. "Nice to finally meet you."

"Same here," Arden said as Turner helped her to sit back against both pillows he had piled behind her.

He retrieved the tray from the bedside table and placed it on her lap. They had brought toast, tea, some canned fruit—"They didn't have anything fresh," he apologized—and some cake. She was so hungry that it did not look like enough food. She found, however, that she was filled up quickly.

While she ate, Turner answered more questions about events of the night before, while Spohn listened from the chair. She balanced the katana between her hands, studying it, which irritated Arden. Why, she did not quite know.

Although they had bound her wound, they called a doctor

immediately upon reaching her hotel room to make sure everything was all right. They knew of one who would not talk, with the right incentive, which seemed more than convenient, given the amount of time they had actually been on Caldera.

"Why did you think it was so important to keep me away from the constable?"

Turner and Bryce looked at each other. She set the tip of the katana on the floor and leaned the blade against the chair arm.

"In Vega City, it's best not to get involved in anything like that," Turner said. "Constable Harris takes a very personal interest in everything that happens in his town. He managed to ban guns of all kinds, but too many people objected when he went after swords and knives."

"Those two had guns last night," Arden pointed out. "How did they get them in here?"

"They have their ways. Those two were professional assassins."

"You're sure?"

"The one you killed had the lilac tattoo of the League on his forearm."

The Assassins' League again. Why? She had thought the two men had intended robbing her. After they killed her, of course. Not even a constable could keep a professional assassin from getting a gun somehow, although their weapon of choice was more often a blade of some kind. Maybe the gun was to make it look like robbery in the final analysis.

She told them she had no idea who might have sent the assassins, but not about the earlier attempt on Glory. She drank the last of the tea, then pushed back into the pillows and closed her eyes.

"Anyway," Turner continued, "Harris would have made your life pretty unpleasant trying to find out who you are and why you brought violence to his city."

She nodded without opening her eyes. From what she

had heard of frontier constables, she could believe that.

Turner patted her hand and stood. "You're getting sleepy. We'll leave you to sleep."

Spohn stood and moved toward the door.

"I think I'll take a shower, then maybe get some more sleep," Arden said. "I'm feeling pretty dirty and sticky."

"Want me to stay just in case?" Turner asked.

"No, I think I'll be all right."

"If you get too dizzy or something, give it up," he ordered her. "Most accidents happen in bathrooms."

She opened her eyes and saw from his smile that he was teasing her. She smiled back.

"I will," she promised. "Where are you two staying in case I need to get in touch?"

"Here in this hotel. Room seven eighty-three."

"See you later?"

"We'll check back tonight or first thing in the morning," he said.

"Thanks," Arden said. "And thank you for last night."

Turner turned from the doorway. "You're welcome," he said. "Later." He followed Spohn out into the hall and closed the door, leaving Arden feeling more alone than ever before.

Except for her assignments as a soldier, she had only left Glory once before, when Jessa had traveled to Tareas to represent the emperor in some ceremony. They were accompanied by more than a dozen officials and servants, and she had not been alone once. Now, here she was on a strange world more than two sectors away from home, with someone out there who wanted to kill her. Who would want to kill her?

Arden sat up, then waited for dizziness to pass. When her head cleared, her mind took up the question again.

Someone who didn't want her to find Jessa. Probably a lot of people did not want the princess found, for several reasons she could think of. A few friends who thought enough of her to wish her free. Waran and his people, who might see her as a threat to his inheritance. Were there people who would prefer that the war not be conducted by psychic means? The military, perhaps? And what about Colin Chase, Lyona's protector? Did he love or hate the daughter?

She swung her feet over the edge of the bed and waited again. Consulting with Pac Terhn might answer the question, but it was not worth going under the influence of lifeweave to find out. Not yet. She hoped never.

Slowly, she got to her feet, wavered a moment, then started toward the bathroom. She had to stop often before actually getting into the shower. As the water soothed her aches, she realized it would have been safer if someone were watching and waiting in case she fell, but years of independence made it impossible to ask. Besides, once she returned to the bed, she could say that she had done it herself.

All scrubbed and dried, she lay down on the bed naked. The waterproof bandage had lived up to its billing, and although the wound hurt a bit, it would be healed soon. Where Spohn and Turner had gotten the necessities she could only guess. That they had not taken her to a hospital was a matter for which to be grateful. Jessa would not arrive in the city for another few days, plenty of time to shake off the effects of the shooting.

The warmth from the shower began to dissipate, and she pulled the covers over her. Sometime later, she woke to the sound of the comm buzzing. Drowsily, she started to reach for the receive button but the pain in her side brought her up short. That further awakened her to the memory of the assassination attempt.

The comm buzzed insistently and, moving deliberately, she managed to sit on the edge of the bed and key it on.

"Where have you been?" Abbot Grayson said.

"Hello to you, too. What's up?"

"A thing or two," the familiar voice said. "Are you all right? You sound tired or something?"

"You woke me up, but that's all right. What thing or two?"

He cleared his throat and there was a moment's hesitation. It must be something pretty important.

"Did you tell Vey or any of his people that you were going to Caldera?"

"No, you're the only one who knows. Oh, and Brother Bryan. It's possible a couple of the other brothers know. Why?"

"We had some visitors not long after you left the monastery. Vey sent them to find out where you had gone. I couldn't reach you while you were in hyperspace. I did try to get through to Titan when you were supposed to be transferring there but I just missed you. Then I tried again yesterday."

"You're on the secure line now?" Arden asked.

"Yes."

She thought a moment. Why she had not wanted Vey to know before she left Glory was not clear. It had been deliberate, although based on instinct, a step toward self-preservation. Surely he would not have sent the assassins to kill her. He wanted the princess found. Suddenly, she thought of Turner and Spohn. Was meeting them coincidence?

"Would any of the brothers have told where I was going?" she asked.

"It's possible. Few of them knew why you were going or that they shouldn't say anything."

"I guess it doesn't matter," she said, thinking out loud. "I'll have to call Vey once I've made contact with Jessa in the next day or two, anyway."

"Just watch your back. When is she supposed to arrive?"

"In three days it looks like. I couldn't determine the exact time so I'll have to keep a check on the port. I might wait until the next day so I won't have to make several trips or calls."

"All right. Now, tell me what happened." His voice was firm, indicating he would brook no more half truths, and she smiled at its familiar tone.

She began by telling him there was no need to worry, that she was all right. She told the whole story as she knew it. When it was done, Grayson remained silent for a moment. First, he asked if her wound had been properly tended to. She assured him that her rescuers had access to all of the latest medical supplies that it had required.

"Watch out for those two who rescued you," he said at last. "They might be as dangerous as the two who attacked you."

"I will."

"And the assassin who got away might not have given up. Members of the League rarely do."

"I know."

"Is there no way to go to the police there?"

"It could make getting to the princess while she's here more difficult. I might even have to tell them who she is or something. I want to keep this as uncomplicated as possible."

"I'll do some checking here and see if I can figure out who might have sent them. Take all the precautions you can against a second attempt."

She grinned.

"I will, Father."

"You better. If not, I just might have to come there and kick some ass myself."

"Oh, you and your antiquated sayings."

He chuckled. "They always come back into style, my child. I'd better disconnect. I mean it, though. Take care."

"I promise. Let me know if you find out anything."

He promised he would, and the line went dead. Hungry again, or maybe still, she commed for dinner to be brought up. When she hung up the handset, she noticed the netsuke lying on the bedside table. She picked it up. The coolness of the small figure felt good in her hand. While she waited for room service, she checked it over to see if it had been damaged in the fight.

The first thing that had occurred to her while still talking to Grayson was that Spohn and Turner could not have been sent from Glory since they would not have known where she was bound until after she left. Her route was the fastest for at least the next three weeks. Unless, of course, they came on a fast, private ship.

They could have been working somewhere nearer to Caldera, and a commercial ship from there might have gotten them here before her. If they really did work for some agency, that was entirely possible.

The more difficult question was who would have sent them. If one assumed that Vey really did have the emperor's interests at heart, he was not a candidate. At present, she had no way of knowing the prime minister's loyalties. Although loyal to the imperial house herself, she never had been political, leaving that to others. Her role had always been as a warrior, protecting that house, those politics. Actually, when she stopped to think about it, it did not matter who sat on the throne, as long as he—or she—had a legitimate right to be there.

A knock on the door ended further speculation.

"Who is it?" she called from the bed.

"Room service."

"A moment."

Slowly, Arden stood and slipped on the brightly striped caftan that had been lying across the foot of the bed. Just as slowly, she walked to the chair and retrieved her sword—something she should have done earlier, she told herself. The distance from there to the door was shorter, but seemed to take as long to cover.

Shielding the sword and herself behind the door, she unlocked it and pulled it open. A young man in a waiter's uniform stood in the hallway. She invited him in, holding the sword behind her. He set the tray on the table near the window and handed her the check board and stylus for her to sign the bill. She asked him to hold it while she signed, explaining that she had hurt her left arm. Once he was gone, she sat at the table and ate. The wound in her side ached, distracting her from the question of Turner and Spohn, and she concentrated on moving the fork from plate to mouth.

She grew tired before she was full, pulled off her caftan, and slipped back into bed, making sure that the katana was near to hand on the nightstand. In moments she was fast asleep.

Arden woke with a start. A noise somewhere nearby had wakened her out of a dream. Sweat dampened her skin and bedclothes. She tried to listen, but her heart hammered in her ears. She told herself to relax. She shivered, pulled the second pillow to her, and hugged it tightly.

There it was. A light tapping on the door. She slid from the bed, crouched beside it, feeling for and finding the sword lying on the nightstand. The door slid open a crack, admitting a long sliver of yellow light. Still crouching, she moved to stand behind the door and raised the sword over her head.

Concentrate on the shadow cast by the intruder and the arm reaching through. At the end of the arm a pistol pointed toward the bed. She brought the blade down, cutting through the forearm. The gun fired. The man screamed. The severed limb dropped to the floor, twitched, the hand still clutching the gun. A body fell against the door with a thump.

Footsteps pounded through the hall in a matter of seconds, getting louder as people rushed toward her room. Hotel security coming to punish the fool who disturbed the other guests, who were curious now to see if anyone had been killed.

Arden returned to the bed and sat down. A pair of hands pushed the door fully open. The would-be assassin moaned. A uniformed hotel security guard entered her room. Arden touched the light panel, and soft light bathed the scene before her, yet leaving her in shadow.

She lay the sword on the nightstand, letting the hilt slam down, so no one wondered where the weapon was. The approaching security man's jaw muscles twitched under the skin. He looked unhappy and, since the assassin was in no condition for abuse, he might think she would do as a target for his anger. He stopped short, however, when she stood up. His jaw dropped momentarily as he realized that she was naked except for a bandage on her side.

From the foot of the bed she retrieved the caftan and pulled it over her head. Then she walked to the closet and pulled her identity disc from the pocket of her brown travel jacket. She handed it to the guard who seemed to be only then remembering why he was there.

While he studied the disc, a commotion rose in the hall and a second security guard, who must have entered the room while her back was turned, moved away to see what was going on. He disappeared for only a moment, returning with another man in a constable's uniform. The new arrival headed straight for the man holding her ID disc.

"Miss Grenfell," the guard said after referring again to her disc. "This is Constable Harris."

At last, she was meeting the man whose name she had heard so often. Arden nodded to the newcomer, wondering at the same time if it was the uniform or the selection process that made all men of the law look so much alike. Maybe it was the lifestyle: moving every five years, losing wives and children because families cannot manage to remain together on inhospitable worlds.

The security guard handed the disc to Harris and stepped back against the wall out of the way.

"Miss Grenfell, what is your home world?" Harris asked.

He looked over fifty years old, but that could have been an illusion brought on by the exhaustion evident in his eyes. Frontier constables were notoriously honest but hard-nosed.

They had to be to control the goings-on so distant from centralized control and discipline.

"My home is on Glory."

"Never heard of it." He looked back at the disc.

She shrugged. Not many people from other places had heard of it, and those who knew of the place thought of it as the world always at war with its neighbors. A few others knew it as the world that used more lifeweave than any other. It was a cinch that very few people on Caldera used lifeweave.

"Do you know the man who was trying to get in?" Harris motioned toward the door.

"I haven't even seen his face yet," she replied, although she felt sure it was the man who had escaped the night before.

"Perhaps you had better take a look, then."

Arden shrugged and moved toward the door. A medic stepped out of the way. The would-be assassin lay unconscious on the carpeted floor of the corridor. The severed part of his left arm was wrapped in cloths and had been placed on the stretcher that waited on the other side of the hall. The cut was clean, so they should have no difficulty reattaching it. The sleeve on his good arm had been torn up to his shoulder by the medic, revealing a lilac tattoo on the upper arm. Another League assassin. Thus far, it would be hard to call him a professional. He was a small man who could sneak in and out of crowds and hotels.

"I've never seen him before," she said.

She turned back into her room and took a seat on the sofa.

"Why would he be trying to kill you?"

"How do you know he was trying to kill anyone? Or that it was me he was after?"

"That gun isn't the kind used by thieves or for self-protection. It's an assassin's gun, and he bears the mark of the Assassins' League. I think you know that."

After two attempts on her life she could certainly recognize the type of gun. She also knew that officials would only get in her way as they tried to find out who was behind the attempts.

"I do," she answered coolly. "I know a lot about weapons." She picked up her sword. The man's blood was already drying on the blade. "I carry this at all times, and I'm an expert with it. I also know how to use numerous kinds of guns."

He showed no reaction as he made notes on the handheld sensor screen.

"As for the choice of target," he went on, "their assassins don't make mistakes like killing the wrong person."

That certainly was a given if all she had ever heard about the League was true. But, so far, the ones sent after her had not been very good at their jobs.

"Do you plan on staying in Vega City long?"

"Oh, I want to see more of the volcanoes and such. A few more days."

"Can we expect any more such incidents?"

"I don't know, Mr. Harris." True enough. "If you're wondering if I need a bodyguard, the answer is no, I do not. I can take care of myself in most cases and I will not have anyone else placed in danger on my account." If only she felt as confident as she sounded.

"Nevertheless, we will keep an eye on you, Miss Grenfell. For your own protection, of course."

Of course, she thought. *And to see if you can find out anything.* Not to worry, though. She knew how to give people the slip when necessary. Except for lilac-tattooed members of the Assassins' League. Not much luck in that respect so far.

Harris asked more routine questions, then went silent as he studied the notes he had already made. With a request to let him know anything else she might think of, he left. The night manager of the hotel entered just as everyone else was leaving. Maids had arrived earlier and between them and the guards, the mess was being cleaned up, the manager said. He apologized for the lax security and told her that another room was being readied for her if she would care to move.

Security was being strengthened, he explained as he escorted her up the elevator to the fifteenth floor. A guard was already posted outside the door when they arrived at room 1557.

The manager opened the door, apologized for the lax security once more, handed her the key, and departed. The new room was identical to the one she had left. She looked at her bags and decided to put things away tomorrow. Alone at last, she poured a small drink from the decanter provided by the hotel. The smooth Calderan brandy warmed her from the inside and, in a few minutes, calmed the jitters that had settled in her stomach. The bedcovers warmed her from the outside as she slid between them.

Sleep evaded her in spite of the brandy. At quiet times like this, fear and doubt beat at her confidence, and she remembered all the things her father used to say. Right then, he would say that she was not handling this task as well as she should, but she was only a woman, after all. It certainly was becoming more complicated.

Then there were the dreams about Pac Terhn, her cell, the man in the lifeweave square she had not yet met, and often about Jessa. They had come unexpectedly, while she was still en route to Caldera. Some nights, they robbed her of sleep, sapped her strength. Worse, they raised even more doubt about her ability to carry this whole thing off.

Worries and memories came one after the other. Push them away. Relax. Listen to the silence. Sleep.

The sky was barely light when she awoke, sitting up in bed. Sometime while she slept she had taken the loom and a yank of lifeweave from the bedside table. It lay in her lap, wound with another completed square.

Tears welled up, flowed down her cheeks. Lyona was dead. Arden had seen that in a vision, in a dream, whatever had come to her in the dark.

She reached for the light switch on the console beside her bed. The fingers of her other hand still clutched the loom. She brought it under the light from the lamp, studying the pattern that shone in rainbow colors, and in colors that were invisible to her. Perhaps her mind could still detect the latter. Perhaps her mind built something into the pattern that was not really there.

Whatever the reason, Lyona's face, eyes closed in death, shone from the square. Behind her, a figure stood, hovering protectively.

Arden stood still, arms extended, wrists poised, shinai balanced in the air. For an hour she had been practicing with the bamboo sword made specifically for that purpose. Being lighter, it did not make the same demands on her arm and shoulder strength that the katana did, in deference to the wound that was slowly returning to normal.

She pulled the shinai back into the rest position, took the mandatory five steps backward, bowed, squatted on her heels, and placed the shinai in the scabbard position. Arden sat back and closed her eyes. She was so tired. The alley incident had sapped her energy and made it impossible to practice for two days.

And now, practice helped get rid of the anger roused by Constable Harris on his second visit. He wasn't happy about the occurrence of a second altercation involving her. How he had heard about the first one was anyone's guess.

"People are trying to kill you and you have no idea why?" he had bellowed when she answered his question.

"Don't you think *I* would like to know?" she said.

"It doesn't seem so."

For a few minutes, he had sat quietly in the chair he'd pulled up to the small table. Dirty breakfast dishes waited on the tray at one side to be picked up by room service. His mustache nearly bristled as he resumed berating her for endangering herself by not reporting the first attack.

"I could have assigned a deputy to stay with you," he

said angrily. "That would have prevented this from happening."

"If it will make you feel any better, Mr. Harris, I am in the process of employing some private security. Perhaps that will ease your mind and make things easier on your deputies."

"I thought you said last night you didn't need any bodyguard."

"I did. However, if you insist, I would prefer one of my own choosing."

"Like who?"

"Jackson Turner."

"Never heard of him."

He knew about the attack in the alley but not the names of the people who rescued her?

"He has apparently been working here on Caldera for a short time for one of the mining companies. He finished that job recently and has been waiting for a ship to take him and his partner off."

"I'll be checking up on him," Harris said, making it sound more like a threat than a promise. "What's his partner's name?"

"Spohn Bryce."

He wrote both names down on the sensor screen.

"If things don't work out with those two, you let me know," he ordered. "I'll assign a deputy to you. Meanwhile, book passage on a ship out of here."

He stood up, indicating the matter was settled.

"As soon as possible," she had agreed.

All she needed was one of his men following her around for the next few days. They might just decide to interfere if Jessa decided she did not want to go home.

Hiring Turner as a personal bodyguard might not be a bad idea. However, she wanted nothing to do with Spohn. When she and Turner stopped by earlier that morning, the feeling of distrust had been as strong as the first time. His surprise at the night's events had seemed genuine; hers had not. Of course, that feeling could be a result of her suspicions rather than any real reaction from the woman.

Maybe the only way to know about the two detectives was to consult with Pac Terhn. Arden shuddered at the idea. Each meeting left her with greater emotional tension than the last, not to mention a slight hangover from the effects of the lifeweave. There were questions, too. Questions about her supposed control within the visions, and about the long-term effects she might suffer. Lyona's helplessness, her blindness, and her death always became significant each time Arden woke with the loom in her hands.

The comm signaled and Arden answered the call. Jackson Turner was on the other end.

"I'm downstairs," he said. "Would you care to join me for dinner?"

"In the dining room here?"

"Yes."

"Sure. Give me a few minutes."

She checked herself in the mirror. Her hair was growing out again; she might have to get it cut before leaving Caldera. A glance at the katana. It probably was not considered polite to carry a sword to dinner, but after the two assassination attempts no one could fault her for being careful. If this visit lasted much longer, it might be wise to check into getting a gun of some kind. Too many other people seemed to have one, and a sword was hardly an adequate defense against them.

She slung the strap over her head and across her shoulder, resting the scabbard against her back. It felt good and natural to have it there.

Stepping into the hall, she first locked the door, then checked both ways. The elevator car arrived and she got in. It took her smoothly to the lobby floor, from where she made her way to the dining room. Turner had already gotten a table, and he waved to get her attention.

"I didn't know what you wanted to drink," he said as she sat down.

"Calderan brandy is fine," she said as she removed the sword and set it against the table beside her chair.

He waved the waiter over and ordered brandy for her and whisky for himself.

"I just can't believe that a world such as this can possibly produce grapes that would make a fine brandy," he said as they waited. "Or a good wine even."

"It really is quite good," she said. "Thank you for the invitation, by the way."

"You're quite welcome. I thought it might do you good to get out of that room for a bit. How is the side?"

"A little tender but healing quickly. I'm glad you had that medical kit."

"I always carry one. You never know when it might come in handy."

"You must travel with a load of stuff."

He laughed. "Yes, I suppose I do. But the company pays the expenses, so it's no problem for me."

His voice hit that chord inside her as they talked about his travels. She had heard it before, or one very much like it, but no recollection would come beyond that. It must have been many years ago, and probably did not matter. It was probably someone with a voice quite like his. She tried to shrug it off mentally, but could not quite.

Their drinks came, and they ordered dinner. The brandy burned slightly going down, leaving a warm glow in its wake, relaxing muscles that always seemed too tight anymore.

"Where is Spohn?" she asked.

"She said she had things to do and would eat later."

"Have you worked with her before?"

"No, this is the first time. I never met her before." He looked at her sideways. "I get the feeling that you don't like her very much."

Arden shrugged. "I don't have any feelings either way. I guess she does make me a little uneasy."

She deliberately changed the subject, turning it to his exploits on a myriad of worlds. It was easy to envy him the adventures that he described so casually. She had always thought herself content with her life as a soldier on Glory, but that was because she knew of so little else. At least in part. The realization hit her that if Jessa returned with her, her life would not change. Pac Terhn would hold her to their agreement.

Dinner arrived, and they talked more as they ate. Turner asked her questions about her life and her reason for being on Caldera, but she dodged most of them. She did describe her life in the monastery. He thought it must have been very odd to be the only female there most of the time, and she agreed it was.

The waiter came to take away their dishes. They ordered another drink each and sat back, sated and comfortable.

"I guess I never really learned how to be a woman," she mused. "I learned to be a warrior and how to meditate in the monastery. Later, I learned to be . . ." She had started to say, "to be loyal to the imperial house," but thought better of it. Turner raised an eyebrow as he waited for her to continue.

"You seem woman enough to me," he said after a time. She felt herself blush. "With some it just comes naturally."

Her face grew hotter. It would be best to end this discussion before it went any further.

"I thank you for dinner," she said. "Right now, I think I could use a good night's sleep. I have work to do tomorrow."

He stood as she did and suddenly took her hand in his.

"Thank you for joining me," he said.

"It was my pleasure," she said, barely managing not to stutter. It had been such a long time since there had been any need to observe the rules of polite society. "Thank you for asking me. Good night."

She slid her hand loose and nearly dashed for the elevators. No man had ever held her hand quite like that, nor looked into her eyes as if seeking the depths of her soul. In a few minutes, she stepped into the hallway on her floor. No sign of anyone. She took the magnetic key from her pocket and silently unlocked her door. As it opened a crack, she had the impression that things were not as she had left them. Her hand reached over her shoulder for the hilt of the sword, and she eased the door open a bit farther.

The light was turned low. A figure stood before the built-in storage chest, and one of the drawers was pulled out slightly. There was a familiarity about the figure and in the way it moved.

Arden slipped through, pushing the door nearly closed. She stayed between the figure and outer door, blocking any escape.

"Can I help?"

The figure whirled, blonde hair wrapping around to one side. Spohn crouched tensely. In her hands the small bundle of fabric squares nearly opened.

"Put them back." Making the words come out cold and hard was no problem. She was prepared to take the bundle away if necessary. Too much time and effort had gone into collecting them.

"What are they?"

Of all the nerve! Someone caught stealing asking for an explanation of the booty.

"They're mine."

"What are they made of?" Spohn persisted.

"Lifeweave."

"The most expensive fabric in existence. Few can afford it, but you have a supply for your amusement. At least people from Glory have heard of it."

"Then you know where I come from?"

Spohn smiled then. "Of course. Why do you think I've been hanging around?"

"You were waiting for me?"

Now the uneasiness and mistrust were justified. It had been the sense of the woman lying in wait that had been under the surface all the time.

"For several days. It turned out to be easier to get close to you than we anticipated."

"You and Turner," Arden said. Spohn nodded. "Did you set up the attack in the bar?"

"No. We didn't have to. You have attracted strong opposition with this quest of yours."

Arden stepped closer, held out her hand for the bundle, and Spohn handed it toward her. She certainly was being cooperative.

"Who opposed it so much that they sent you?" She took the bundle and slipped it under her belt.

"I can't tell you that. It would be unethical."

"How much do you know about what I'm looking for?"

Spohn grinned again. "As much as you do. Are you going to tell the police about this?"

"Not if you promise to go back where you came from."

"Think you can trust me?" She stood.

"No. I guess not." Arden circled around toward the bedside table and reached for the comm. The katana did not waiver.

"I can't let you do that, I'm afraid."

Spohn stood up. The gun in her hand emphasized her words. One moment it wasn't there, the next it was.

"What now?" Arden asked.

"I can accomplish my assignment by killing you as well as any other way."

"And that assignment is?"

"From where I stand, there's no need for you to know that."

"Arden?" Turner called from the hallway.

The door banged open and he stepped inside. For an instant, Spohn's eyes shifted toward him. Arden dropped and rolled, knocking Spohn's feet from under her. The gun fired as it flew out of her hand, the beam hitting the wall above Jackson's head.

"Shit!" he said, and dove for the corner.

The gun lay on the floor. Arden lunged for it on all fours. Spohn kicked out, catching Arden in the side. The blow caught the earlier wound and she collapsed from the pain. Gasping, she looked up from the floor in time to see Spohn disappear through the doorway. Turner sat on his rump to the right of the door, looking dazed.

Arden got to her feet, holding her side with one hand and picking up the sword with the other.

"At least *you* can talk to the police," she said.

Security sent two men in answer to her call, took her statement, and hauled Turner away. The hotel manager appeared again, looking more than a little upset. This was, after all, the second time she had been the center of violence in his establishment.

Eventually, everyone was gone, including Constable Harris who promised to return. She surveyed the events of the past few days. The lifeweave squares were nearly stolen. The thief got away, but her apparent partner was in the local lockup. Half of the hotel's staff had seen her naked. The local constable saw her as the cause of too much violence and just might lock her up for everyone else's safety, if not her own.

Soon, she had to go to the port and see if the *Starbourne* had arrived yet. She could only hope that the rest of her mission would go more smoothly.

It was nearly one in the morning when a knock came on her door. She slid out of the bed, sword in hand. No way was she going to believe that a friend had come calling in the middle of the night.

6

The *Starbourne* limped along the edge of the planet's atmosphere. The thrusters had been damaged by the sudden eruption, as well as other parts of the ship, and they had barely been able to get even that high. Without the air resistance, and probable winds, the ship was easier to control, although without much speed. At this rate, it was going to take all of three days at least to reach Vega City, a trip that would normally require only a day.

Jessa and Tahr were doing most of the work of keeping her moving, while Liel oversaw everything, giving advice and coordinating between the bridge and maintenance. Vida had her hands full trying to hold it all together.

Rafe found himself remembering the two downed Glorian ships a little too often. A natural worrier, he needed to be active to forestall too much thinking. Now there was nothing for him to do except worry and encourage the crew he had hired for their proven expertise. *Let them do their jobs*, he told himself over and over. *That's why you hired them. Remember?*

For the past ten minutes, he and Liel had sat talking in his cabin. There were other problems that they needed to prepare for.

"We could tell the authorities nothing," Liel was saying.

"There's a good chance the ships will never be found."

"Except the scout ship did contact its base," Rafe said, bringing his attention back to the conversation. "We have to assume that Lan gave them our ident numbers at least. If they were thinking of accusing us of piracy then, what will they do once the second ship doesn't report back?"

"What good will it do for us to tell anyone in Vega City? Hell, we'll be in and out of there so fast they won't have time to get any feedback on us."

"Maybe. But if they do get feedback, and we've been up front with them, we might get them to ignore any report they get."

They sat in silence a moment. It could become a ticklish situation. At least they had the ship's tapes showing the extent to which they had endangered the *Starbourne* in their efforts to rescue any survivors from the scout ship. However, that came after they were ordered to land. That was on the tapes too.

And there was the lifeweave. Millions of credits worth.

"We'll have to tell them about the first ship," he said. "Why else would we have been on the other side of Caldera when the ship was damaged?"

Liel sighed. "That's true," he said. "That kind of hull damage wouldn't happen out in space unless we were attacked by another ship. That might be even harder to explain."

"We'll play it by ear regarding the scout ship. If the port authorities ask to see our tapes, we'll have to tell them the whole story."

"At least Vega City is pretty wide open. This is still something of a frontier world. The one thing in our favor."

"Yeah," Rafe said as he stood up and stretched his arms up toward the ceiling. "We might be able to grease some palms. We certainly can afford it."

Liel grinned. "You got that right," he said. "For once in our careers, we don't have to bring our own profits up short to pay someone off. It's a nice feeling."

"Sure is." Rafe shook his head. "Wouldn't you know it, though? Our first really big strike and we've got more trouble than we can handle."

"Maybe. But it's a fact that the amount of work to achieve something is in direct proportion to the size of the reward."

"And who told you that?"

"My daddy."

"Ah," Rafe said. "The pauper philosopher."

"The only kind a drunk can be."

The captain nodded. He had heard the story of Liel's youth, at least the high—or perhaps the low—points. Since he had grown up with so little, it was no wonder that his exec was so mercenary. It was just one of the factors that made Liel good at the business he was in. Rafe's own past was quite different, but nonetheless as good a one to push a person into picking up what those who were better off had lost—then thumbing his nose at them when they complained. Once in a while the opportunity presented itself for even ransoming the found goods, something that irritated the original owners even more.

His own father had been aggressively ambitious until other more powerful interests took everything he had. Something he did not want to think about at present, and he closed down the memory before it reached the vision of William Semmes's leap from the tenth-floor window.

"Let's check on the bridge," he said, and opened the door.

Liel stood up behind him and followed down the hall. The *Starbourne* lurched, throwing both of them against the wall. If the ship did not hold together, worrying about what to report in Vega City would be a waste of energy.

The terminal was incredibly quiet at midnight. The one on Glory was busy at all hours. People coming and going on business and for pleasure. Military people heading for their postings on one of the moons or outlying worlds. Diplomats and other government representatives coming and going. The crowds made it very easy to get lost, to avoid detection, to slip in and out at will.

Spohn walked through the main terminal as if she belonged there. Down a long hallway, then through a door to the tarmac, and she could see the ship she wanted. Turner's ship, right where he left it.

She had come to Caldera on a Glorian scout ship. It let her off in Vega City, then went in search of a cargo transport that had been lost in the sector. Captain Lan had never told her what the transport carried, but if it was important enough to send another ship to look for it, the cargo could only be one thing: lifeweave. As far as the Glorian government was concerned, it was just about the most important commodity these days.

Well, that was going to change. Even Turner did not know that.

When she was ordered from duty on Dubbins to this backwater, she was told to contact Jackson Turner of the Wilson Detective Agency. Had they thought she would not recognize him? They probably did not worry about that. She was a soldier, accustomed to obeying orders and not asking questions.

They met three days before Arden arrived. He had used his own personal runabout, fast and sleek, that had brought him from another world closer than Glory. She had not let on that she knew who he really was, but he probably expected that possibility, although not everyone from Glory would have. Right now, he was probably mystified by her actions.

The attack on Arden had been more fortuitous than they could have expected. What an opportunity to get in her good graces. So far, though, she had not been able to find out who sent the assassins. They had certainly wasted their money. Had the League thought Arden would be so easy to dispose of? That might have been true had she and Turner not intervened, but it was just as possible that Arden would have taken care of things without help. If it had not been for Arden's wounded side, Spohn might not have escaped herself.

Unfortunately, it was all ruined. Turner must not be quite the romancer he thought he was. He might have tried harder, though, if the search of Arden's room had been his idea. All she had needed was a few more minutes and the search would have been finished. As it was, she found nothing to tell her exactly when contact with Princess Jessa was to take place.

Getting out of the hotel and to the port had proved easy enough. Word had not gotten to the port authorities, as far as she could tell. Spohn hurried to the little ship dwarfed by its neighbors. Picking the lock would be no problem; she had managed more difficult ones. Marooning him here might actually give her and her people more time to decide on another course of action. This was one battle they did not intend to lose.

Making her way across the tarmac, Spohn had to hide once from a guard patrolling the area in a three-wheeled scooter. As she suspected, picking the lock took only a few minutes. She climbed inside and its systems turned on as the computer sensed her presence.

"Unauthorized entry," the computer announced.

"Override 'Echo Tango eight seven five,' " she said.

The computer paused, then said, "Password."

"Parcq."

"Password recognized. Computer standing by."

"Hmph."

He had not changed his password in more than six months. He might be very intelligent and have all the latest in technology, but it did not do him one damn bit of good if he couldn't follow security protocol.

She took the pilot's seat and began initiating systems both with voice commands and activating switches. Only when every other system was on line would she activate the engines, thus delaying notice by the tower. At last, the time came. The engines roared, warmed, and she pushed the levers forward slowly. Suddenly, the comm sounded.

"Alpha Baker Charlie, you are not cleared for takeoff."

A pause as the ship rose slightly.

"Alpha Baker Charlie, liftoff from the parking tarmac is not authorized. Loss of license will result if you persist."

As the runabout rose higher, she could imagine the scorching of nearby ship surfaces.

Sorry, fellas, Spohn thought. *No time for proper authorizations this time.*

"Alpha Baker Charlie, if you persist we will be forced to fire on your ship."

That they would not do as long as she was near other ships. Falling on them would result in numerous lawsuits for damage. As long as she stayed directly over the parking area, they would take no action. That is, until she was high enough that falling debris would cause less damage. By then, she planned to hurry out of the way.

She checked the altimeter. Just over five hundred feet. No time like the present. Quickly, she entered coordinates into the computer, took a deep breath, and activated high-speed acceleration. The engines roared. Below, a mid-sized ship tipped to one side. The skins of several ships blistered. The blast burst against the ships, breaking antennas, plastiglass windows and shields, and rattling hulls and hatches.

A small fighter ship came into view just as she made the jump into hyperspace. It disintegrated in the backwash.

7

Turner's eyes widened when the sword point nearly touched his throat. He spread his arms out to his sides, showing empty hands.

"What the hell are you doing here?"

He smiled. "I wanted to let you know that the constable released me."

"Why?"

"He's satisfied that I had nothing to do with Spohn searching your room. The fact that she stole my runabout pretty much convinced him."

"You had your own ship here?"

The blade did not waver. With that lie exposed, her inclination was to slit his throat and let the constable clean up the mess.

"It actually belonged to the agency," he said, "but she knew about it. Apparently, she went into hyperspace before she'd even cleared the atmosphere, and nearly wiped out half of the ships on the parking tarmac. The whole port has been shut down for the time being."

"Shut down? Nothing in or out?"

"Could I come in? It's probably not a good idea to be discussing this out in the hall."

He certainly had nerve. However, he was right about that

one thing. She let the sword point fall slightly and backed up, keeping it directed toward him. He stepped inside.

"Have a seat," she told him.

He moved to the table and sat down in one of the chairs. She stood just out of his reach, strongly inclined not to trust him, maybe to even send him on his way. If she did that, however, she would always be looking over her shoulder to see if he was sneaking up on her.

"Look," he said. "I never met Spohn before we got here. I had nothing to do with her searching your room. I was told to keep an eye on you after I finished my original assignment. Spohn was supposed to have been sent by the agency. She had all the proper I.D. *And* I saved your life in that alley."

"Or nearly cost me my life," she reminded him.

"You have to admit that it was damned dark." She nodded. "So, the possibility that I could not see who was doing what is pretty strong. Right?"

"Right."

Although the argument about his saving her life was a very strong one, the one about having him where she could keep an eye on him was stronger.

"What do you suggest we do?" she asked.

"Tell me why you're here. Why someone sent assassins after you. Let me work with you."

"Why would you want to do that?"

"Well, for one thing, I don't have a way off this hunk of rock now. My runabout is gone. The port is closed down, and no one knows how long it will take to clear the damaged ships. In other words, I don't have much else to do for the next few days and I have a vested interest in making sure no one shoots you in the back."

The part about having nothing to do seemed more in character than wanting to protect his investment, in spite of his having saved her before. It would not do, however, to tell him much about the reason she was on Caldera. Just enough, maybe, to make him think she was beginning to trust him.

After a pause, she sheathed the sword and laid it across the far side of the table. Sitting down opposite him, she began telling him a little about herself, starting with the fact that she was from Glory.

"I was sent here to meet someone. I can't tell you who or why, but it is very important."

"Are you part of the imperial guard or something?"

"Why do you ask that?"

"Well, the sword, for one thing. Most civilians don't walk around with a weapon like that, even in wide-open places like Vega City here. One like that katana of yours does attract a lot of attention. A little above what an ordinary soldier would carry, wouldn't you say?"

That was true enough. Yet she hesitated to admit even that much. Instead, she told him that she was an ordinary officer fortunate enough to have inherited the sword that had been in her family for generations.

"I do want to go out to the port tomorrow and see if the ship I'm expecting has come in," she said. "I'm not exactly sure when it was due."

"As I told you, nothing is coming or going right now."

"I need to check anyway in case it landed just before Spohn made her getaway. Do you want to come along?"

He nodded. They talked more about what they might expect to happen at the port and what they might need. Before she knew it, talk had turned more personal, mostly on his part. He began by telling her about his assignment on Caldera and what he had learned about its officialdom. He started backtracking, comparing this assignment to others he'd had. When she reached up to rub the side of her neck, he came behind her and massaged the stiffness out of it. His hands moved to her shoulders, kneading, bringing warmth to the surface there. And elsewhere.

The intimacy of his touch made her self-conscious and she considered asking him to stop, but it felt so good. Every aspect of it. The feel of his hands, strong but tender. The warmth that was both relaxing and arousing. It had been such a long time since Arden had experienced intimacy.

"Lie down on the bed and I'll rub your back," he said.

She did so without hesitation. Her body relaxed under his ministrations. Her mind raced loosely around the reasons she should be wary. Most of those came down to the fact that she did not trust him. Letting him get too close to her would not be wise, maybe dangerous. But it had been so long and he was so handsome and had such wonderful hands. And she had always been attracted to dangerous men.

As his hands began to touch more intimate places, she moaned and let loose the doubts, drifting along the waves of passion. He proceeded slowly and tenderly. Before long, both of them were undressed and he was lying beside her. Even though she wanted to shout for him to hurry, she let him set the pace. Let him control the ebb and flow until at last their passions exploded together. Thinking she was more sated than she had ever been, she drifted slowly into sleep, every bit of tension gone.

Just before dawn, Turner slipped from the bed and started dressing. She raised up on one elbow and watched in the dim light. His was a nearly perfect body, made for pleasure, or so it seemed at the moment.

"I'm going to get some sleep before I shower and change clothes," he said when he was ready to go. I'll meet you in the dining room for breakfast at, say, nine."

"Okay," she agreed. "I have a rented rover in the garage. We'll take that out to the port."

"Good." Turner stepped to the side of the bed. "Anything you want me to bring?"

"Whatever you might think would be a good bribe for the port authority superintendent. I understand it is sometimes difficult to get the sort of information I'm looking for."

"I can handle that. Good night. Morning, rather." He bent down and kissed her, then moved to the door. "See you in a bit." He opened the door and was gone.

Arden lay awake for some time, going over the events of the past few days several times. Nothing had occurred to make her trust Turner; in fact, quite the contrary. Yet what had happened between them tonight seemed right. It had not changed her mind about him, but she did hope there would be more nights like this one.

Clamped into the repair bay, the *Starbourne* looked like a trapped animal. The aft burn pods were blackened by heat not their own; small bits of cooled lava clung to the titanium skin.

Rafe, his inspection complete, returned to the control office. Williams, the port repair supervisor, handed over the damage list his own crew had worked up.

"That doesn't include anything on the inside of the ship," Williams reminded.

Rafe nodded. Liel would supervise Tahr, Owen, and Vida in repairing the wiring and guidance systems. No use in giving strangers access to the ship and, possibly, spreading the word about the cargo. It was bad enough they had to dock in the first place.

Bad luck or no, they'd been luckier than the Glorians. Luckier than the poor sods whose ships were destroyed or badly damaged on the ground by the escaping fugitive that Williams had told him about. None of those ships had made it to the repair yard yet. Workmen still had to separate them from one another, insurance companies had to survey the damage, checks had to be issued, before any of them would be repaired. Clearly, some of them were beyond that.

As he had waited for the inspection of his own ship, he had walked through the parking tarmac, as well as he could. Much of the area was unapproachable, the paths blocked by large chunks of metal and polymers. His timing could have been a lot worse as far as getting the *Starbourne* scheduled for repairs. As it was, work would begin on it within the next day or two.

When they arrived over the city, things had not looked quite so positive. The port authority had at first refused them permission to land because of the disaster. Once the damage to their own ship had been fully described, however, permission had been given.

The debate with himself and Liel over telling anyone about the crashed scout ship had continued, even though, as captain, the decision was his. Liel's perspective was always from a skewed angle, and he had contended that people might become too curious, especially bureaucrats who usually made something out of nothing. But what if someone had survived? The crash had occurred only three days ago, after all. It was possible.

Not likely, according to Liel. There were no life signs from the ship and, while they watched from the *Starbourne*, lava had surrounded its metal victim, rising to nearly one-fourth of the ship's height. The heat alone was deadly, not to mention the sulphur fumes.

Just before docking, Liel had changed his mind when he was reminded that, if the authorities were notified, the wreck technically belonged to the *Starbourne* for the next year, and they could someday return to salvage whatever else might be aboard. It would be a good idea to notify port authorities, he decided. Then it turned out that no one showed much interest. They had experienced their own disaster, and that of the *Starbourne* and its crew just was not important enough for anyone to ask many questions.

"Will anyone be checking out the Glorian ship?" Rafe asked the supervisor.

Williams shook his head. "Not much chance anyone survived. And if the lava rose as high as you said, most anything of value will be melted by now. Or so deeply embedded in cooled lava it wouldn't be cost effective for regular salvage."

Liel would either be disappointed by that fact or challenged by it. No use telling him; he'd figure it out for himself eventually.

Before heading into town, Rafe called the ship. The first officer reported that repairs were proceeding slowly and they might stay on board overnight. He'd let the captain know if they needed rooms in a hotel.

Jessa had gone ahead to find rooms for the two of them. Rafe promised to let Liel know what hotel.

"Of course, sir," Liel answered with unusual politeness.

"Make sure you know where everyone is at all times," the captain said, ignoring the grin in Liel's voice. "Let Jessa know when you need her to calibrate the navigation equipment."

He hung up, wondering why Liel suddenly assumed that some sort of flirtation existed between him and Jessa. Oh, he was just being his usual lewd self. Not that Jessa wasn't attractive.

Don't get carried away. Sure, she was nice to look at, in an otherworldly way.

He stepped into a car of the shuttle train that would take him into town. It was nearly empty, and he took a seat near the door.

Would keeping Jessa as a part of the crew prove dangerous down the line? She had shown no hesitation about possibly fighting the Glorians. If there were to be future conflicts, would she always make the same choice? He had never abandoned a member of his crew and wasn't going to start now. Neither would Liel. Mercenary though he was, the first officer didn't tolerate interference from outside. It was always a good idea to consider all the things they might come up against.

The rest of the crew were, as far as they had ever been tested, loyal to one another. Outsiders on their own worlds, their home was the ship, its walls a barrier against the rest of humankind when they wanted to shut everything out.

The train started with a jerk; then the ride smoothed out on a cushion of air. A dull hum and the passing panoramas on the outside of the windows were the only indications they were moving at a hundred miles an hour.

Rafe smiled, returning to thoughts of his crew. Even grumpy Tahr, whom nothing ever suited and who had been with them more than five years, was loyal. In fact, he, more than anyone else in the crew, had attached himself to Jessa in sort of a protective way. It had been most noticeable when they were offloading the lifeweave—not from anything Tahr did overtly, but from a sense of his watching, anticipating, in case the lifting and carrying might prove too much for her, or her foot might stray too close to a red stream of lava.

The train slowed and he rose. As he walked toward the door, he shook his head. The best thing would be for him and his crew to get on with the work and get the hell off Caldera.

As he stepped onto the platform, he saw Jessa waiting nearby. No, she did not appeal to him in the way Liel kept implying. More like a younger sister.

"Did you notice how that man kept looking at me down in the garage?" Arden asked.

She guided the rover into the sunlit street that ran beside the hotel.

"Yes."

"He certainly had more than a passing interest."

Turner laughed. "You are getting paranoid," he said. "It was pretty obvious that he found you attractive."

"I hardly think so," she said with irritation.

"You are just being paranoid," he said again.

"Is that surprising? There have been two attempts on my life since I got here."

"If you're going to survive this affair, you'd better learn the difference between danger and lust." His tone had become more serious. "I know you must be a very good soldier. In this kind of adventure, however, you have no experience. You have no idea who has sent the assassins after you. And I have no idea why you're here."

They were now on the road leading to the port. Traffic

was thin, and she accelerated. He was fishing for explanations. She started to tell him that it was not within her right to tell anyone about her mission, but he cut her off.

"I am not asking that you tell me now. However, I have offered to help you in this adventure and I intend keeping my word."

The port was several miles beyond the outskirts of the city. The land in between was planted with grapevines that might be the ones that supplied the grapes used in making the brandy she had come to enjoy so much.

"Look," he continued. "I'm a simple man. I know how to survive under most circumstances. I understand people of the low orders, if you will. I'll admit I don't know everything and most of what I do know didn't come from school. I've been doing this kind of work for a lot of years. Maybe too many."

He shook his head and averted his eyes, giving the impression he feared having said too much. She could hardly believe that he had called himself a simple man. A man whose tastes ran to the very best in clothes and food, and who flew a private ship, even if it did belong to his employer, could hardly be called that.

There was nothing she could say to any of what he said. She was grateful for his offer of help, while at the same time leery of his motives. She could not shake off his knowing Spohn and thinking they could have been working together against her in spite of the logic of his arguments, and in spite of what had happened between them.

"I can tell you that I'm here to find a woman," she said. "She is Glorian and her name is Jessa. Her family needs her to return home."

She left the reasons unspecified.

"Is there a chance she might not want to return?" he asked.

"Yes, there is."

"Are you sure she's arriving today?" Turner asked.

"Yes. Well, no. Just that she will be here today. She

could have arrived late last night or might arrive tonight."

"So, if we find someone named Jessa, how can we be sure it's her? Is the name common on Glory? I admit it's not one I've heard before, but that doesn't necessarily mean anything."

He fiddled with one of the buttons on his white linen shirt. He had worn the same outfit the first time he walked into her room, even to the soft leather boots reaching to mid-calf. Expensive stuff that looked as if he'd had them tailor-made. The way he dressed was one of the things that attracted her to him. Admitting that, even if only to herself, made her feel flustered. She could almost feel herself blush. She had best get her mind back on the conversation at hand and the task coming up.

"True," she said at last. "But how many civilians would be traveling from Glory to this sector during wartime? You know how a war economy can be. Besides, I know the name of her ship."

"You didn't tell me that."

"Didn't I?"

Arden guided the rover into the parking lot, easily found a slot near the entrance, and parked. It occurred to her that the moment had passed in which she might have learned even more about her self-appointed protector. Turning the conversation around would have been easy enough for some people. He had been right about one thing: she was not very experienced in subterfuge.

They stepped from the rover and headed for the terminal. It was nearly empty of travelers. She reminded herself to check with Constable Harris and see what he had learned about Turner's background as soon as an opportunity presented itself.

After checking the route on the map displayed on a monitor, they made their way to the port authority office quickly. Getting in to see Janet Logan, the immigration superintendent, took longer, but eventually they were seated across from her. She was slightly built, almost bony, with long, slender hands and short, flat hair of an indiscriminate brown color. Her immediate interest in Turner was clearly not of an official nature.

"Only two liners carrying passengers arrived prior to the disaster on the field," she said, barely able to take her eyes off her male visitor to check a list on the computer screen. Her voice was high-pitched and petulant. "And one salvage ship. The *Starbourne*. Let's see ... Seventy-eight passengers all together: fifty replacements for the mines, three engineers, eight new business employees, one entrepreneur ..."—she chuckled at that one—"... and six tax accountants." She sneered at the latter group, apparently without any realization that many people considered her profession on a level with tax collection.

"When did the salvage ship arrive?" Arden asked.

"Very early this morning. It suffered some kind of damage and was allowed to land. Apparently it needs extensive repairs."

"How about the crew?" Arden asked, trying not to show the growing dislike she had for this official. "Did they remain with the ship or have they gone to a hotel?"

Logan leered at Turner and checked the screen again.

"Six members. Most stayed on board. Looks like they are working on the internal damage. The captain and astronavigator went into the city. Usually we do not let crews stay on board. Our techs are very good at what they do, but with this mess we have ..."

"Might I have a printout of the crew names and whatever else you have on record?" Arden interrupted.

"We really would appreciate it," Turner added when Logan hesitated. She smiled and bobbed her head.

The printer was an older model and took nearly a minute to finish the job. No one said anything. It was amazing how easily the superintendent accepted the explanation that they were looking for someone whose father was ill on Warrick. But given the way she kept smiling at Turner, any explanation would do.

The printer stopped and Logan tore off a sheet of paper, handing it to Turner with an even broader smile. He in turn handed it to Arden, his face without expression except for a raised eyebrow.

The list contained the six names, with the name of the ship at the top.

"Thank you, Superintendent," Arden said. The two women shook hands and, when they parted, one held a twenty-five credit scrip.

"Is her name there?" Turner asked after they were seated in the rover.

"Yes, it is."

There it was, halfway down: Jessa Parcq, astronavigator. Logan had said that the astronavigator had gone into town with the captain.

How had she managed to avoid detection for so long when she used her real name?

"Well?" Turner broke in.

"Now we need to find what hotel she's staying in."

They hastened back to her room, where they took turns calling the hotels in Vega City.

"I've got her," Turner said, his hand covering the mouthpiece. "She's at the New Hilton ... Yes?" The last word was spoken into the mouthpiece. "Thank you very much."

He disconnected the line.

"She and her captain—uh, Semmes—checked in about an hour ago. Separate rooms."

Arden jumped off the bed, straightening her jumpsuit.

"Let's go talk to her."

"Just like that? Don't you think you might call first?"

"Why?"

"Clearly, she is not expecting you. You have no idea what happened to their ship. How it was damaged. It could be they are running from someone. If they don't know you, they might be spooked if we just show up."

She shrugged. Jessa should recognize her—letting the princess know her former bodyguard was here might be the very thing to spook her. Showing up abruptly, without warning, would be best.

"No, we'll do it my way," she said. "It might not be perfect, but it will be best."

"Have you considered whether or not it's to her benefit to go back?"

There was a question that scraped against raw nerves. Jessa left in the first place because staying was anathema to her. Going back would not be any more attractive. That thought was not a good one to contemplate at the moment, however.

"Yes, I have considered it," she said. "I have no choice in the matter."

He couldn't possibly understand. Although it might be easier to work it out with his help, she did not need his understanding.

"Look," she said. "If you're going to work with me, don't ask questions. I have a job to do, and I intend to get it done. If you can make it a bit easier for me, your help will be appreciated. If not, get out now and leave me to my job."

"Whoa," he said, holding up both hands, palms toward her. "I just asked. It's a bit difficult to know how to handle any of this without all the facts."

She shook her head. "It's for me to decide how to handle this. I still haven't figured out why you want to help me."

"Because I find you attractive, too."

Her head jerked around, and she looked at him for a long minute. He was alluding to the man in the garage earlier. "Of course you do," she said, putting as much sarcasm into her voice as she could.

It was not much of a mystery that he found her attractive. They had spent enough time on those feelings to reach that conclusion. However, she did not for one moment believe that he ever did anything for purely emotional reasons. She sighed. Even having him with her was not going to make keeping him under control very easy.

Jessa flopped down on the bed. A real bed at last. It seemed years since the last one. Abruptly she sat up, stopping the memories that started. Another New Hilton, on Pembroke. And again on Warrick. Jonas was hard to leave behind. Even harder to forget. They kept in touch as much as they could, but between his business and her travels, it was difficult.

Jerking open the knapsack, she dumped the contents on the bed. Civvies for a change. Just for a day or two, though. Once the others got the electronics back on line, she'd have to begin calibrating the navigation equipment. Until then . . .

She felt like partying. Go out, have a good time, and forget. Forget. Gods, would she ever forget? Preparing to fight her own people, or seeing their ship engulfed by all of that red-hot lava. It had been bad enough boarding the cargo ship and finding it was Glorian. Passing by the bodies. She might even have known some of those people. Chances were good she would not have. People who worked on cargo ships rarely had the chance to meet a princess of the blood.

At least those first four were already dead. The crew of the scout ship died almost right before her, helpless to save themselves, just as she had been helpless. Silent in their deaths, at least as far as the *Starbourne* was concerned. She and her shipmates had witnessed their dying, but, except for her, they had died alone. No one else may ever know.

She had not inherited any telepathic abilities, but she had felt their dying. Did it keep them from being so alone? Jessa had only the ability to feel others' emotions. Empathy, some called it, and all that she had inherited from Lyona.

She started shaking out the clothing one piece at a time, hanging things up, anything to stop the train of thought.

Why had she suddenly become so maudlin about Glory? She had been gone for six years and, until recently, she had never felt the slightest desire to go back. Fear of what might happen to her was enough reason to stay away. Add to that the sorrow of watching what was happening to her mother, and here she was. Almost as far away as she could get, seeking a life that would not be possible on her home world.

However, for the past month Jessa's thoughts had often turned toward home. She had wondered how Lyona fared, how many more pieces she had woven in the service of her emperor. What was the cumulative effect of all that lifeweave? Jessa hated the stuff. It had been part of her life from the day she was born. It would be part of her mother's death. It stopped there!

As much exposure as she had to it, one would think it only natural that she would develop even greater extrasensory abilities. Especially since she was her mother's daughter. But that had never happened. One very large blessing for which to be thankful.

Still, she could not shake off the uneasy thoughts of Glory and wondering what was going on there. The thoughts of home were gloomy at best, as if someone had died. And that was best kept to herself. It would not help anything to have people suddenly believe that she could know such things without being told.

She took the clip out of her hair and let the long tresses fall to her waist. How like her mother's hair when she was young. How sad to see Lyona's black hair turn to grey prematurely, those fiery eyes become dulled. How the love for a man turned to lust for—not even a drug—a costly fiber that took as much as it gave.

Why couldn't Lyona see what it was doing to her? Oh, why, Mother?

Searching through the debris from the bag, Jessa found a four-foot by three-foot piece of lifeweave. She clutched it to her breast, wanting to feel the power that drew so many to spend fortunes on it. To her senses, there was nothing. It felt soft; the colors danced as she moved it before her, holding it with both hands. This, her first baby blanket, woven by Lyona herself, before total addiction took over. Jessa had lain under it for a thousand nights or more, and her senses had never changed.

How gentle were the hands that wove the piece of cloth, how soft the voice that had soothed the crying of her only daughter. A voice never to be heard again, hands never to hold again.

Jessa rubbed one eye as she opened the door. She had fallen asleep without meaning to, and the sudden knocking on the door had startled her. Captain Semmes stood outside, his usual cheerful but wary self. He always seemed to regard his surroundings as containing a possible threat. However, he did not comment on her sleepiness.

"Liel called," he said without preamble. "He and a couple of the others decided to come into town for dinner. Tahr is staying on board to keep an eye on things. Where would you like to eat?"

"I wouldn't know," she answered and yawned. "I've never been in Vega City before."

"Maybe the desk clerk can give us an idea."

She nodded agreement. Both were silent as the elevator glided from the twelfth floor to the lobby. Rafe kept fluttering the forefinger and middle finger together on his left hand, a habit of long standing when there was nothing for him to do but wait.

It was a strong hand—medium-sized and solid like the rest of him. A few dark brown hairs grew on the back of his hands, darker than the hair on his head. No warning there of the temper that occasionally flared. She had always suspected, however, that the temper was used to good effect more than being an uncontrolled reaction.

Yes, the captain was a controlled individual, for the most part. A man of good common sense, rumor was that he had learned to pilot a ship in some merchant service. That was where he and Liel had met. One was supposed to have saved the other's life during some unspecified adventure. Somehow she suspected that might have worked both ways, and more than once.

Part of his swagger probably came from the fact that he wasn't very tall. Shorter men tend to compensate. But she liked a man she could look directly in the eye.

Better stop that line of thought. It smacked of romance, something for which she had little time and no wish to start up. Especially with her captain. That could lead to all kinds of complications. And, truth to tell, she was not attracted to Semmes in spite of his being the type she usually was drawn to. That could be due to the age difference. More likely it was because her feelings led to someone else.

The door opened, and they stepped from the elevator. Halfway across the lobby, Semmes slowed for a moment and stared at a woman seated a few feet away. She looked up at that same moment, a surprised expression passing across her face; then she turned away quickly to speak to a blond man seated next to her on the sofa. Jessa had a momentary thought that she had seen the woman somewhere before, but her attention was immediately drawn to the desk clerk, who was giving Semmes directions to a very nice restaurant just down the street.

"Thank you," the captain said, and he drew her toward the main door of the hotel. Before they went out, he looked over his shoulder one more time.

Liel, Vida, and Owen were waiting outside. Rafe told them he had heard about a really great steak place down the street, and they all turned to follow him. The features of the woman in the lobby came back to Jessa, although not clearly, since she had not gotten a good look at her. Then Vida started asking her how the hotel was and launched into a description of how the repairs were going.

Considering the conditions at the port, the *Starbourne*

was being repaired quickly. It would be ready to fly in four more days at this rate.

In spite of her earlier desire to party, Jessa found that news comforting. She was always better off when she was working. Less time to think and worry about things left behind and over which she had no control. That was why she left Glory in the first place, and there was no need...

Arden Grenfell. That was who the woman in the hotel reminded her of. It was not likely that her erstwhile bodyguard would be on Caldera, of all places. She was probably still in prison, if not dead, after letting her charge go off on her own. That was something Jessa had not felt guilty about since Arden had let herself be persuaded, for whatever reasons of her own.

Jessa shook her head, and Vida looked at her strangely. She ignored the cook's look and walked on as if nothing had happened. All of these memories and feelings, usually hidden behind her professional duties, were recurring suddenly. She could do without all of this introspection.

All right. She had seen the princess. It was her. Arden sat on the sofa next to Turner and kept wishing she had not turned away. She should have jumped right up and introduced herself.

"Let's get something to eat," Turner said, and she nodded.

They rose from the sofa, and she let him lead her in the opposite direction from that taken by the crew of the *Starbourne*. He had said nothing about her inaction, although his expression had been one of amazement. Her own feeling exactly.

She had walked into the lobby of the New Hilton, at first determined on a course of action. However, as they sat waiting, hoping that Jessa would appear, sure that would happen since it was dinnertime, her resolve had weakened. She was still ready to accost her once she appeared, but...

The man with the princess, Captain Semmes, had looked

her in the eye and she had become almost paralyzed. Arden remembered swallowing hard and thought she remembered blushing, something that had not happened since she was very young. She could swear that her heart had skipped a beat. There had been a look akin to surprise on his face at the same time. Whatever in the world could that mean? They had never met before, she was sure. Yet, she had seen that face.

In a picture. That was where she had first seen that face, in the picture she had woven in the first square. She could only have learned his name in one of the visions. The feeling of recognition had drained all strength from her limbs. The feeling in the pit of her stomach that meant she wanted to know him better. The weakness had lasted several minutes. Turner kept casting sideways glances at her as they made their way down the street. Once her strange euphoria dissipated somewhat, she found his glances ominous. Once more she felt uncomfortable in his presence.

She became conscious of the sword settled across her back and a strong desire to know what about him had changed. Sitting across from him as they ate in a restaurant away from the hotel, she studied him. She saw the blond hair that set off his face, such a handsome face, and wondered why this seemed like a new discovery. He was tall and lean, but well muscled, his skin almost golden. All of that and the fine clothes he wore, the ease of his movements. So very nice looking, but his glance had never brought the same reaction she had felt when encountering Captain Semmes in the flesh. Turner's touch had excited her, but Semmes had done more with a look.

There was a tenseness now in Turner, even a coldness in the blue eyes, but both dissipated as they ate and talked. His voice warmed, and she realized the change was a matter of control. He was definitely angry, and she did not understand why. She could not help finding the shorter, darker man more fascinating. And somehow Turner knew that.

After dinner, they returned to the hotel together, then

went to their separate rooms. She continued worrying about his mood for a time, then pushed it out of her mind. There were other things to do. Like calling Don Vey and letting him know that she had at least found Jessa. He would probably be angry too, because she had not kept in touch since she left the palace. There were reasons for that, but none that he would like. Among them, the most important: She had not wanted Vey to know where she was until things came together. That way he could not force her hand before she was ready.

She looked at the comm panel and began pacing. This was perhaps the last chance to change her mind. It would be very easy to walk away, leave Jessa to the life she had chosen for herself. That would leave Arden with two alternatives: return to Glory and take her chances, or try to lose herself among the settled worlds. The latter would mean giving up things that meant too much to her. Especially Abbot Grayson and his monastery. The only home that meant anything to her. That was a lot to lose.

So was her life.

She stopped pacing and sat on the edge of the bed next to the nightstand. After a moment's hesitation, she pressed the key that opened a line and punched in the special number.

"Connection made," the almost female voice reported.

Arden pressed the confidential button, heard the clicks on the line, then a beep.

She cleared her throat, then said, "Mr. Vey, this is Arden Grenfell. I have found Princess Jessa. She . . ."

She had started to tell him where the princess was but stopped. He might already know that, but if not, telling him took even more control over the situation out of her hands. Besides, he could find out anytime from the comm records.

She looked at the comm. There would be no blank space on the message. The recording had stopped when her voice did. Vey would be expecting more, though.

"She has been serving on a salvage ship called the *Star-*

bourne. I will be in touch again when I have finalized our plans."

What else was there to say? Nothing, she decided, and pressed the button labeled "end."

"Please select routing," the voice instructed and she said, "Urgent." The line disconnected.

She raised her right hand from the console and felt surprise that it did not tremble. Rubbing her hands together, she resumed pacing. Would Vey suspect that she had doubts about bringing Jessa back to Glory? He certainly should after her prior behavior. She did not doubt that he would carry out the sentence of death.

A knock came on the door and a voice called out, "Arden, it's Turner."

What did he want at this time of night? It occurred to her to pretend to be asleep, but that seemed cowardly. What did she have to be afraid of?

Her eyes sought the sword, finding it leaning against the nightstand as usual; then she opened the door. For the first time since they had met, he seemed unsure of himself. His hands were folded in front of him, and he shifted slightly from foot to foot.

"I'm sorry to come by so late," he said. "I just could not let the day end like this."

"Like what?" She stepped back. "Come on in."

He crossed the threshold, moving more like a little boy than anything else she could think of. He looked from the bed to the chairs on either side of the table, finally choosing to sit in one of the chairs. Arden poured a little brandy into two glasses and handed him one. He grinned his thanks and took a sip. The warmth spread through her body just as it must be doing the same to him. Whether that was what loosened his tongue she did not know, but he began talking.

First, Turner told her that he had been serious when he said that he found her attractive. Their night together had been important to him. Very important. As he continued in the same vein, she realized that he was expressing jealousy over her reaction to Semmes. He had read that reaction clearly, and was saying that what existed between him and her was more real.

He did not wheedle or whine. The words came out just right. And she realized that he was trying to manipulate her. Not out of any real feelings for her, but in his desire to control her. Finally, she stopped him.

"I don't find you any less attractive than I did before," she assured him. "But I'm not in love with you. What exists between us is very pleasant and fulfilling and I, for one, have no intention of terminating it. I'm not in love with Captain Semmes, either. Hell, I don't know the man. I may never know him. Although I confess that I've never experienced anything quite like the reaction I had when our eyes met today."

Turner reached over and touched her hand. Clearly, he wanted to hear no more about how another man had made her feel with just a look. She let him kiss her, let her arousal begin, took charge this time and made love to him. When he rose from the bed to return to his own room, she lay still, feeling his side of the bed cool with her outstretched hand, and wondered how it would have been with Semmes. What secrets did he know that would surprise her, make her desire reach a crescendo of passion? For a moment, she let herself hope that she might actually have the opportunity to find out.

8

The hour was early, the sun not quite above the horizon. Arden moved quickly around the room, flicking the shinai with her wrists, striking at pieces of furniture with the tip as if they were weapons pointed at her, without quite hitting them. She had learned to practice right after getting out of bed in the morning when her mind was more uncluttered and a little less controlled. At least when she practiced alone. This morning was unusually early since she had slept little, finally giving up just before four.

She had tried morning practice once on the ship, when a young crewman had volunteered to practice with her, but that had not gone well. Although she still was unable to reach the red haze after so many years of no practice, the lack of control had made her more aggressive at the same time. The poor man had to endure the pain of a very large lump on the side of his head for several days.

Afterward, they agreed to practice in the evening, when she was a bit less dangerous. He was brave, she had to give him that, and not too bad with a sword. In the end, he had improved considerably, and she had kept limber and improved her reactions.

Practicing alone helped her to improve her focus and stay limber. As in the prison cell, however, it did nothing to keep her reactions keen. However, it did help her to avoid thinking about facing Jessa.

She had not thought it would be so difficult. She was not as sure about this adventure as she wanted to be.

Dammit! It was a simple matter of the survival of one or the other. Her return to the world—and her own survival—depended on getting the princess back home. Vey had promised. And she had promised Pac Terhn.

What kind of survival would it be for either of them, if Jessa was chained to the loom and made to weave lifeweave for the rest of her life? Both of them would be prisoners in that room, the princess taking Lyona's role and Arden taking Colin Chase's. Was that any better than a smaller cell in the prison? Was it any better than death?

Arden dropped panting into a chair. In the end, getting up so early had not prevented her mind from wandering into unwanted territory after all. She picked up the towel from the table and wiped sweat from her face, holding it there as if to block the world from her senses. If she can't see, hear, or smell it, maybe it did not exist.

She leaned back suddenly, letting her hands and the towel drop to her lap. Someone was going to get hurt— that thought kept intruding again and again. It was not fair. Life was not fair. And now she was sounding like a child.

There is another choice, her inner voice told her once more. *Let Jessa go her own way.* And she need not return to Glory herself. She might even be able to return home when both Don Vey and the emperor were dead. Chances were, though, that Grayson would be dead by then too. Nothing gained there except her own freedom. Maybe.

Vey was not above sending assassins after her himself. However, he would choose better than the person who had already been after her. He could afford to.

Maybe there would be no problem once Jessa knew her mother was dead. She might want to return home then, the loving daughter seeing to her mother's affairs, taking her place.

What would Vey do if Jessa could not take her mother's place at the loom? As a girl and a young woman, she had never displayed any such abilities. Could lifeweave create what was not there, or enhance what was too weak to otherwise detect?

What of her own experience with lifeweave? Grayson had given her a shawl made of the stuff for her fourteenth birthday. A strange choice under the circumstances, yet she had slept with it that first night and experienced her first vision. It was a year or more before Pac Terhn appeared. That had been a terrifying experience, indeed. But was it a confirmation of suspected latent extrasensory abilities of Glorians?

That was not a subject for consideration just now. Contact with Jessa had to be made today. The course of action had to be decided once and for all. First she had to take a shower and get dressed. Breakfast at nine.

She jumped to her feet, determined to get the job over with as soon as possible. At least as much as she could do today.

A sudden thought hit her. The port was closed, and there was no way to tell how long that would last. Her choices for leaving Caldera were therefore limited. Jessa, however, was not so stranded, since she served on an independent ship. Her departure choices were limited only by the amount of time it took to repair the *Starbourne*.

Maybe Janet Logan could help by making sure the repairs went more slowly, or at least were not reported correctly to Semmes. The superintendent would probably do anything Turner asked of her.

Arden shuddered at the thought of Turner and Logan together. She suspected Turner would be equally appalled at such a thought.

The streets and sidewalks were crowded even though it was near midday. That was one of the amazing things about Vega City, and Arden suspected about any frontier town:

it was open twenty-four hours a day. The mines operated all three shifts, all fully manned.

The word "manned" was not a misnomer by any means, either. The number of men was far greater than the number of women on this world. The stores, restaurants, hotels, and bars employed quite a few of the fairer sex. The mining companies, however, did not. Oh, there were female miners, and a lot of women working in the offices, but as far as one could see on the streets and read in the statistics, only about one in ten.

Arden had expected a more even ratio for whatever reason. Not because of her own experience, that was sure. After three years, there had been only three women in the imperial guard back on Glory. The ratio had been greater in the regular army, but not by much. Somehow, she had believed that the civilian sector was more even-handed.

Searching the passing crowds as she walked along the main street had brought this realization home to her. She was seeking a woman's face in a male-dominated population. Jessa should be quite easy to spot under the circumstances, even with her long black hair coiled tightly to her head as it had been yesterday.

Arden had called the New Hilton right after breakfast and gotten no answer from Jessa's room. The same result when she tried Semmes. Either the two of them had gone back to the port to check on their ship, or they were taking in the sights. Once she had decided to confront the princess, she wanted to get it over with. Her own best route had seemed to be sending Turner to talk to Logan while she checked through the streets. There was only a random chance of success in the streets, but if that did not work, they could meet at the hotel later in the day and visit Jessa in her room together.

She maneuvered along the sidewalks crowded with company men heading to lunch somewhere or to hotels for a quick nap. Every once in a while someone would brush too close, touch her a little too intimately, but under the conditions, it was impossible to tell if the touches were accidental or not, and she ignored them.

More than a few of these people would probably stop off at one of the bars, before or after dinner. They might end by drinking themselves into a stupor, waking in their own beds when it was time to go back to work, having been picked up during the night, identified, and delivered.

No, she was being too hard on them. After all, how could they get to work each day if they got drunk every time they were off? Most of the men passing were hard-working and lonely, away from families and homes. All they wanted was to work out their time here and get back with more credits than they had ever seen in the preceding years of their lives.

Yet the money itself couldn't be the only thing that drove them. There must be plans on what to buy with the money, or who to marry when they got back. So many choices. There would never be enough to pay for everything. Maybe they should set their sights a little lower.

Arden paused, realizing that she was thinking of herself. Did she really want so much? Certainly not more than most people wanted. She was fifth-generation Glorian, descended from a line of farmers. Her ancestors were practical people, not given to flights of fancy. She supposed her cousins still were like that, but had no way of knowing because she had not seen any of them since her father died.

A daughter should never be glad when a parent died. But she hadn't been glad at the loss of Madison Grenfell. She had mourned him deeply; even remembering now brought a lump to her throat.

No, it wasn't losing him to death that had hurt so deeply. He was never hers to mourn after her mother died, and that was what brought pain. He had blamed himself, and rightly so. She had succumbed to his passion for lifeweave. Small bits and pieces of cloth and unwoven fiber.

He had collected the fragments, buying more when he had saved up enough credits, and storing it in the attic of the house. The farm was isolated, and his hobby had become known in the district. The thieves had caught Melinda home alone—Madison and Arden had been in the field— and the thieves were never caught. They shot Melinda once, and she was dead when husband and daughter returned late that afternoon.

Her father's death came less than a year later. It at least gave purpose to her own life. Even though she was his only heir, the farm did not come to her. Instead, it went to his younger brother, who had enough children of his own, and no particular interest in another girl to raise. Thank goodness for her father's old friend, Abbot Grayson.

That had been an unlikely friendship. The stolid farmer and the sophisticated churchman.

A sudden glimpse of a familiar face brought Arden's thoughts to a stop. So much woolgathering, and she had nearly walked past. Jessa was going into one of the shops, and Arden hurried to follow. Near the back, strolling between shelves, Jessa showed little interest as she inspected items displayed for sale. Semmes was nowhere in sight. A good time to approach her erstwhile charge.

Arden approached slowly, wondering if there might be a look of recognition this time. All around, the sounds of voices waxed and waned, blending with the soft rustle of feet on carpet. Occasionally one voice would rise above the general din, but she didn't try to find the source, concentrating instead on the object of her search, the girl—no, young woman now—who had played such a large part in her own life, even if sometimes indirectly.

She was tall, at least as tall as Arden, who was five feet eight. Her black hair was once more pulled tight on the back of her head. The thin, teenaged body had filled out, not quite to plumpness, but there was little physical strain in being an astronavigator. Men would probably admire the curves.

It was the face, however, that drew Arden's attention. Lyona could never have denied being Jessa's mother. Except for the heavy eyebrows that were inherited from the emperor, she was made in the same mold as the seeress.

Jessa raised her head, and their eyes met. There was no hint of recognition in the bright green eyes. Arden felt herself smile at the sadness that touched her mind. And at that moment, the princess's eyes widened and her lips formed Arden's name.

"Hello, your highness."

Jessa's eyes darted from side to side, making sure that no one had overheard.

"Please don't call me that. No one knows, and I want to keep it that way."

"All right. Jessa."

The princess regarded her one-time liberator for a long moment, then looked back at the piece of lava rock she had picked up. Her hand shook slightly. Very carefully she replaced the souvenir on the shelf. Once it was safe, she exhaled loudly.

"I don't suppose you're here by accident."

"No, I was sent to find you."

"Why?"

Jessa had no idea, did not know about her mother, and Arden suddenly felt sure that Jessa had no psychic powers at all.

Turner retraced the path to Janet Logan's office. The superintendent was waiting for him. She smiled as he entered and closed the door.

"My friend and I need your help with a rather delicate matter," he said after they exchanged greetings.

"I'll do whatever I can," she said.

Her voice was as loud and oily as it had been the first time. Her eyes practically undressed him as they scanned from his blond hair to the tips of his brown alligator-skin boots. He had no doubt that she understood the wealth the boots alone represented. She also knew exactly what she wanted. Unfortunately, he did too.

"You remember the *Starbourne* that we checked on?"

She nodded without taking her eyes off him for a moment. "We don't care how quickly the repairs proceed on the ship. However, we would like to make sure the crew does not know they are complete until we give the word. I know this is very unorthodox, but we must make sure they do not lift from Caldera until we have what we need."

"And what is that?"

He smiled and could almost see her heartbeat quicken.

"I cannot say at the moment, I'm afraid."

"That's okay. If you want, we could make sure the repairs are not completed for a while."

"Actually, it might be to our advantage if the repairs were done very quickly. We might want them to leave immediately after our business is finished."

Logan nodded, then licked her lips. He wanted to laugh at her attempt at being seductive. Few men she met turned her down, given the power of her position. He would love to destroy the delusions that had given her. Right now, there was no time. He had to check to see if Princess Jessa was on her ship, then get back to keep an eye on Arden.

That part of his visit to Caldera had proved pleasant enough. Thank goodness Logan need not be included in those activities.

She checked the computer, then said, "They're pretty close to completing the repairs. The cost of keeping that from the crew will be very high."

"I thought it might be."

"I'm usually here until very late every night," she said. "After nearly everyone else has gone home."

"I love a woman who is devoted to her job," Turner said.

"Give me a call earlier in the day. When you'd like to come by and discuss this further."

"That will be a pleasure," he said, and stood. "I don't think it will be very long before I do just that."

Logan held out her hand, and he took it in his own. To seal her doom, he raised her hand to his lips. She giggled.

He winked and left her office, heading for the service arm of the terminal.

The woman had actually giggled. No wonder she had been assigned to a backwater world like this.

The shop had a coffee bar in the back, and they sat waiting to be served at a table in a far corner. Arden had suggested they go back there so they could talk. No one could see them through the windows of the gift shop. Chances were they would not be disturbed.

"So," Jessa said. "I would guess that my father or Don Vey or both want me to return to Glory."

"Yes, both of them want that."

"Of course my mother expressed no opinion. She hardly knows whether it's day or night."

Her voice was low, controlled, without a hint of emotion. Maybe she had stopped caring during the years she had been away from home.

"When I left, your mother was dying," Arden said gently. "Your father thought you might want to see her before she is gone."

Jessa's mouth tightened slightly, and she blinked rapidly for a few seconds. Signs of tension that Arden remembered from what now seemed a very long time ago. For the moment, she had no intention of telling her that Lyona was already dead, especially since there had not yet been any confirmation of that.

A waitress brought their coffee, saving both from having to say anything else right away.

"I thought you would be dead shortly after I left," Jessa said evenly after the waitress left. "I think that's why I didn't recognize you when I saw you in the hotel lobby."

"I almost was."

For a moment, Arden considered telling Jessa that if the princess did not go back to Glory with her, her execution would probably follow shortly after she returned home. However, that smacked too much of being a sympathy ploy, and she doubted that the reaction would be sympathetic. Besides, Jessa must know that would always be a possibility.

"I heard a rumor once, not long after I left home," Jessa said. She stirred cream into her coffee. "They said that a faction had risen that wanted me to be empress, based on my being older than the heir apparent. That would probably be as much a prison as being chained to that loom."

"I couldn't say whether there was such a movement or not," Arden said, choosing to ignore the last part of the statement. "I got very little news during the past six years."

"Six years. Hard to believe it has been that long."

"Seems longer to me."

They drank their coffee in silence without looking at each other. Arden had no idea how to proceed, what words to use that might convince Jessa to return with her. There would be no sympathy directed toward her, but what about the mother?

"She is blind now," Arden said. "Her hair has turned totally grey. There's a guard, Colin Chase, who hovers about, protecting her as if she were his own child. He and the servants have to do everything for her."

The space between Jessa's eyebrows wrinkled, and she took a deep breath. There was feeling after all.

"The lifeweave did that? Blinded her, I mean?"

"That's what they say."

Jessa raised her head and looked Arden full in the eye.

"And you want me to return to that? Take her place, suffer the same? Who will be my Colin Chase?"

The questions, the fearful tone, all reminiscent of the young girl who had talked Arden into letting her leave Glory.

"Are you so sure it would happen to you?" Arden asked. "Have you ever shown any talent in that area? I don't remember any. What if you returned and you were unable to weave one thing that was helpful? If you proved that you could not foretell anything, wouldn't they have to let you go? You would stay a year at most. Then you could escape to the life you have now."

Jessa's face brightened a moment; then she frowned.

"You haven't discovered any talents, have you?" Arden asked.

"No. Nothing like that. It doesn't seem likely, though, that the emperor or Don Vey would release me, does it? I mean, would they want me going around telling people what had happened? Could they afford that?"

"You could promise to say nothing..."

"They might even believe that I was faking it. That I could do the weaving, but pretended as if it did not work. Even if I did manage to get away, Captain Semmes would have replaced me. I couldn't go back to work on the same ship." She drank the last of her coffee, which was cold, and set the cup firmly on the table. "I like what I'm doing now and the people I work with. I won't leave it all behind. I've worked too hard at making a new life for myself."

Arden had been leaning forward in her chair, forearms on the tabletop. She sat back now and exhaled loudly. So much for gentle persuasion. The only course left was coercion of some kind. Could she—would she—force Jessa to return?

Suddenly, Jessa straightened, her eyes on the entrance to the coffee shop. Arden turned to the left to see what had caught her attention.

Semmes was rushing toward them, his attention on Jessa. He came up to the table and seemed to barely stop in time to keep from running into it.

"We have to go," he said to his astronavigator.

"What's wrong?" she asked.

"Glory is going to issue an arrest warrant for the crew of the *Starbourne*."

"For what?"

"Piracy. They claim that we forced down the Glorian cargo ship and took the..."—he glanced at Arden—"...

cargo. The local constable will probably have the ship locked in stasis soon. We have to get to the port as soon as possible and try to lift off."

Jessa stood, ready to follow him out of the shop. At that moment, Turner walked in, blocking their way.

"You aren't going anywhere," he said shortly.

The princess was found at last. Any difficulties getting her back were secondary to that. Granid Parcq glanced at his prime minister, who, having delivered the message, waited for his emperor to speak.

"This Grenfell woman is being difficult?" he asked.

"Perhaps, sire. She let the princess escape from Glory the first time. She may be thinking of not bringing her back. However, I think she will obey in the end. She has no choice. We are taking steps to ensure that she does as she has been told."

The emperor nodded.

"How long before Lyona's daughter will arrive?"

"Less than a month, I would think."

"A month?"

Don Vey lowered his head, gazing at the parquet floor.

"Caldera is moving away from the shorter route. There are fewer gates in that sector. It will be a rather long journey now."

"There must be no delay. If Captain Grenfell is not cooperating, find a way around that problem. My mind is set on this course."

"Yes, sire. We have people in the area who will force the issue."

The emperor nodded and dismissed his prime minister. Vey looked unhappy as he left the room. Well, he would get over that soon enough. The man had no vision. He saw only the immediate problem. No, that wasn't quite true, either. It was the overall picture he couldn't see. He never understood that the future wasn't just Glory. Granid Parcq would one day be emperor of the entire sector. He even had plans for controlling Weaver. With that wealth to support him, he intended to expand further. Lifeweave was more sought after than any other product. Once its production was totally in his hands, this would be the most powerful dynasty in all the galaxy. Waran would inherit a grand empire, certainly greater than what he himself had inherited.

As the fifteenth of the Parcq dynasty, Granid had damned his father, Erthin, for leaving all the work of empire building to others. He never possessed any more foresight than Vey.

His own son was different. Granid had always worried about having only one son. Shortly after the boy's birth, several advisors had even suggested repudiating him as a bastard because there was little of the Parcq in his appearance. However, since there were no other sons born, and the empress bore no other children at all in their eighteen-year marriage, Granid had no regrets at not following that advice.

It was in ambition where they matched. Both were dedicated to winning the war, to enlarging their empire. At any cost.

"You know, father, that she will have to be confined every moment," Waran had said of Jessa when they discussed her return. "Those who work for peace see her as their leader."

"They dream, Waran. They have no idea how she feels about the war, or even Glory, for that matter. She abandoned her home and has done nothing to support her home world when it needed her most."

"The peace party does not take that into consideration. Father, as long as Jessa lives, I will be in danger. You will be in danger," Waran had added after a slight pause.

The young man was ambitious. That was all right. Only an ambitious leader could finish such an undertaking. Not that Granid planned to leave much work behind.

"Once she is put to work at the loom, there will be little danger from Jessa."

"You have no doubt that she is like her mother?"

"No." A twinge of sadness arced through both Granid's mind and his body. "As a child, she was like her mother in so many things."

The door chimed, chasing away memories. Don Vey entered when it opened.

"Sire, it seems that Arden Grenfell may be refusing to obey our orders after all. We just received a message from her. She and the princess may be joining forces."

Fear now stabbed through Granid Parcq's body. His hands curled into fists at his sides. Suddenly, all he felt was exhaustion.

Damn that woman. Damn all women. Lyona dying at the worst possible time. Jessa leaving without any regard for her family or her people. This guardswoman refusing to cooperate. Even the empress for not giving him other sons! At least she had been a cooperative and submissive woman in every other way.

It was time to teach these independent-thinking women a lesson.

"Don Vey, send your best men—however many it will take—and teach this Grenfell woman a lesson. Doesn't she have family here we can bring pressure on? Do whatever is necessary to get Jessa here."

"Yes, sire."

Vey bowed and left the room. Granid could have sworn there was a slight grin on his face.

9

The reply was terse. Arden listened with the handset to her ear, not wanting everyone else in the room to know what Vey had said. Not just yet. She should never have sent that message telling him she had found Jessa. She should have waited until everything had been settled here.

Dammit!

"You will bring Princess Jessa back to Glory at the first opportunity," Vey's recorded voice said. "I have taken steps to ensure your compliance with your orders. Not only on Caldera, but also here. I expect to hear from you by tomorrow morning that the two of you are on your way."

That was the end. She immediately disconnected and tried to call Abbot Grayson. The line to the monastery was busy. She instructed the system to keep trying and ring her back. A direct call was incredibly expensive, but she had to know that he and the monks were all right. They were the only ones Vey could possibly have meant by "also here." As for steps taken on Caldera, they had already surmised that he was the one who brought charges against the *Starbourne*'s crew, having the ship locked down, thus ensuring that no one could leave. He was quick, she would give him that much.

She sat on the edge of the bed, worried and feeling more

helpless than ever before. Two forces were pulling her apart, both larger than her and neither caring what happened to her.

She looked around the room. Turner and Rafe sat in the two chairs at the table, talking in low voices. Liel and Jessa sat silently in two folding chairs Turner had gotten room service to bring up. Vida sat on the foot of the bed facing the table.

Arden had finally told them why she had come to Caldera, which meant that everyone now knew who Jessa was. At first, they were stunned by the revelations, everyone looking at the princess in total surprise. When the full implications got through, they had convinced Arden to try to call Vey and see if she could somehow get the *Starbourne* released.

"He wants Jessa," she said at last. "Nothing more, nothing less." Glances were exchanged, then dropped to floor or tabletop. "And me, of course."

She sat and watched for some reaction. Except for Turner, the consensus was that Jessa would go back only if she wanted to. Turner expressed no opinion himself, leaving it to those most closely involved.

"I guess the first thing we must do is get on the ship and get away from here," he said into the silence. All eyes turned toward him.

"How?" Rafe asked.

"We have a friend in the port authority." He winked at Arden. He meant Logan, of course.

"And what do you propose once we're away from here?" she asked harshly. "I'm left under a sentence of death. Vey and the emperor will continue trying to get Jessa back."

The comm signaled before she could continue. Arden jerked up the handset, then exhaled loudly when she recognized Grayson's voice.

"Is everyone all right?" she asked.

"So far," he said. "Vey sent about twenty of the imperial guard to watch over us."

"That's not very many," she started, but said no more. Even secure lines could be trusted only so far.

"It's enough," Grayson said, and she knew he also understood.

"I'm working on righting things on this end," she said. "I just wanted to make sure you all were in good health."

"We are and intend to stay that way. Do what you must, daughter."

"I will. Be well."

"You too."

She disconnected. Twenty soldiers, even from the well-trained imperial guard, were not enough to control the monastery. That did not mean that more could not be sent. Vey could, and probably would, send a whole army if he needed to. However, for the moment, the monastery was largely undisturbed.

One weapon Grayson could use was public opinion. Although few in number, the religious orders were considered sacrosanct for the most part. That would only go so far, but the abbot was clever, and not without his own personal sphere of influence. He had meant for her to quit worrying about him and the monastery and do what was necessary for herself.

And for those who now surrounded her, she realized. Although outnumbered, she could find a way to get Jessa away from them and back to Glory. Especially with Turner's assistance. Unless he wanted out. His was the only name not on the warrant.

She had noticed how he now looked constantly at Jessa. Abbot Grayson would have said that Turner was smitten. An old-fashioned term at best. Jealousy had raised its ugly head, but Arden beat it down. Sure, Jessa was younger and definitely prettier, and that hurt a little. But love was love and she certainly envied them this opportunity, if it was mutual.

It would be nice—even wonderful—if the strange feeling she got in the pit of her stomach every time Captain Semmes looked at her was love. It was a feeling unlike anything she had experienced before. A little like what she had heard described. It made her forget what she was saying or doing for a moment. However, even if it was remotely connected with love, he clearly didn't feel the same way. Especially after everything that had happened.

Something they must deal with soon.

Arden realized with a start that Vey had said nothing about Lyona. Clearly, he did not think her knowing of the death of the seeress would spur her to the proper action. That meant there was no need to tell Jessa. Yet.

"We can't just sit here and bemoan what's happened," she said into the heavy silence. "At least I'm not. First, I would suggest that we get out of this hotel and the New Hilton. Captain, Jessa, you need to get your stuff. Next, Turner and I'll check on the *Starbourne*—who's in charge there, whether guards have been posted. And, most important, I need to find Janet Logan. We know she can be bought."

"We'll need another place to stay in any case," Rafe said.

Arden rose and went to sit on the bed. She opened the hidden door in the wall beside the bed, took out a credit disc, and tossed it to the captain.

"Use this," she said. "It's in the name of Leesan Knohr. It would take days for anyone to trace it back to me."

Turner looked at her, nodded in approval. "I should get the rooms, though," he said. "They aren't looking for me."

"I don't think so," Arden said. "Your name isn't on the warrant. You need to consider how involved you want to get."

He considered that, then shrugged. "We'll need to get that alias listed on a ship's manifest or in the rolls," Turner said. "They might be checking all names and credit use."

"We'll take care of that with Logan," Arden said.

With a plan, even a short-term one, beginning to form, she had their attention. Without a doubt, she could get them off Caldera, but the new credit disc would not get them much farther than that. Funds had to be gotten, but that was something to worry about later.

She called Janet Logan's comm at the port authority but was told the superintendent would not be in until next morning. Arden made an appointment to see her in the name of Leesan Knohr. Meanwhile, some of the others scattered on different errands, with the express goal of removing every possible trace that any of them had been on Caldera.

It seemed all right for Turner to take Jessa to the New Hilton to get her and Semmes's things with Owen tagging along. Semmes had taken the credit disc in search of a new hotel. He returned before any of the others, while Arden was still packing her own things, room cards in hand.

"I got four rooms right together."

"What hotel had that kind of vacancy?" Arden asked.

She fastened the suitcase she had been packing and set it on the floor. Vida, Liel, and Tahr continued a card game they had been playing while the rest were gone.

He smiled. "A very cheap one. It seems that the first hotels built have been crowded out of the mainstream by the newer and bigger ones. They're desperate for customers."

"I suppose it's dirty and smelly and..."

"Not really. It's not as nice as this, but it will be comfortable. And, hopefully, we won't be staying there long."

She pulled the woven lifeweave from the drawer, keeping her body between it and the captain. He paid so little attention to her that she could have packed it openly and he would not have noticed. Still, no sense being careless.

That completed her packing, and she sat in one of the folding chairs. They sat next to each other in uncomfortable silence. He looked at his watch every minute or two.

"Captain," Arden said.

He looked up a little too quickly.

"I am sorry about all this," she said. "When I left Glory, all I could think of was not going back to prison or being executed. I thought it was going to be easy—I had my orders. I'm a warrior, accustomed to doing no more."

"Except when you let Jessa leave Glory in the first place," he reminded her.

"Yes, except then. If I hadn't, none of this would be happening." She made a sweeping motion with her hand. "You wouldn't be in danger of losing your ship..."

"Or my freedom."

"Or your freedom. I wouldn't have lost six years of my own life."

She shook her head.

"I'm a warrior," she repeated. "I have no head for subterfuge. Before I saw you and Jessa in the New Hilton lobby that time, I tried very hard not to think of you as people. Well, even after that for a little while.

"I'm strong when it comes to martial arts, but with anything else, I just get confused," she went on after a short pause. "I've never had to understand such things. I had to fight hard to be accepted in both the army and the imperial guard. Women aren't given much credit on Glory. It may get better one day."

"Is there a point to all this?" Rafe asked without rancor.

"Yes." But what was it? Did she want to be friends? That wasn't very likely to happen. They were going to have to work together for a while. She said as much.

"I just want you to know that I'm not a bad person," she went on. "You may never come to like me..."

The door banged open and Turner and Jessa walked in, suitcases in hand.

"The constable and several deputies are right behind us," Turner said. "Let's get out of here."

"How?" Arden said.

"The staff exit."

"Won't they have that guarded?"

"No, those doors are locked. Only hotel staff have keys."

"How do you expect to use that exit, then?" Rafe broke in.

"He's an investigator," Arden said. "He's got all sorts of skills."

She grinned at Turner, and he answered in kind. Hurriedly, they sorted out the bags and left the room, careful to double-lock the door. The staff exit was in the opposite direction from the elevators—that would buy them a little time. Turner put down the bags he carried, pulled a small tool pouch from his jacket pocket, and went to work on the lock.

The elevator bell announced the car's arrival.

The rover sped along the bypass toward the port. One day this road, built to go around Vega City's congestion, would itself be congested. Businesses would be built along its route, maybe homes, canceling out the good intentions. If Caldera held together long enough.

But Arden Grenfell wouldn't see any of those changes. Oh, no. She would still be in prison for kidnapping a princess—which she didn't do, and for helping steal a rover, which she did do.

For a moment, Turner turned his attention from driving the vehicle to look at her. The half-smile still turned up the corners of his mouth; clearly he was pleased with himself. In spite of protestations to the contrary, he was enjoying all of this.

"Are you going to offer Logan scrip, or a spool of lifeweave?" he asked.

She fingered the roll of bills in her jacket pocket. Although Rafe had offered the lifeweave, she had insisted on drawing out cash using the Leesan Knohr credit disc that had been among the clothes that Abbot Grayson kept for her. The possible need to escape from Glory had occurred to her some time before the need became reality.

The fiber was the more elegant bribe, but could prove difficult to sell. Logan might be too pragmatic for that, anyway. Of course, if she was greedy, it might take both to budge her.

"We'll see how it goes," Arden answered.

Escaping from Caldera might prove more difficult than escaping from the hotel had been. That had been quite exhilarating. Turner had unlocked the staff door just as the elevator bell rang. Hanging back to let the others fight their way through, she had heard the elevator doors slide open, sounding much too close for comfort. Turner pushed her through the doorway, then squeezed through himself.

"Her room's down this way," Constable Harris had said. "She's got a sword, so be careful."

Turner pushed the door closed, shutting out the constable's voice and what little light came through from the main hall. The smaller hall the fugitives were in was quite a bit darker; they moved carefully, two abreast, while their eyes adjusted. Turner moved ahead to lead the way. An elevator stood closed at the far end. He pushed the up button and waved everyone out of sight to either side. Hiding was unnecessary, as it turned out—the car was empty. They piled in with less pushing this time, and Turner punched the button for floor seventeen.

"Why up?" Arden asked.

"There's a freight elevator to the loading dock on that floor," he explained.

No mirrors on the walls like those on the guest elevators. Plain it was, but at least Arden couldn't watch herself fidget. No other decorations to study. She could turn around and study the faces of her companions, but probably sharing their danger had not made them like her any more. She sighed, and Turner looked around at her.

The car stopped and the door opened. No one waited outside. They peeled themselves off the walls while Turner stepped out, checking right, left, then motioned for them to come out. They moved to the freight elevator and went down. Workers looked at them curiously when they stepped out, then went back to their tasks.

"Which hotel?" Turner asked the captain.

"The Royal."

Turner nodded, then led them down an alley, turning into another, and another. The bags were getting very heavy. Her stomach churned from the smells of raw garbage. The farther they went, the more refuse they encountered, lying everywhere. Didn't these people have auto trash bins?

At last their leader slowed. Rafe, who had been bringing up the rear of the small retreating force, moved up beside him.

"Since no one's looking for me, I'll go check the hotel," Turner said. "Wait here." He motioned with his head. "I'll check to make sure the way is clear and come back for you."

"Okay," Rafe said.

Turner went down a side alley, his footsteps echoing back through the man-made canyon, and disappeared into the street. They lined up against the building wall.

"Look casual," Rafe said softly.

Arden stepped away from the synthetic brick wall and glanced right and left. For innocent people, they sure looked like a guilty bunch. She moved past Tahr to stand in front of Rafe. He blinked, his eyes downcast a moment.

"I'll get your ship back," Arden said. "You were not supposed to get involved this way. Somehow, it will all come right."

Jessa had turned to watch them. Her expression was not as neutral as his.

"You thought we would just watch as you took Jessa away?" he asked in a flat voice.

"I truly thought she would go with me to see her mother before she died."

Footsteps echoed down the alley again. She turned and, although the figure was in shadow, she recognized the walk.

"It's him," she whispered.

As he came near, Turner shook his head.

"Good thing there isn't anyone else in the alley," he said, looking them over. "Plastered against the wall like that, you look anything but casual." Everyone looked appropriately sheepish. "Let's go. The hotel is just to the right. The rooms are ready and everyone is checked in. No need to go by the desk."

Getting everyone and their luggage into the hotel and settled took half an hour. There were four rooms together on the fifth floor—two connecting and two separate. Jessa and Arden had just finished testing their double bed when a knock came at the door.

Arden whirled, sword in hand.

"Who is it?" she called.

"Turner."

At least he didn't say "me."

Jessa let him in. He nodded approval when he saw they had not unpacked. Quick getaways might become their strong suit with more practice.

"I'm going to hang around the New Hilton and see what's happening." he said to Arden. "We can't use your rover or the train to get to the port tomorrow, so we will have to find our own transport."

Liel and Vida went out to pick up dinner for everyone while he was gone. He was in a very good mood when he returned three hours later.

"I think the constable and his men will be a bit preoccupied for a while," he said. "It seems there was a major robbery at one of the mines."

"What did they take?" Arden asked.

"A month's payroll."

The thieves had headed into the interior, he explained. Apparently there were several oases scattered across the surface of the planet.

"Why didn't they head for the port and get off world?" Rafe asked.

"The port is still closed and Constable Harris got the roads blocked pretty quickly. His whole force is on the move into the interior. I don't believe the thieves have a prayer."

"How fortuitous," Arden said.

Much too fortuitous, it might seem, and she looked at Turner with a new respect. Because of the robbery, she and her new companions would be able to get to the port without worrying about any roadblocks. If they made it out within the next couple of days.

Arden said as much about their need to act fast. Turner told the others about Logan and said he and Arden had an appointment to see her the next morning. The intent was to bribe her to release the *Starbourne* the morning after. He had little doubt that they could convince the superintendent to go along and that their exit would be in good time. It was at that moment that Arden started to distrust him.

Early next morning, he knocked on the door. She was up and waiting. He told her to leave the sword in the room and, reluctantly, she complied.

Waving awkwardly to Jessa, Arden turned and followed him out. It was not the time for petty bickering in their ranks, but she did not like the way he was taking control of the adventure. If it hadn't felt so urgent to get away and hide, giving vent to irritation at his imperious manner would have been such a pleasure.

The irritation increased when she had realized what he meant by "find our own transport." She had come close to leaving him there on the street, jump-starting a rover. If only they didn't need to get off Caldera so badly.

They arrived at the terminal without incident and parked the rover in the garage. As they started inside, Arden tried to remember exactly when she had changed from taking Jessa back to Glory to helping them escape from Caldera. The two goals were not necessarily mutually exclusive. She could still get Jessa back, just in her own time and in her own way.

Turner was looking over the other parked vehicles as they walked, and she asked him what was up.

"We will have to find another one when we're ready to leave," Turner answered.

"Is stealing transportation what makes you a good investigator?" She passed through the doorway and into the terminal proper.

"Just one of my many talents."

A policeman stood halfway across the terminal with his back to them. A woman was giving him an earful about something that had upset her. Arden hooked her arm through Turner's and snuggled close.

"It's *my* face they're probably looking for," she said against his white shirt sleeve. The linen felt soft against her cheek. Not as soft as lifeweave, but it had properties that made it as wearable. She inhaled a slight scent of spices and tobacco although she had never seen him smoke. And the scent brought memories of night passion.

"See, I told you they were more interested in those bank robbers," Turner said as they sauntered past the officer. The man never looked up.

Once they were in the corridor leading toward Janet Logan's office, Arden released his arm. His strides were much longer than hers, and clinging to him had made keeping up difficult.

"You could have kept hold of the arm," he said with a grin.

"Who are you, really?" she asked, ignoring his teasing. "Ever since we've been under more pressure, shall we say, you've changed. This is the kind of action you like, isn't it?"

"It's better than sitting around waiting for something to happen," he answered.

Yes, it was true for her, too, she realized. Having a specific task brought more action, although dodging policemen and stealing rovers was not what she would normally choose to do. All of these things Turner was clearly very practiced with. Last, but not least, would come the escape from Caldera, on board a ship the law everywhere was probably alerted to and which was currently locked down in stasis. If they were very lucky, it would be an escape and not a disaster.

Turner stopped just in front of her. He pulled open the door to the immigration offices. Arden snuggled up to Turner again, before noticing the lack of interest of people working at the desks they passed.

They walked directly into Janet Logan's office. The superintendent looked up, eyes wide in surprise. She made no move toward the comm station or her computer.

"What a surprise," she said. "I was expecting Leesan Knohr."

"That's me," Arden said. "I suppose you've heard." Logan nodded. "Does anyone know I was here before?"

"No one has asked," Logan said. "They sent your picture over the network, of course. But I suppose they had no way of knowing that we'd already had dealings. Besides, there aren't enough deputies and soldiers to cover everything, what with that terrible robbery and all."

She paused, then gave Turner one of the looks that said so much and now made Arden's skin crawl.

"What can I do for you today?" she asked.

"We need to get off Caldera," Arden said. "The ship..."

"The *Starbourne*."

"Yes. Is it ready to go?" Logan nodded. "Good. Is there some way you can see that it's free of stasis and that any guards are withdrawn early tomorrow morning?"

"We would appreciate it," Turner said. He never took his eyes off the woman behind the desk.

"There are ways," the superintendent said. "How early?"

"Two-thirty," Arden said.

"How much?" She turned at last to Arden, as if she and

Turner had silently struck their own personal deal and it was time to talk cash.

Practical or elegant? Try the cash first. The cost would be less.

"Three thousand."

"No." Logan sat back in the chair, lacing her fingers together across her flat abdomen.

"How much, then?"

"Six thousand. Not a penny less."

"All right," Arden agreed.

"And you"—Logan pointed at Turner—"be here at two-thirty to check that everything is set."

He smiled and nodded. Arden concentrated on pulling just the right number of scrip notes from her jacket pocket to avoid letting Logan know she could have had twice the amount. She kept her eyes cast down, too. No use letting Logan see the disgust in her eyes. As much as she felt it inside, it had to show.

Arden handed over the scrip. She and Logan shook hands. Turner extended his hand, and the superintendent lingered over the feel of it in hers.

Suddenly, Arden realized that she didn't hate the woman for her brazenness. She actually pitied her confidence. A confidence based on a false belief in her charms, when it was what she could do for them that men courted.

The two walked out arm in arm. Twice, they passed policemen. One checked their ID, and she felt like she should stop breathing while he looked the cards over. He waved them away, accepting their false identities. At last, they were in the parking garage. Fewer eyes to recognize them, but now they would have to find new transportation.

As they walked between rows of rovers and ATVs, Turner checked for an easy mark.

"Did you get it?" she asked.

"Yeah." He opened his right hand. A flesh-colored strip barely showed, stuck across the palm. "Voice and palm print in case she tries to change her mind."

He'd shown Arden the strip as they drove to the port. Activated by pressure, it could record almost five minutes of sound. And when Logan shook his hand, her own palm pressed against the surface, its print transferred by body heat. And she certainly had displayed plenty of that.

"We will check the ship at two-thirty to see if she has kept her word," he said. "Ah, here's one." Both doors of the rover were unlocked and they slipped inside. "If the ship is free . . ." He went to work with the magnetic probe. "I will meet Janet Logan in her office as agreed."

"Won't she be mad if you're late?"

"I think she will be willing to wait."

"It doesn't bother you?"

He laughed silently. "I have a few tricks that you haven't seen yet. She will wake later in the morning believing that it was a great moment."

He guided the rover out of the garage and toward the bypass. They rode in silence, she absentmindedly counting the poor trees lining the road. On this nearly treeless world, well-meaning companies had shipped in hundreds of different species, more beautiful in their minds than the leaner indigenous specimens, testing to see which ones might grow in the volcanic soil. So far, no one had quite gotten the right combination. A few of the distorted trees still stood, still green, and still the same height as when they were planted two or three years earlier. The rest were brown sticks poking upward, bare, dead or dying. Native trees, grasses, and mosses had not yet revealed the secrets of living in this soil. They might never do so. Then again, given enough time . . .

"No one's discussed what we're going to do once we leave Caldera," Arden said.

"Any suggestions?"

"No one ever expected everything to get so out of hand."

She had repeated that sentiment to herself many times in the past few days, but it said so much. How easy to fail when everything one cared about was so concentrated: one world, one monastery, one everything. Except the people. Just under one hundred counting monks and a few other workers, if she remembered correctly. It sounded like a lot of people, given that they lived in a single complex of buildings.

"What was it like growing up Arden Grenfell?"

His question startled her, seeming to imply that he had been reading her mind. In their short relationship they had not discussed much about her past, and only his professional past. What to answer?

"You mean as the only female in a monastery, and the only child?" Childhood and girlhood seemed so far away, both in distance and time. "They treated me as an equal—one reason it surprised me that it took so long to establish a pecking order when I became a member of the imperial guard. And it took even longer to realize that women were not welcome into just any profession."

"But you made friends?"

"Yes. A few. I concentrated on being very good at what I do." She chuckled. "For the most part, the men didn't welcome me in their ranks, and when I ignored them and turned to practice and work to take up my spare time, they were even more displeased with me. Thanks to me, though, two more women have joined the guards."

They had reentered Vega City a short while ago, and the streets and buildings were starting to look familiar. The hotel was probably not very far away. Surely Turner wasn't going to park the rover right there. They both remarked on the continuing lack of roadblocks. Perhaps with the port shut down, Harris believed they could not get off-world and was content to bide his time.

"Are there only monks and soldiers in your life?"

She laughed. "Mostly."

"No romance?"

"Sure, there have been a few men. Nothing ever lasted long. I do have one friend, though. That's more than a lot of people can say."

The fear of what would happen to Abbot Grayson and his monastery returned to overwhelm her momentarily. If Vey and the emperor decided to take it all over, there really was not much chance of fending them off without some other kind of support. She made a silent prayer that Grayson's highly placed friends would not abandon him.

Turner stopped the rover within sight of the hotel.

"I will let you out here," he said, "and drop the car a few miles away. I'll be back soon." She started to get out, but he stopped her with a hand on her arm. "We are going to be together for a bit longer than we thought at first," he said. "Frankly, I still want us to be more than friends."

"I don't . . ."

"You do." He reset the controls on the steering wheel. "When you get back to the room, start everyone discussing where we go from here. If they haven't already."

She got out and shut the door. He sped away. Once more she wondered how much she could trust Jackson Turner.

The hangar was quiet. Only a few night workers went about their tasks, and they were concentrated around and on top of a freighter at the far end, where the lights were brightest. Only ships needing work were hangared. If they stayed at Caldera, they usually deposited cargo, passengers, crew—or all of these—then lifted into a parking orbit off-planet. Most didn't even stay, making their drops and going on their way to the next port.

They would find out the hard way if repairs on the *Starbourne* were actually complete.

The hum of the stasis field died at exactly two-thirty. The *Starbourne* was free. No guards outside. Rafe silently made his way among tool chests and crates of spare parts. No one gave an alarm. He glanced behind him but couldn't see any of the others. He opened the hatch amidships, froze at the sound of escaping air, then climbed inside.

He made his way to the bridge. No locks on the controls

and no guards there, either. He put on some headphones, then made a quick sweep with the detector Turner had given him. No tracers or monitors. Methodically, he progressed to the cabins. Even if a device had been attached to the outer hull, the little piece of electronics in his hand would detect it.

They were expensive pieces of equipment. He had never used one before, but he had heard of them many times and knew their reputation. Rafe stepped into the galley and the detector pulsed in his ear. Strange sensation. Physical as much as auditory. Got your attention when something was present.

Something was present.

The signal was strongest near the water tanks. He opened the cabinet door. The space was small, crowded with tanks and tubing. He checked the signal again. It came most strongly from the left side of the right tank. He reached in, searched with fingers and the palm of his hand. There it was: metallic, round, and apparently attached magnetically. He left it as agreed. Removing it might send a signal that someone was on board, and attracting attention was the last thing they wanted.

He checked the rest of the ship. The others waiting outside for his signal must be getting more than a little jumpy by now. Once they came inside, each had an assigned task. He didn't envy the investigator his next assignment. From what Turner and Arden had said, Janet Logan wasn't ugly, but she wasn't subtle either.

Arden is a strange one, he thought suddenly. Although she seemed genuinely sorry about the trouble she had brought them all, she made no real apologies. She explained her reasons. She had *said* she was sorry and meant it. However, he was sure she would act the same way in the future if given the same choices. Whatever the reasons, she looked out for her own interests first. Not unlike the rest of them, true, but hers was a single-minded self-interest. Trusting her would be difficult—impossible if her own interests conflicted with those of the group.

She was still determined to get Jessa back to Glory, and getting herself reinstated in the guard; that was clear enough. Doing so would solve her own problems, but she had to be convinced, somehow, that her interests must be made to coincide with his and Jessa's and the rest of the crew's.

The sweep completed, he headed for the hatch. Once they took off from Caldera, there would be more time to get to know the former captain of the imperial guard and, maybe, to influence her.

While he waited for the others to get on board, he checked the arms locker. The guns and swords were gone.

When Rafe disappeared aboard the *Starbourne*, Arden sighed in relief. She then checked the workmen to see if they had heard anything. Watching Turner fidget did not help her own nerves.

He peered around one side of the enormous tool chest they hid behind, then went around her to peer from the other side. He was unusually restless, perhaps dreading the meeting to come with Logan. He might also be nervous about stealing into the hangar, although it had been accomplished easily enough. Arden had been nervous about that herself, unsure that Logan could manage to pull the guards away. The ease of their invasion had only increased her tension. With a warrant issued, there should be more security, in spite of the search for the robbers.

That must be what was making Turner so jumpy, too. He certainly had taken the teasing from the others in stride. Except, he had never answered Liel's pointed question about how far he would go to get free of Caldera.

Shouts from the workmen froze her thoughts, and Turner ceased moving behind her. A quick glance showed the men shouting instructions back and forth. Sounds carried far in the big emptiness, but without clarity.

This was one of five hangars, each capable of holding five medium-sized ships. With such limited facilities, Rafe and his crew would have been lucky to get the *Starbourne* in right away under normal circumstances. Getting it out as easily was what she prayed for now.

The captain reappeared at the hatch and waved both arms over his head, the agreed-upon signal that everything was all right with the ship. Turner waved back, then touched Arden's shoulder.

"Get everyone aboard," he said. "I will get back as soon as I can."

"I know, Turner. We've been over it a dozen times."

"Yeah," he said and moved toward the door that led into the office section off the hangar.

"Have fun," she called softly after him. He waved without turning around, and she looked toward the workers. No attention from them. As much noise as they and their equipment made, it was unlikely they heard anything beyond twenty feet, unless it was an explosion. Like a ship taking off.

She shook off the fear that rose in her throat and looked at her watch. Two-forty-five. Work to do.

Jessa appeared from behind an array of boxes that hid the rest of the crew. She carried her bag. Arden left her shelter, cutting across the concrete at an angle to meet the princess.

"Stay along this line," Arden said, pointing. "That should keep you out of their line of sight." What if the workmen took a break?

Vida came next. She reached Arden just as Jessa disappeared through the hatch. Tahr followed, carrying Semmes's bag and mumbling under his breath as usual. Only a few words—"killed," "tortured," "new job"— could be heard as he passed. Owen came next.

Liel came last. She already knew that was like him. Make sure everyone else was safe before he got to safety himself.

His crew was his responsibility, but she was not. Nor would he expect any help from her.

Just as he got inside, a movement caught her eye. She dropped to sit on her heels and looked left. A port policeman sauntered down the ramp into sight. He stopped, lit a cigarette, and glanced around. If she moved, he would surely see her. If she stayed perfectly still, he might not see her in the dim light. Or were her clothes too brightly colored? Her hair too shiny? Something would give her away. Her heart pounded. She couldn't hold her breath much longer, and when she did breathe again it would be too loud.

The policeman looked at his watch, turned, and started back up the ramp toward the terminal. He had just come out for a smoke, wasn't even looking for her. Them.

She sat another moment, making sure that he did not suddenly return. When she did rise, she first glanced around to make sure no one else was coming around a corner, then started toward the ship. Liel looked from the hatch, probably wondering what was taking her so long. Or had he been watching from the shadows? Did it matter?

No. Only getting out of sight mattered. Six years had taken a lot out of her.

Twilight in the hallway. Silence, too. Funny how he had not noticed the noise during the day, but now, in the night, the absence of noise made him remember. Better to think of that than what lay ahead.

Janet Logan was not the first; there might never be a last. He hoped not. Many times as an investigator, it had been necessary to utilize every weapon in his personal arsenal at one time or another. Too often the weapon of choice had been his good looks. The agency had recognized his strong points, and hired him for that reason, even though they knew so little else about him. Sending him on this case would have been logical: one woman was known to be involved; a second was probable. It was set up like any other job. Afterward, however, the masquerade was most likely over forever.

But now there was Logan to deal with. Not planned for but not unexpected, either. Making love with Arden Grenfell had proved to be a pleasure, in spite of her inexperience. Enough so that he was beginning to think long-term. Bedding Janet Logan would be a chore, if he actually had to go through with it. However, thanks to a long-ago visit to Janis IV, that would not be necessary.

The Janissaries—as they liked to call themselves—were a sensual people whose population, unfortunately, consisted of half as many men as women. Some problem in their genetic makeup. In order to keep the women satisfied, their scientists had perfected a potion that created sexual satisfaction rivaling anything a man could accomplish.

Turner patted his pocket. It sagged with the weight of a small bottle of wine. The potion had already been added with a syringe through the stopper. An old technique, but still effective.

The door to her office opened as he raised his hand to knock.

"You're late," she said accusingly, eyes shining. Her short hair was brushed straight back. Her cheeks were flushed. She wore a one-piece jumpsuit, easy to remove.

"I hoped you would wait," he said. He lifted the bottle free. "Glasses?"

"Yes." She moved to her desk, opened a drawer, and set two tumblers on top.

He uncorked the bottle as he moved nearer, then poured each glass half full. He handed her one, took one for himself.

"To us," she said.

"Of course."

They touched the glasses together. He held her eyes with his own, watched as she drank, his own glass only held to his lips, although the potion would have no effect on him. She reached to undo the fasteners of her suit. Gently, he pulled her hand away, lifted her in his arms. Her arms went around his neck, and she kissed his ear. As he placed her on the pallet she had made up on the floor near the wall, she moaned. Her breathing became rapid and her eyes rolled upward.

She would not be aware of anything except her own body for the next fifteen to twenty minutes.

Quickly, he moved to the computer. He sure did miss the voice-activated machine in his own office. Many businesses and residences now had them, but in a backwater like Caldera, any computer might show up.

The machine was already online but the screen was blank. He touched a key and a display appeared. She hadn't bothered to exit, even knowing that he was due any moment. The order had been sent; the important part was right there.

"The crew of the *Starbourne*, along with Arden Grenfell, will make an attempt to retrieve their ship at approximately three A.M. A force of twelve men should be sufficient to take them into custody. Stasis will be automatically reestablished at two-fifty-five . . ."

Damn. Two-fifty-three by the computer clock.

Frantically, he exited that program and searched the menu. Nothing there to lead the way to turning off the stasis field.

A gasp escaped from Logan. He wasn't surprised by her betrayal, nor by the fact that she had arranged it all so that he wouldn't be caught with the others. The problem was that she had planned the betrayal a little tighter than he anticipated.

Two-fifty-five. A notice flashed on the screen. The stasis field had been reactivated.

He found the diagrams for the hangars and pulled them up. After a moment's study, he saw what he wanted: the location of the stasis control. Working from there would be easier than trying to find his way through the online menus. He keyed in command after command, working his way to the one database that would give him what he needed. If he did not get this done, no one was going anywhere.

Logan moaned, her body writhing in ecstasy.

"That's as good as it gets, they tell me," he said, looking down. She neither heard nor saw him.

The last window appeared on the screen. He keyed in the last command. The stasis field was disabled and would not come back online for half an hour.

Carefully he poured what was left in both glasses back into the bottle and replaced the stopper. No use in leaving it behind; it still could come in handy again.

Turning, he left the office and relocked the door. Logan would probably sleep for an hour or more after the potion wore off. No need letting anyone barge in on her. Although the embarrassment that could cause would be good for her soul, the alarm she might raise would not help him one damn bit.

He ran back toward the hangar, the soles of his shoes squeaking against the painted concrete floor. As he drew near his goal, the sound of swords echoed along the corridor.

"We'll need to restock," Vida reported to Rafe. She had just checked the food stores and found they had not been replenished. Of course, no one had planned for any of the crew to get back on board.

"Okay," Rafe said. "Take Tahr and break into the store's locker. It's over against the east wall of the hangar." Vida started off. "And for God's sake, do it quietly."

He had just finished checking the lifeweave. Surprisingly, it was all there, probably because the Glorians had planned to come and take it all—ship and cargo. Not if he could help it. He had also found his personal sword in the hidden drawer under his bunk.

Liel and Owen went through preflight checks. Jessa worked frantically to get the navigation system recalibrated. It was a one-person job, but Rafe stood nearby, overseeing, worrying. Last he'd seen of Arden, she had planted herself at the hatch, watching. For Turner to return? For some kind of trouble to appear? Both, more than likely. After a while, he made his way to her, looked outside, saw nothing unusual as yet.

"How long has he been gone?" he asked.

She looked at her watch. "Six minutes."

"You expect him back already? He must be fast."

"Not always." She grinned up at him. "Not when it counts."

No evasion. He liked that. Not that she had any reason not to be honest about the relationship. Some women just did not admit their affairs; a holdover from more sedate times, he supposed.

Vida came into sight, followed by Tahr. Between them they carried a sling with a dozen or more canisters of food for the replicator. They had been quiet, just as he ordered. They were still quiet as they moved quickly with the heavy load.

Arden stiffened, then pulled her sword from its scabbard still slung across her back.

"What is it?"

"I'm not sure," she answered softly. "A noise. A movement. Something in the shadows over there."

She indicated the entrance ramp where the policeman had appeared earlier. Nothing there at the moment. He looked back at the two thieves. Halfway to the ship, willing them to hurry.

"Go!" a voice yelled.

The word echoed around the cavernous hangar. Heavy, fast moving footsteps followed. That sound, too, echoed, coming from everywhere at once. But those making the sounds suddenly appeared on the ramp. Rafe drew the sword he had taken from his cabin, knowing how inadequate it would be against guns.

Two lines of men in uniform split to either side of the

entry with swords drawn. Four of them rushed toward the two loaded down with booty. Tahr and Vida ran a little faster, a little more crouched. Arden jumped down to the concrete floor.

"Hurry, Tahr," Rafe yelled.

He hit the comm button beside the hatch. "Liel, speed it up. We've got company."

"The stasis field just went back on," Liel reported.

Arden looked up at Rafe. Her eyes were green—he hadn't noticed that before.

"What happened to Turner's plan?" he said.

She shrugged and hefted the sword. "Guess he needs more time," she said.

Vida and Tahr were very close. The captain had only another moment to wonder why the soldiers were not using their guns. He jumped down, following closely after Arden.

She raced to get behind the crew members, but one of the soldiers reached Vida bringing up the rear. His sword flashed, striking her hip a glancing blow with the tip as she dodged. Vida stumbled and fell. Tahr stumbled to his knees from the full weight of the sling falling toward him. Arden stepped between the soldier and Vida, slashed with her own sword, and the soldier dropped, blood pouring from the cut across his torso.

"Get the sling," Arden called over her shoulder.

She backed up to Vida and straddled her as a second soldier attacked with his straight sword. Why didn't they use the guns they were carrying in holsters at their sides?

"Can you stand?" she asked Vida. She took two strikes against her own blade.

"I think so," the cook answered.

"Get to the ship," Rafe said. He picked up the end of the sling, practically pushing Tahr to hurry.

Liel leapt from the doorway, picked up a fallen sword, and helped to defend against the leading soldiers. Suddenly, a shot was fired from the corridor leading inside. Arden could not look. However, a soldier went down. It must be

Turner, returning. Where in the hell did he get a gun? Arden guided Vida behind the other two. Two soldiers started toward the corridor, the rest toward Arden. Tahr stepped a little quicker. Another shot from the corridor, and another soldier went down.

With Owen pulling, they shoved the sling inside. Tahr then helped Vida climb in. Tahr scrambled off and returned a moment later with a sword. Owen had already found one. They both joined the fight.

Why were the soldiers still not using their guns? Even when Turner had hit two more of their number, they stuck to swords. Arden and the others continued fighting, finally managing to push most of the soldiers back toward the ramp. Two more lay on the floor.

"Get inside," Rafe yelled. He started toward Arden, who was holding off two soldiers.

"Go ahead," she yelled back. "You're closer."

The soldiers broke contact and backed up the ramp as if chased away by the gunfire. Rafe turned and ran toward the ship. He jumped through the hatchway to lie prone in the entryway. The others stood just inside. He sat up and spun around. "Come on," he yelled to her.

Turner suddenly ran for the ship, firing several times over his shoulder. Arden sped toward the hatch. He kept firing to one side of her, keeping most of the soldiers at bay.

A soldier, wounded and quite still, suddenly reached up and gripped her ankle. She went down hard, the impact knocking the wind from her. She lashed out with the sword while gasping for breath. The man's hand relaxed, and she climbed to her feet. Holding one hand against her side, she wobbled to the hatchway, but could not pull herself up.

More shots were fired. They were using their guns now. Something hit the side of the ship, near the hatchway. Arden ducked instinctively. Rafe reached out, grabbed the waist of her jumpsuit, and pulled her in. She gasped when the landing forced more air from her lungs and a sharp pain in her side. Once inside, she rolled out of the way, but to where she could look out. Turner was nowhere in sight. What might he be doing as they got shot at?

"Where is Turner?" Arden asked through gritted teeth.

"I don't see him," Rafe said.

"Is he hit?"

Her words came out a little choked. She twisted around so she could see out.

"Keep down," he ordered, and knelt beside her.

Tahr appeared from somewhere in the ship. "I'm going to the escape hatch on the other side," he said. "I'll look for Turner there. Just in case."

An explosion rocked the ship. Rafe put his arm over Arden to keep her from being tossed against the bulkhead. She gasped again.

"He blew up the stasis field," Liel shouted over the comm.

The engines hummed through the ship, creating slight vibrations in the deck. Rafe released Arden and stood, keeping as close to the bulkhead as possible. He keyed the comm.

"Get us out of here," he shouted.

"What about Turner?" Arden cried.

"We can't wait," Rafe said.

The explosion had sounded close, but on the other side of the ship. With the soldiers' steady firing now it didn't seem possible for him to get back around and into the ship.

"There he is," Arden said.

"Tahr, where are you?" Rafe called.

"Right here," came the answer right behind him. "Turner blew . . ."

"We heard," Rafe said.

They watched as the detective raced for the ship, keeping low, dodging side to side. He fired over his shoulder, then dove into the hatchway.

The taxi engines fired. No need in using the reaction drive yet and blowing everything up, including the hangar.

Turner bumped against Arden and she cried out. He called her name.

"Get the hatch closed," Rafe yelled. He hit the comm button. "Liel! Go!"

With everyone on board and the hatch closed, the police guns could not do much harm against the ship itself. It rose suddenly and hit the roof, which gave way. Free of the hangar, Liel kept it in the atmosphere so that they could all get to acceleration couches.

Rafe stood and reached down a hand to help Arden to her feet. Turner took her by the shoulders and turned her away from the captain, heading down the hall.

"Where are our cabins?" he asked.

"There's only one extra," Rafe said. "Tahr, show him."

"Sure."

The pilot led the way down the aisle. Rafe watched them. A little while ago he was worrying about trusting Arden. The private investigator would bear watching too.

10

The ship sat ready for takeoff. Every item necessary for the voyage had been stowed and all of his personal items put away. Colin Chase waited patiently for those who were to accompany him on this mission: Farrell, Marat, Zierah, and Thoms. Handpicked for this mission. All former mercenaries, they had found their niche in Glory's wars and had served under Chase more than once. Spohn, a fellow Glorian, whom they would pick up on the way, would be second in command, as usual.

"Hey, Chase," a familiar voice called from behind the command chair. "Good to see you again."

Chase turned from the ship's console to face Farrell entering the bridge. His bulk filled the entry, his dark red hair touched with grey at the temples, his smile wide and genuine. Farrell could drink any one of them under the table while piloting a ship through the eye of a needle if necessary. Chase rose and they embraced, clapping each other on the back.

"Let us through," said another person from behind the pilot. Both men moved aside and Zierah pushed through.

"Gods, you two take up too much room in here," she said sourly. "What does a woman have to do to get a little space?"

"She could act like a lady," Farrell retorted, then laughed until all the empty space seemed filled by the sound.

Zierah let loose a string of invective mostly aimed at his ancestry.

"Chase," she said, turning to him. "It's good to see you again."

They clasped hands, and a warmth spread through his body. Their friendship had never been more than that—his desires had lain elsewhere—but the woman before him was one of three who meant a great deal to him.

She reached up and kissed his cheek, an uncharacteristic show of tenderness.

"I thought of you when I heard," she said softly.

Farrell looked appropriately subdued, and Chase wondered how much he knew. Better not let this go any further.

"Thanks," he said. "Let's get to the salon. The others should be on board soon."

"This sure is a small ship," Farrell commented as they made their way along the gangway.

"She's built for speed," Chase said. "We will be a very small group. Our mission is to be completed quickly and with a minimum of fuss. That doesn't mean we don't have firepower, though."

Neither asked what the mission was. They knew he would tell them when the rest had arrived, that such things would always be done in his own good time. That was one reason he liked working with this team.

Of course, the main reason was that they were very good at what they did. Good soldiers; good spies when necessary. The long war had honed their talents, made them survivors, whose loyalties were aimed slightly lower than the emperor.

The two arrivals tossed their bags into a corner of the salon while Chase ordered drinks from the drink service. He handed them over, and all three took seats at one of the tables.

"I was glad that I was able to get hold of all of you," he said once they were settled.

"Did you get everyone?" Zierah asked.

"No. I couldn't get Sidar, he was off on a cruiser somewhere. And Kehrie was killed at Sidonia."

Farrell winced visibly. "I'll miss her," he said.

The two had enjoyed a fling on furlough a few years back that had meant a great deal to both of them. In their line of work, however, it was hard as hell to keep in touch.

Chase's own sense of loss flooded through body and soul for a moment. Although his love had been unfulfilled, Lyona's death had hurt as much nonetheless.

Loud voices announced new arrivals, driving away sadness. The others had finally come on board.

The door flew open, and the last two entered. Marat never told anyone where he came from, but he had the dark looks of a Sidonian. Thoms, short and stout and nearly bald, was from Carrell in the Jedan system. Greetings were exchanged, more bags were thrown on the pile, and more drinks ordered up. A crewman appeared.

"The captain is on the bridge," he reported to Chase.

"Fine. Tell him to lift off when he's ready."

The crewman saluted and departed. All of the team looked at him in surprise.

"This may be a small ship," Chase said, "but we've got a crew to run it. Barring any unforeseen events, you should not have to lift a finger. To run the ship, that is. I expect each of you to keep in shape, of course."

He winked at them, then got himself another coffee and settled back into the chair. Four pairs of eyes watched without staring. Good. Strong, silent types, just as he remembered. Although they shouldn't have changed that much since the last time; it had been only three years ago, after all. But, then, war can make things happen so fast. How cruelly it had killed Lyona. Beloved of Colin Chase, her bodyguard, companion, and avenger.

Liftoff from the space station went almost unnoticed. For

a short while they caught up on each other's lives, swapped a few stories. No group of people had ever been closer, and Chase welcomed their presence: the sounds of their voices, the teasing and bickering that meant only companionship. They played the game of waiting for him to speak in their own way.

The time came but, before starting, Chase got a second round of drinks. It was okay; nothing alcoholic had been stocked on board. His rule on a mission. Always. The group had fallen silent, sitting alert, expectant, unhurried. He returned to his seat and cleared his throat.

"As you know, the seeress Lyona died a short time ago," he began. He took a sip of coffee. "Without her, the war will start going badly."

He explained about the lifeweave woven into pictures and diagrams. If they didn't already know, they had guessed a little. Only Spohn and Zierah knew his feelings for Lyona. He felt sure that neither had ever told anyone else, although the others must have guessed. That he had been willing to give up the war to take care of her had been a mystery to them, but he had once been pledged to her family. His sense of failure at not being able to save her *no one* knew about.

"Our job is to get Jessa back to Glory. Now we know where she is and who she's with. The people with her have been charged with her kidnapping among other crimes. That way the law is on our side in case we need them.

"I don't foresee any problems on this assignment. The crew of the *Starbourne* are scavengers. They probably know little about fighting, with the exception of the Grenfell woman. However that may be, we will treat this as militarily as any other assignment."

Chase uncrossed his legs and wiggled the toes of his right foot. A sign of getting old, his foot going to sleep like that. Zierah and Thoms took advantage of the pause to get fresh drinks.

"You may remember Arden Grenfell. She's the imperial

guard captain who let Jessa get away from Glory six years ago. Even if they get off Caldera somehow, we can track them. We have a man on the other end.

"As far as I'm concerned, we can kill the whole lot of them. With two exceptions: Jessa and our plant. The princess owes Glory—and her mother—a lot."

He put his hands together, rubbed once.

"Okay. That's our mission. Now, let's check out the weapons. Everything I ordered was brought aboard, and I think you'll all be pleased."

"My favorite part," Marat said.

They followed Chase to the weapons locker and went to work. Small and large arms were soon spread across the floor and propped against the walls. They inspected each one, assuring themselves of its workability and that there were plenty of loads.

"I'm hoping to take them all alive," Chase said. "Or most of them anyway." He hefted one of the new laser rifles. "One thing for sure," he went on. "Princess Jessa is not to be harmed."

They all nodded agreement and continued checking out the weapons. By the end of the day their routines were begun: exercise, rest, eat, sleep, study the plan for action on Caldera, and discuss options if the quarry had left the planet. The second day out, a priority message came through. The *Starbourne* had left Caldera, destination unknown.

The ship was night quiet; everyone slept except the two or three crew members on watch. Now that she had completed her daily journal entry, Spohn heard the pulsating silence of a ship in space. People who had never been in space before couldn't hear it. They were too accustomed to lots of noise and, to them, this was total silence.

She listened a moment longer, then switched off the recorder, stood, and stretched. Muscles were still too tight. The day's news had come right after she transferred from the shuttle, and it had made everyone tense.

The *Starbourne* was on its way somewhere with both Jessa and Arden Grenfell on board. The princess interested Spohn most, but Arden could prove to be a serious problem.

The biggest problem was going to be Chase. Why did the route to the princess have to be with him? He trusted her—she'd never given him any reason not to. He was the one person whose opinion she valued but, in this case, their interests were totally at odds.

Jessa was not to be returned to Glory as Lyona's replacement. No matter what had to be done.

Short of murder? One could hope.

She opened the door and stepped out into the corridor. Her cabin was about midway among the passengers' quarters. It was not as comfortable as the one on Turner's private runabout, but few were.

Spohn made her way to the galley. Unlike her companions, she needed little sleep, a great help when a job required sleepless nights. Not that the others couldn't handle them when the need arose.

Having a ship to herself, more or less, was one of the things she enjoyed. No telling why. Even empty of people, there was little elbow room.

"Water, water everywhere, nor any drop to drink..." she recalled from a poem she had read once. Sailing an ocean. Sailing through space. Very much the same thing. A person could drown in either one, and be lost forever.

The salon was dark except for a light over the beverage replicator. She entered the code for coffee with cream and sugar. The mug filled, steam rising, bringing the scent to her nose. Even though the drink was artificial, the smell was nearly the same. Of course, she was used to the fake stuff but, having had real coffee once or twice, she understood the pleasure of expensive tastes.

"Couldn't sleep?"

The voice came from behind her. Her muscles tensed, and she fought the impulse to grab a gun where none was, to whirl around prepared to shoot. Pick up the steaming mug instead, turn calmly. The voice was familiar. No need to panic.

It took a moment to make out Chase sitting in shadows in the far corner.

"I guess that makes two of us," she said as she walked toward him, relaxing as she went.

Usually, nothing disturbed his sleep. But then, she had not seen him since long before Lyona's death.

He touched a button on the wall next to him, bringing the lights up a little. Sitting in the semicircular booth, feet crossed on a chair on the other side of the table, he looked calm enough. She sat down next to him and put her feet up beside his. He played with something in his right hand. She could almost swear it was a piece of lifeweave.

"Are you sure the tracker can keep up with the *Starbourne*?" she asked.

"Yes. As long as Eli can stay close. Last report, they weren't in any big hurry once they got out of Calderan space."

"Where did you get such an old tracer? One with that low a frequency and signal must be a hundred years old."

"Almost. Glory's armories house a great variety of equipment. Eli takes whatever he needs from it. He likes odd bits."

Eli was a tracker they had both worked with in the past. He came and went, a rather mysterious figure, seeming to work when he felt like it. Some people even thought he was over a hundred years old. She had never met him face-to-face.

"Why was he there in the first place?"

"He'd been tracking—or trying to track—the lost lifeweave shipment," Chase said. "I was told to get in touch with him when we learned that Jessa was there. He put the tracer on the *Starbourne* in case they got away. Law enforcement on such out-of-the-way places is notoriously unreliable."

The last part was said with bitterness, but she ignored it.

Instead, she simply nodded agreement. She had expected little better out of the port officials when she had retreated from Caldera herself; however, inefficiency is a way of life on remote worlds.

"Any ideas on where they'll go?"

Chase shook his head. "There are several possibilities, of course. If they're smart—and I think they are—several can be eliminated right away."

"Like?" she prodded when he went silent.

He took a drink from his cup and grimaced. The coffee was probably cold.

"If they're smart," he reiterated, "they won't go to Glory, of course. In fact, none of their home worlds. Best guess is one of the trading posts where they can sell the lifeweave. We can't commit ourselves until we at least have a better idea of their general direction."

"Meanwhile," she said, moving her feet out of the chair and to the floor, "we head thataway." She set her feet on the floor and waved her arm toward the stern of the ship. Chase grinned and shook his head. "You know what I mean," Spohn said, and clapped him on the shoulder.

"Yes, I know what you mean: chasing our tails." He sighed. "They sent that Grenfell woman looking for Jessa because all they knew was the princess 'was out there somewhere.' I don't know how she did it. Hell, I don't know how they expected her to do it. Money, I suppose. But she found the princess and let Don Vey know where she was—somewhat by accident. Someone else told him that the lifeweave was on the *Starbourne*; Eli, I would guess. That gave him the lever he needed to try to take control of the situation."

He picked up the mug, started to drink, thought better of it. Instead, he picked up the piece of cloth and rubbed it between his hands.

"What do you think made her change her mind?" Spohn asked. "What could be worth becoming a fugitive? Or losing your whole world?"

"Who?"

"Arden Grenfell."

Probably not the same thing that made you turn your back on your world and guard a blind woman instead, old friend, she thought. *But then, that Jackson Turner was quite a man. He could have made me . . .* She left the thought unfinished. It was a moot point now, anyway.

He shook his head. "I thought you might mean the princess. I don't have a clue about Grenfell." He stood up, ran his fingers through his salt-and-pepper hair. "It's getting late. I better get some sleep. You still stay up 'til all hours?"

She nodded. "I'll be up a while longer. Good night."

He was already walking away. He waved over his shoulder. She stood, picked up both cups, and took them to the chute. They disappeared silently. It was a nice ship, but she would miss that runabout.

She made her way to the bridge, looked in, waved to the crewman on duty. From there she walked every foot of corridor and communal area. There was a lot to think about. Like, how *did* Arden track down Jessa?

The breakfast call came over the comm system next morning. Two hours sleep. Enough to get by on. Not enough to make anyone like morning. Hard to believe that this time of the day felt bad even when there was no "day" to speak of. One of the few constants of life.

Everyone in the tactical group was already in the galley when she stepped in. Loud talk. Hands waving food and utensils in the air as Farrell and Zierah described an adventure the others had not been part of. The smell of coffee helped clear her head a little. The taste—and caffeine— would finish the process. None of that waker-upper pill junk for her. And, apparently, not for anyone else that morning.

The rolls looked fresh. Better than the meat pastries. The tall tale continued as she joined them. Zierah nodded while Farrell carried the tale.

". . . the bastard brought that fighter right down at us." His arm indicated the angle of flight. "We dove for cover. Any cover we could find."

"Sleep well?" Chase asked close beside her. She caught him in the ribs with an elbow. "Oooh, I forgot. Don't talk to you before you've had three cups of coffee."

"Four," she corrected.

"You never change, do you?" he said, grinning.

"Why should I? I know who I am. I've always known. And liked myself."

"All of us change a little," he pointed out.

"None of you has changed much from the first time I met you."

"More than you realize. More than you."

"And you think that's a bad thing?"

A female crewman appeared and spotted Chase. She hurried to hand him a comm slate, waiting while he read the message. The storyteller went silent.

"Can we get astronav charts on that monitor?" he asked her, pointing to a comm screen in the far wall.

"Yes, sir. Shall I access them for you?"

He nodded.

"I'll let you know if there's an answer," he said. She finished setting up the monitor, then left without another word.

"It seems that Eli has been in touch this morning," he said to everyone in general. "He sent us their position as of"—he glanced at the slate—"three hours ago."

He got up and went to the larger screen set into the wall. He keyed in coordinates. When he had the one he wanted, he turned to the group of people surrounding him.

"They went through stargate five-alpha," he said. "That's here." He indicated the spot with a finger. "Caldera is here." He pointed again, then became silent. Something had occurred to him.

"You know . . ." He rubbed his chin with his right hand. "I think I know where they might be heading."

"Sudden insight?" Spohn asked.

"Yeah. They will need money. They have millions in lifeweave on board. What trading post in that sector will most likely buy it quickly and without asking too many questions?" Spohn shrugged, and the others looked at each other. "Miga. They don't ask many questions under any circumstances. There, you can buy anything you might want. Unless there is a closer trading post, I'll bet that's where they are headed."

"I've heard the name . . ." Spohn began.

"Let me check the charts," Chase interrupted, turning back to the screen.

Chase keyed in several queries. A few minutes later he announced the answer. At that moment, Miga was the nearest of five trading posts in that sector to Caldera. It was also relatively close to Glory and their own position.

"What makes you so sure they will head for a trading post?" Spohn asked. "Seems to me there are probably a lot of places they are familiar with that we wouldn't think of. The *Starbourne* is a salvage ship, after all."

"Exactly. They've probably figured out that it's not safe to use anyone's credit disc. But they need credits. Everyone needs credits. Where else would a salvage ship go but to one of the ports where they customarily sell their goods? And they believe no one has the slightest idea where they are headed."

"You are positive they still have the lifeweave?" Farrell asked.

"Eli saw it when he placed the tracer on board."

Chase became silent, thoughtful. Everyone backed off; time to be quiet and let him plan. Spohn stood back and watched them all. Still too soon for her to make any specific plans herself, and no way to get in touch with her other comrades. They'd left everything in her hands at this stage.

"We may be able to get there ahead of them," Chase said with a big grin.

"What if we commit ourselves to Miga and they aren't going there?" Spohn asked.

He looked at her a moment. Difficult to tell from his expression whether he was angry at her questioning him or simply considering the possibility. He turned to the crewman who had returned.

"Tell the captain I may have new orders for him in a moment," he said.

The woman left and Chase returned to his chair, followed by the others. After a moment he jumped up, went to recheck the chart, then returned.

"Miga is as good a place as any for us to start," he said. "Anyway, we should know in a day when Eli gets in touch again. At this distance, we can alter course without losing too much time."

He glanced back down at the slate, nodded, and touched the transmit button.

"Captain, set course for Miga. Flank speed."

Spohn listened and worried. If she lost the princess because he guessed wrong... She took a deep breath and tried to relax. Chase's instincts were always good at times like this. Often, he almost read the prey's mind. If she didn't know him better, she might believe he used lifeweave. Needless to say, he could not afford the stuff. Except for that one small piece she was sure he had held last night. Lyona may have given it to him, or he might have slipped it from one of her caches. She would not have missed a few yards now and then.

Hard to imagine a man of his large size using a hand loom to weave a square for himself. Those hands often had difficulty pressing a single button on a comm slate like the one he held at that moment.

Hand loom!

A stack of lifeweave squares.

Chase offered to get her another cup of coffee but she begged off. It was time for her meditation, she heard herself saying. Back in the cabin, Spohn tried to slow her breathing and the thoughts racing through her mind: Arden wove lifeweave. She had seen the hand loom and squares hidden in a drawer. And the former captain had found Jessa Parcq soon after being released. Those squares were important, over and above their intrinsic value.

As far as anyone knew, Jessa had never displayed any talent for prediction. The emperor only hoped his daughter had inherited her mother's abilities.

Now they may not need the princess at all. They need only be told of another. This plan could be completed on Glory. And, while Arden was tested, there would be time for Jessa to prepare to take her place as empress. Others of her persuasion would carry out the other plan: getting rid of Granid Parcq and his equally militant son.

Government officials and generals sat closely packed around the circular conference table. All aides had been banished from the room moments before, and the talk had turned to strategic planning.

Granid Parcq sat in his high-backed chair. How does one determine the premiere position at a circular table? With a more impressive chair, of course. He chuckled to himself, garnering a look from Don Vey sitting to his left. The emperor turned to his right, where Waran should be sitting, fiddling with the pages of the report lying in front of him as he did on those rare occasions he actually attended.

The heir presumptive didn't care for these meetings, attending only occasionally at his father's insistence. How else would he learn? This war could go on for another generation, maybe longer. And if it wasn't this war, it would be another one. Eventually. However, once more, the prince was nowhere to be found. Few people on Glory even knew what the boy looked like anymore. Although the prime minister probably knew his whereabouts.

It was upsetting how well the two got along, the prince relying on Vey's advice on every matter. Something should be done about that before the relationship turned into a situation. That brought up another question: how to conduct an assassination without anyone finding out, particularly when the intended victim was also in charge of security?

Voices rose, attracting his attention. The emperor listened for a short time as the discussion of the latest setbacks and advances became heated. Suggestions were rattled off concerning how to strike back where the setbacks had occurred and how to take best advantage of the advances.

The war was going surprisingly well without Lyona's foretelling. However, without that tool in his arsenal, it was difficult for him to approve any plan with any sense of surety. *Guessing* what to do next, or worse, *guessing* what the combined enemy might do was not to his liking.

Yet it could be said that these advisors and leaders—and those doing the actual fighting—had learned a great deal, both about themselves and their forces, and about the enemy. The military lessons, the habits already formed, were standing them in good stead. Yes, the war went well, but he looked forward to the return of Lyona's daughter, which was imminent, he was told.

That bodyguard—Colin Chase—had welcomed the assignment of leading the team to bring the princess Jessa home. Strange man. His devotion to the seeress had bordered on an addiction itself. If Lyona had not been totally subservient to the lifeweave, a relationship might have developed.

He tried to bring his attention back to the discussion, but the emperor liked these meetings only slightly more than did his errant son. Shortly, General Hsing presented the plan for approval. Granid read it over, made sure it did not include any of the provisions that he could not approve, signed the paper copy, pressed his thumbprint on the infocube, and departed as soon as was polite.

Back in his sitting room, he ordered a large brandy. As he sipped it, he paced before the fireplace. Wood smoke gently scented the air. Not many people on Glory could afford wood just to burn, with so few trees. That damned monastery owned the largest remaining forest and sat right in the midst of it to make sure no one trespassed.

God, would he never be warm? The outside surface of his tunic was warm to the touch, but that warmth didn't penetrate the cloth, much less his body. He held out his hand, but warmth eluded the fingers. Flames jumped, flickered, back and forth, up and down, teasing, luring.

Come closer and you will be warm at last, they seemed to say.

Small hairs on his knuckles withered. The smell of burning hair saturated his nostrils. He drew back, set the glass down on a table, and rubbed his hand. Warmth for an instant. Only an instant. He could just see the smirk on Waran's face, mocking his father's cold nature.

He dropped into the chair and picked up the glass from the table beside it. Ordering a drink and getting it sometimes seemed the only thing he could count on anymore. Cliques and groups vied for power all around him. Waran and his supporters, the war party, counted some of the generals among them, or so it was said. Waran wanted the throne *now* and, encouraged by the military men, favored waging war without foretelling.

Then there was the group that wanted peace. Only recently, word had come to him that they favored having Jessa as their empress. But the princess had been gone so long, no one could know what her policy might be. These people assumed she would favor a peaceful conclusion. Fools! She was a Parcq. She would . . . He had been about to think that she would follow her father's policies. Like she followed them clear off the planet.

She had been away six years. No one knew anything about her at all anymore. Had any of them considered that the generals might not follow a woman, which would make war be a moot point anyway. If she took the throne, there would be no choices. Therefore, the peace group would have what they wanted without having to make any real decisions. Peace by default.

Or through a lack of war.

Children! They were every bit as unreliable as wives and friends.

Glory would lose, and everything he and Lyona had...

She came into his dreams almost every night. They started less than a week after her death. In the beginning she was beautiful as in the early days, eyes bright, all-seeing. Hair black, thick, long. A man could get lost in either if he looked long enough.

Slowly she donned layer after layer of lifeweave robes. With each, the eyes dimmed, the hair greyed, the skin withered. In the end, just before he jerked awake, the seeress, his old love, withered to nothing. Lifeweave shimmered around the dried hulk, the fabric's colors accentuating grey death.

Granid shook his head, chasing away the memory. He had discarded all lifeweave from his wardrobe and bed. Still, the dream came, now haunting him when awake.

If there was someone he could trust. Just one.

There was one, but he had sent Chase away. A loyal man, even if Lyona was the object of his devotion, the loyalty had spread to the emperor through association and long habit.

Or...

How could he know?

Maybe, when Jessa returned, she could be convinced to back her father. If she favored the war, or even if she had no prejudices either way, she could be his best ally. It might be accomplished, particularly if she never learned of the movement to put her on the throne. That could be prevented if things were managed properly.

Would she look like her mother?

Please, no.

That would be unbearable.

11

"Come. I will show you the way."

The spirit turned, started away. Arden's body was too heavy; nothing would move.

"I can't," she said.

It turned, regarded her a moment. Unlike earlier spirits that she had encountered, which always appeared smoky as if their life essence swirled in a void of its own, this entity sparkled with cold fire. It was more frightening because she knew it less.

As if deciding she told the truth, it nodded and moved toward her. It picked her up easily, yet nothing pressed against her skin. No sensation from the hand that wrapped up and over her knee, nor from the other hand gripping her upper arm. Arden floated forward, tense and afraid.

This spirit not only looked different, its frame of existence was unlike any other. Before they were always bound to their own worlds, unable to leave, firmly anchored even while they flew above, sometimes through, material objects. This one existed in nothingness, seemingly lost between worlds, as if an exile. Or had it never known boundaries? How does one ask such questions? After another glance at the being, she decided it might be best to learn as things developed.

She turned from studying it to considering their surroundings, although there seemed little to see. But she discovered that was wrong. They moved among millions of stars, each glowing in its own little conceit. One shone brighter as they drew nearer. No, not a star. A planet. Cries of pain and sorrow rose from a small area on its surface, to be heard even in the vacuum of space. Tears came to her eyes. How could people suffer like that and go on?

Wait. She knew that world, that area. The monastery. Home. What had happened?

"No!" she shouted. "I don't want to see. It's my fault."

"Not until you know the enemy," the spirit said. "I will show the way."

Laughter, starting low as if far away, came out of the darkness behind her. It rose in volume, drawing nearer, then stopped abruptly.

"Aren't you in a fix now? See what you've done."

Pac Terhn was somewhere behind her. She tried to look around, but the creature holding her would not move.

"You didn't keep your promise," Pac Terhn continued.

She tried to beat at the creature, but her hand passed through. "Put me down!" she ordered.

"You promised to take care of the princess and stay with her until she dies."

"What part of that have I not done?" She continued to struggle, trying to get free, but it was hopeless.

"You aren't taking her back to Glory."

"There was nothing in our agreement about her having to return."

"It was understood."

"But not stated. It doesn't count unless the term is stated."

"That was the task set you prior to our agreement. It was a preexisting condition. Only by doing that can you save your precious monastery from the ravages of the emperor's troops."

"That hasn't happened yet?" She stopped struggling and

looked back down on the scene in the forest.

"No, not yet. It will happen if you don't comply."

"I really don't have much control over the princess's fate at the moment."

"Find a way."

Arden sighed. She was tired of her own conflicting emotions and of others demanding that she comply with their commands or needs. Everywhere she looked, she was outnumbered.

"I'll try," she said.

"Don't try. Do!"

Arden closed her eyes, tears squeezed between the lids. Voices spoke around her, but the words were unclear. Their tone encouraged and soothed. Sleep came, wrapping her in darkness, protecting her from dreams and spirits. And from the trickster, Pac Terhn.

Turner had stayed close to Arden for most of two days and a night that they had shared the cabin. He had no function on this ship. Leave its operation to its crew. Instead, examine what had happened.

Because he had not been careful enough, both Jessa and Arden could have been killed. It was bad enough that the wound in Arden's side had reopened. He had thought to help the group, thereby accomplishing his mission, but that was a bit of a miscalculation. One that would not recur.

Arden had been very restless just a few minutes before, but now she slept quietly. How pretty she looked. She was the only woman he had ever known to actually look pretty in sleep, a thought that occurred to him every time he saw her like this.

A knock on the door; then Jessa came in at his invitation.

"Oh, I thought I heard Arden cry out."

"She is sleeping now," he answered. "How is Vida doing?"

"The cut on her hip is healing quickly. She should be back to work in the galley soon."

"I'm glad it wasn't more serious." Turner made room for her to sit down on his bunk. "Have a seat."

"Does she always sleep so soundly?" Jessa asked.

"Sometimes. She has dreams that are very real. That's when she does these."

He reached over and touched the hand loom that Arden held in both hands. Jessa stiffened.

"Why does she do this?" the princess asked.

"Things come to her in the dreams," he said. "Arden weaves pictures so she will remember what she saw afterward."

"She might not want to let anyone else know she can do this."

"Why not, for God's sake?"

"If my father and Don Vey find out she has this ability, they might decide they don't need me. Especially since, I have never exhibited this talent that they want so badly. If this is any indication"—she pointed to the loom with its lifeweave square—"Arden can do what they want. They might settle for her if they ever find out."

Although he knew the reasons Jessa was wanted back so badly, he had certainly never made this connection. Arden's weaving had been for her own use and something she didn't exactly control. Except . . . the squares answered a question—her own question.

Other questions could be made vital in much the same way the search for Jessa had been. Why hadn't he seen this before?

Arden raised her arm over her head. In another moment her eyes opened. She looked at the two standing over the bunk.

"What . . . ?" she said.

"Good morning," Jessa said, smiled down at her, and left the cabin.

"What's the matter?" Arden asked.

Turner picked up the hand loom lying on her thigh and showed it to her.

"Not again," she said. "I'd hoped that part was done."

"It may be a bigger problem than you think."

"How?" she croaked.

Turner got her a glass of water from the tray on the dresser. Arden sat up and drank almost all of it; then her head fell back on the pillow and she rubbed her side.

"Why might this be a problem?" she asked, waving the loom.

She sat up and stretched.

"Jessa is afraid of what might happen if Granid Parcq and Don Vey find out about your weaving."

"Why would that..." Her eyes widened. Turner nodded. "I see," she said. "But... I don't exactly work to order."

"No. However, your unconscious weaving—now, at least—was brought about by pressure from them. Your needs coincide with their needs. They might learn to control you in the same way, at any time, given the right incentive."

Arden closed her eyes and sighed. Turner waited a short while, then asked, "Are you tired?"

"No," she answered quickly. "Just thinking. It would seem that my safety could depend on Jessa's return to Glory more than I knew. I couldn't live like that, Turner. A loom and lifeweave my only existence, the visions my only memories. I'm not addicted. Maybe I'm somewhat immune. Jessa sure seems to be immune. I just don't want to take that chance. If... Promise me you wouldn't let them have me."

"What?" he said. "You are asking that I..."

"Yes. Kill me if I can't manage it myself. That way I couldn't be blamed. The monastery must be saved."

"All right," he said with seeming reluctance.

"Don't look so gloomy," she said. "There has to be a way for all of us to get what we want. Or most of us, anyway. I've promised to help find a solution, and I mean to do just that. Still..." She sighed.

The loom was still in his hand. Turner started to lay it on the dresser, but something about the pattern caught his eye. He turned it to face him, twisted it slightly to catch the light. There. Spohn's features stared from the shiny cloth.

Arden paced the corridor between her cabin and the far end. After more than a week of confinement in the ship, the side that was wounded in the alley and reopened in the fight in the hangar, was beginning to tighten from lack of exercise, as were all of her muscles.

She had thought often how easily she could have been shot again in the hangar. True, she had recognized early on that this adventure was not her strong suit. Desperation makes people do things they would not ordinarily tackle. That truth was also difficult to cope with. Her situation was made desperate by someone else who didn't give a manton turd what happened to her. Even if she failed, they could send someone else.

If only they'd done that in the first place. Someone else could have found the princess. Using lifeweave wasn't the only way to track someone down.

Finding Jessa was the only thing she had done right so far!

She leaned her forehead against the cool metal wall and shut her eyes tight. This was one of those times when she almost wished that she had been born male. And yet, dammit, she was tired of apologizing for being female. To whom? Abbot Grayson certainly did not mind. Being the first female in the imperial guard had made it necessary to work harder, to be better than the men, and that was something to be proud of.

If she owed an apology to anyone, it was to the crew of this ship, and that had nothing to do with her sex. Of course, they still blamed her for their current plight, and rightly so. However, they appreciated her courage in helping get them off Caldera. Rafe had said as much on one of his rare visits to her cabin.

The future was still a problem, for all of them. Rafe had, of course, been thinking about what to do, and he'd explained to her on one of those visits that salvagers work two ways. First, they work within the law, everything aboveboard, which meant having all licenses and permits. That way you never had to look over your shoulder to make sure the law wasn't closing in. You never had to worry about a cargo being confiscated or not being able to sell it.

Or they could ignore the laws, taking cargos that might not be legal, and always selling on the black market. Few major trading posts worked that way. However, Miga was one that worked either way. It was also the closest. Even though the cargo of lifeweave was obtained legally, word had surely spread about the warrant, and it was hoped the people there would look the other way. Unless, of course, they got there ahead of the warrant.

Arden asked Rafe only once why they had to be in such a hurry to sell it. Couldn't they wait until things had calmed down a bit? Everyone else was of the opinion that if they did not sell quickly, that might lose all chance to do so. They might be lucky enough to get the jump on everyone. If not . . . He had shrugged.

He put a brave face on it, but the thought of seeming to turn pirate saddened him. It was plain not in his words but in his eyes. Although other feelings had sometimes shone from his eyes during his rare stops over the past two days.

Turner had been in the cabin most of the times, although he often stepped out to let the two of them talk. The detective had shown a new dedication to her welfare. Somehow, that change in attitude had also increased the uneasiness she felt about their relationship.

Could Rafe's presence have anything to do with that? Several times she took out the lifeweave square with Rafe's likeness on it. Had its existence preconditioned her to find him more fascinating than she would otherwise?

Every time the captain stepped into her cabin, Arden got that feeling in the pit of her stomach. Pleasant and unpleasant all at the same time. If he wasn't there, she waited for him to appear, hoping he would come. When he did come, one time she might be tongue-tied, almost unable to think of a thing to say. Another time, they would talk like old friends, catching up on things after not seeing each other for a long time.

A new wariness seemed to have developed between the two men, too, in spite of all they had been through together. Another figment of her imagination?

Arden placed her hand on the corner of the bulkhead and turned back toward her cabin. Rafe stood about halfway down, and she stopped short.

"Didn't mean to startle you," he said, and walked toward her.

"It's okay. I just didn't know anyone was there."

Stopping just in front of her, he held out his left arm. His warmth coursed along her skin through the sleeve when she linked her own arm through his.

"Getting restless?" he asked.

"Yes, a little. I need to practice, but there just isn't enough room." They took a few more steps in silence. "When do we get to Miga?"

"Another two days. Maybe a little more."

"Are you sure it's safe to go there?" she asked for what seemed the twentieth time.

"Nowhere is totally safe these days." Her grip tightened on his arm, and he stopped. He looked down and must have read the reason for her distress in her face. "I didn't mean that as a criticism," he said. "Only a statement of fact. As long as that warrant is outstanding, the law everywhere will be looking for us. At least there isn't a reward. Yet. *Everyone* will be looking for us if that ever happens."

They reached her door, and he pushed it open and stood aside for her to enter. The cabin didn't feel quite as confining as it had when she left it.

Releasing his arm, she stretched out on the bunk and propped herself up with the pillow. He sat in the chair once she was settled.

"What can we do to avoid the law on Miga?" she asked.

"There isn't much law there. It's mostly run by the major dealers. I know some people we can deal with. As far as we know, Glorian officials have no way of finding out where we're headed. If everything works quickly, we should be in and out of there in two days at most."

"Then where?"

He exhaled loudly and crossed his legs, without kicking the bunk. He had lots of practice in the small spaces of the ship.

"We've been talking about it," he said, and ran his fingers through his hair. "No one has come up with a good idea yet. We need to clear our names as soon as possible."

"For that we probably need someone as powerful as Granid Parcq."

"People like that are hard to find."

"True. But maybe my friends on Glory can help. The abbot is not without some influence in government."

They sat silently. It was easy to be comfortable in his company. Arden closed her eyes and willed herself to relax. Rafe's presence seemed to be a two-edged sword in that regard.

"Turner told me you haven't mentioned getting Jessa back to Glory since we left Caldera," he said.

"No, I haven't."

"Why?"

"Because of a dream."

He nodded as if he understood. They talked a while longer about their situation and speculated on what they would do after leaving Miga, mostly wild and impractical ideas of how to spend so much money.

The door opened, and Turner stepped just inside. He looked at them with that expression of exasperation with which he always seemed to regard them when they were together.

The chair creaked slightly as Rafe stood.

"I had better get back on the bridge," he said. She reached out a hand, and he took it in his and smiled down at her. Her eyes closed as he released her hand.

Captain Raphael Bedford Semmes, that's me, he thought as he made his way to the bridge. *Salvager, spacer, lady's man—or wanna-be—and ship owner. Outlaw.*

The last word came to mind unbidden. How the hell could everything fall apart in such a short time? Women. That's how. They would always be the bane of his existence. Of all men's existence.

Now, suddenly, there were two women in his life on a serious basis. One a member of the crew whom he was determined to protect. The other... What was Arden to him?

Someone he also wanted to protect. Someone he enjoyed being with. A woman who had put everything he valued in jeopardy, and who would fight very hard to accomplish her task. Even go as far as feigning interest in him?

That last part wasn't fair. His own feelings would not be so strong if she wasn't also attracted to him, at least a little. This was the kind of attraction that was strong because it worked both ways. However, the worst part was, he didn't want to feel this way. He'd been in love before. A dozen times. More than once, anyway. Freedom was better. He would have to shake free of these feelings before they became too embedded.

He entered the bridge. Tahr looked up from the pilot's console and gave him an "I'm overworked" scowl. Jessa was checking coordinates, still a little paranoid about the recalibration she had done so very fast. Semmes sat in his chair.

The captain's chair. It was comfortable because it was where he belonged. From there he watched and commanded as they roamed the known sectors of the galaxy, picking up after other people, and making a pretty good profit in the bargain.

Arden, on the other hand, had been dirt-bound most of her life. She had her own career. Not a lucrative one, but one she valued. She couldn't go traipsing around, searching out wrecks and derelicts. Nor could he settle down on Glory, or anywhere else for that matter.

Whoa, there, son. There he was thinking about her again and making plans. Or avoiding them. And why? Because he had that feeling in his loins, to put a biblical turn to it.

Liel entered the bridge, distracting Rafe from such useless thoughts.

"Captain, we may have a problem."

The executive officer stopped almost in front of him, allowing enough space for his captain to still see the entire ship's console.

"What kind of problem?" At last, a distraction to pull his mind back to business and off the passenger.

"We've picked up a low-frequency signal and can't seem to trace its source."

"Outside the ship?"

"Can't tell for sure, but we think it might be inside."

"Have you made another sweep with a detector?"

"No. But this signal isn't like any tracer."

"Try it anyway," Semmes said. "Not just Turner's, though. Try our old one, too. Just in case."

"That will have to wait, Captain," Jessa spoke up. "It's time to make the next stargate jump."

"How long?" Semmes asked.

"Two minutes," she responded.

"Okay. As soon as we're through, then," he said, turning back to Liel.

"If the signal is coming from inside, we could have trouble getting through the gate," Liel reminded him.

Ships had to cut off all communications while going through a gate. Any kind of broadcast signal could echo back and set up a vibration that would shake a ship apart. However, they had already made the jump through one gate safely. *No need to worry now,* he thought, and he told Liel the same.

Tahr muttered something that no one quite heard or paid attention to. He didn't like stargates, along with everything else he didn't like.

Liel moved to his own chair and Semmes strapped himself in while Jessa announced the upcoming jump over the comm. Looking down, he saw his knuckles were white and made himself loosen his grip on the armrests. No one liked jumping, although each person was affected a little differently. The magnetic field played along his nerves like a xylophone and made his back teeth hurt. The whole process lasted only a few minutes at most, but it was unpleasant enough to remember for a day or so. Especially when you jumped one gate after another.

There had been times the *Starbourne* had jumped almost every other day as they hurried from one wreck to another. Sometimes the wreck would already be claimed by another salvage ship. Working the outer worlds, like Caldera, was easier because there were fewer salvagers. The drawbacks were many, however, including the scarcity of both trading posts and wrecks.

"Jump in fifteen seconds," Jessa announced.

Check the straps. Swallow hard. Loosen your damn hands. It began.

No one understood who had not been through it. Those who had experienced it—even if they had jumped a hundred times or more—could explain what it was like only to someone else who had jumped.

Nothing compared to the thrill—or chill—running up and down legs and arms. Even his throat itched. His toes curled inside the soft boots. Lights danced in his field of vision, while through them he watched Tahr working the controls. Rafe gritted his teeth.

The sensation was gone as quickly as it came, leaving a

residue of feeling that was a numbness like no other. They were inside.

Semmes started to unfasten the straps.

"Everyone stay strapped in," Tahr yelled.

The ship shuddered, then pitched to starboard.

"We've got vibration, Captain," Jessa yelled.

The *Starbourne* shuddered and bucked over and over. The stabilizers weren't responding to computer commands.

"Manual controls," the captain shouted.

They had to get her under control or the ship would shake itself apart, spilling them into the cold airless vacuum. That thought had never scared him as much as it did at that moment.

Liel strained to reach the console. Rafe fought down the urge to unstrap. The exec was closer and knew what he was doing. Liel finally flipped the switch. The ship shook as if it was a rat in the jaws of an immense terrier. Liel was thrown back in his chair. Rafe was whipped from side to side. Jessa cried out.

Liel reached to undo his straps, but he was thrown to the side again.

Captain Raphael Bedford Semmes. That's who I am. Right hand to the strap. Move up to the latch.

Slowly, his fingers pulled along, feeling metal at last, as the ship continued to toss him side to side. A violent lurch, and his hand slipped. He tightened his grip, and a rivet dug into his thumb. It felt sharp as hell and he fought to hold on. In a moment of calm, he grasped the latch, pulled it open, and braced himself for the next buck.

When it subsided, Semmes slid out of the chair to the deck and started crawling toward Liel. *The manual controls. Must get to them.* Another lurch bounced him off the deck. Blood salted his tongue.

Almost to the chair. He grabbed the pedestal just in time to keep from being bounced again. Constant shudders in the deck had numbed his hands, and he had to watch to make sure they didn't slip off. Another quiet moment, and he gripped the chair arm, started to rise. A lurch. He butted Liel in the mouth. Both men grunted. Rafe pulled away. A small trickle of blood appeared at the corner of Liel's mouth. His eyes looked dazed.

Rafe fought the urge to rub his head. He pressed himself upright, turned. The next lurch set him in Liel's lap. He braced again, then launched himself off Liel with his hands on the armrests and fell toward the console. *Don't land on any controls. Make matters worse. Grab the overhead handles.* His right hand curled around the metal, but the left missed. Sharp pain seized his anchored hand and wrist as he spun halfway around.

He clamped his jaws tight and pushed with one foot to straighten himself. Pain seared his upper arm, and he cried out. His left hand grasped the other handle, but he dared not loosen the right just yet. The ship bucked and his feet came off the floor. More pain.

He ignored it and reached down with his good hand to grip the stabilizer wheel. It resisted, and the injured hand protested. If the ship were steady, there would be no problem at all.

At last the wheel moved. He must get the ship stabilized, keep it that way, until the vibration played itself out. It *was* steadying. His feet didn't come off the deck quite so often nor so high. Liel appeared beside him, the blood from his mouth still glistening. The exec pressed the firing button for the port attitude jet, then the starboard. The lurching ceased. Soon, even the shuddering eased and stopped.

Rafe tried to let go of the stabilizer wheel but couldn't. With his right hand he pried the fingers loose. The injured wrist was already swollen, throbbing with pain that reached from fingertips to shoulder. He sat back in Liel's chair.

"Find that goddam signal," he said. "And don't say 'I told you so.'"

"No, sir," Liel agreed with a grin. He wiped at his mouth with the back of his hand. "I'll let Tahr take care of that."

The captain groaned. He glanced over his shoulder. Tahr and Jessa worked at their controls, checking, resetting. Both looked badly shaken. Sure enough, though, he would get an earful as soon as the pilot could take the time.

"I'll go back and check our passengers," he said.

Liel grinned again, as if reminding him that escape would not last long. No, but he had to find out if Arden was all right.

"Better get that wrist taken care of, too," Liel advised.

Lord, that would mean seeing Tahr sooner than he wanted. No help for it, though. The pain was bad enough to indicate at least a bad sprain.

He pushed out of the chair and stopped, pressing his right hand against his chest with the left. When the pain subsided, he made his way toward Arden's cabin, still cradling the wounded appendage.

The door opened just as he caught sight of it, and Arden rushed out, her face even paler than before. She saw him and ran to him.

"You're . . ." she started, then seemed to see his injured hand for the first time. "You're hurt."

"Just a sprain or something," he said.

"Where's Tahr?"

"He's busy getting the ship back in trim."

"Come in and sit down, then. You are white as Amun in the morning."

She opened the door of her cabin, letting him enter first.

"On the bed," she ordered.

"Are you . . ."

"I'm all right."

She practically pushed him onto the bunk. He let her lift his feet up. Gods, he did feel tired. And, at last, his head quit spinning.

"What's Amun?" he asked as he relaxed with relief.

"Our sun on Glory. Named after an ancient sun god of Earth."

She filled a glass with water and handed it to him.

"You know a lot about your world," he said.

He had once known a lot about his own world, but that was long ago. Arden sat down while he drank.

"When your family has lived on a world for several generations, your history and its history are linear and joined. You tend to learn both, whether you want to or not."

He handed the empty glass to her. "More?" she asked.

"Please."

His throat was so dry. He leaned back against the pillow she had fluffed there and closed his eyes. All in all, he was feeling better, but the others on the bridge were probably in need of a break. He had better get back soon. Maybe Turner could . . .

Where was Turner? He asked Arden.

"He went to check on something."

"What? When?"

"I don't know what. Once the ship quit bucking, he said he needed to check on something and left. Not long before you appeared. Were you looking for him then?"

"No, I . . . I mean . . . I just wanted to make sure the two of you were okay."

"I see," she said, sounding disappointed.

She'd probably wanted him to say he was worried about her. He wasn't ready to admit that, even to himself. But this whole conversation was turning in a direction that made him do just that. After all, she was all right and . . .

What could Turner be checking on?

Rafe finished the water and handed her the glass. He laid his head back on the pillow and tried to regain the relaxed feeling that was there a moment ago. However, the realization that Turner was missing—if only for the moment—and the pain in his wrist both shouted for attention when he moved his hand from resting on his stomach to his thigh.

"Do you want me to get Tahr?" Arden asked softly.

"No. I'd better get back to the bridge. We're still a day

and a half out of Miga and there are some things to take care of before we arrive."

"I hope we won't have any more problems like the last one."

She had no idea what had happened. It had not occurred to him that an explanation might be in order.

"No more," he said. "Only when jumping through a stargate. The problem happened because..."

"... a signal of some kind was broadcast from the ship in the middle of the jump sequence."

Rafe started at the sudden interruption. He turned and saw Turner standing in the doorway, his right hand extended. In it was a small, old-fashioned tracer unit. The outer case was blackened from intense heat.

"You know about magnetic resonance?" Rafe asked, but he studied the small piece of electronics.

Turner nodded.

"As soon as everything settled down, I went looking for this. I was sure that neither you nor any of your crew would have made the mistake of using a radio or comm unit."

"Where was it?"

"In one of the lifeweave crates."

"What made you look there?"

Turner lifted his other hand. It held the old detector Rafe had told Liel to use just a few minutes ago.

The three of them speculated for a few minutes on how the transmitter had gotten on board and who put it there.

"Looks like we'll need to hurry our plans on Miga," the captain said. "If someone is following us..."

"I think it was damaged when the ship was trying to shake apart," Turner said. "Unless whoever is trying to follow knows about trading posts, they won't know where we are going. However, I agree," he added hastily, "that we should not take more time than is necessary, but at the same time, we do not need to rush the sale of the lifeweave too much."

Turner handed over both pieces of equipment as Rafe

rose to leave. Owen would need to check it out to be sure it was no longer sending signals and to determine exactly what happened to it. Turner guessed that its circuits blew during all the tossing and turning of the ship.

Once it was in Owen's cabin, the thing came apart quickly, pieces strewn all over the blanket. Liel had joined them and watched with interest to equal Rafe's.

"Yes, Captain," Owen said. "It shorted out."

"Would that have happened when we came out of the stargate?"

"Could have. These older units weren't as tough as the newer models."

"Thanks," Rafe said. "Put that back together but make sure it doesn't work. Let's go," he said to Liel.

Halfway between Owen's cabin and the bridge, the captain stopped. He considered a moment before speaking. New suspicions must always be considered before one said anything. However, this was not something to be ignored.

"If this burned out when we exited the stargate," he began, "how did Turner find it just a few minutes later with this? The detector only works when a tracer is broadcasting."

He held up the detector. Liel's eyes narrowed, and he nodded.

12

The crew went about their tasks, readying the *Starbourne* for landing. Arden watched, admiring the way their movements meshed, as if the four were one person. She had always admired people who knew their jobs and performed them assuredly.

Fascinating as it was, it could not keep thoughts of an earlier scene from her mind. It had been unpleasant, to say the least. Rafe had been so sure.

Turner had just left on one of his walkabouts to stretch his legs. He had become more and more odd since leaving Caldera, and she welcomed time alone to analyze his attitude. Not that any insight had materialized.

The obvious elements: Turner had become more possessive of her, quieter, and more alert. And definitely more secretive.

When Rafe knocked, she had opened the door and felt the now familiar pleasure at seeing him. He and Liel stepped inside without a smile between them. Before she could ask about his injured hand, now encased in a stretch bandage, the captain started asking about Turner: how had she met him and what did she know about him, all of which she had told him before. At first, the grilling had irritated her. This was hardly the time to review Turner's credentials. However, Rafe's earnestness stilled any protests.

She started at the beginning—their meeting in the alley. Spohn's betrayal. Turner's revelation that he was an investigator for Wilson Detective Agency on assignment on Caldera with one of the mining companies.

"Did you check on him?" Rafe asked.

"Of course. I contacted the agency and they confirmed that he worked for them, but not much else. He was born on Warrick II..."

"Warrick II is allied with Glory," Liel broke in.

"True, but he hasn't been home in several years," Arden said. "Surely, that being his home world isn't reason to condemn him."

The two men had said nothing specifically accusatory, but what else could their attitude, and the questions, mean?

"If you have something specific—some reason to mistrust him—tell me," she said.

They looked at each other, and suddenly she felt that they didn't quite trust her, either. This was ridiculous. She opened her mouth to tell them to leave when the captain interrupted.

"You remember the tracer he found in the lifeweave?" he said.

"I remember," she said. That should mean he was on their side.

"It was a very old model, one that his brand-new detector couldn't read. He had insisted that we use the new one the first time. This time, he used one of our old detectors. The trouble is..." He looked at Liel again. The latter shrugged. "The trouble is, he claimed that he found the tracer after the shakeup, and that it was already damaged. If all of that was true, there was nothing for the detector to pick up."

The conclusion that was clearly logical to them seemed pretty weak. There must be a dozen other explanations for what happened. Turner was not necessarily an enemy, a spy, not to be trusted, already trusted too much. But he *had* insisted that they use his brand-new tracer in the original sweep of the ship.

What if he was all of those? They could be heading into a trap on Miga. The princess . . .

Fear for herself turned her stomach slightly. All well and good to be concerned for others, but Jessa's warning still chilled her. And Turner knew about the squares. He knew what they meant. The sudden fear must have shown on her face. Rafe took the two steps that brought them together, put his arms around her, and held her.

"There's some reason this frightens you more than I imagined it would," he said.

She let him hold her a moment, then gently pushed away. He didn't release her completely, keeping his hands on her shoulders.

"You know why Glory wants Jessa back," she said. He nodded. "It's possible I could turn into the target. It seems that I have more talent in that area than she does."

"Captain," Jessa's voice said over the comm speaker. "We are approaching orbit around Miga."

"Very well," he acknowledged.

"We could be walking into a trap," Arden said, voicing the fear that had started plaguing her.

"Perhaps not if we're quick enough," Rafe said.

He kissed her, quickly, gently, and turned to leave. He stopped and turned back.

"You can take one of the couches on the bridge," he said and took hold of her hand.

She followed, stunned into submission by his unexpected display of affection, of caring. All the fear had left her mind and body, banished by that moment's contact.

The euphoria evaporated as they met Turner in the hall.

"Arden's going to watch the landing from the bridge," Rafe said as they squeezed past.

Turner looked puzzled, then shrugged and moved from sight. Where was he as preparations continued for landing? In the cabin, she supposed. Each bunk was equipped with straps for acceleration and deceleration just like the couches on the bridge.

Dammit. She had let her interest in Turner as a man cloud her judgment. She should have been more wary. But he was so charming and handsome. The physical attraction that had been so strong, and was waning now, had been compulsive in the beginning.

Once again, danger was brought to the crew of the *Starbourne* by her stupidity or carelessness. But, then, they would not have gotten off Caldera without his help. Why, if Turner was in on the plan to return Jessa to Glory, had he worked so hard to help them get away? Maybe he had feared Harris or someone else would interfere. Or, it could be that he and his cohorts had a plan from which they did not want to deviate.

Damn! Judgment made, and with so few facts against him. Was she so quick to believe Turner was the enemy because Rafe was sure?

"Entering the atmosphere now," Tahr declared.

The captain looked around from his chair and smiled. It didn't chase worry from his eyes or from her heart. Pressure built up, and the ship began to vibrate. He turned back around. Arden squeezed her eyes shut.

I'm too tired for this. All of it. I just want to go home.

Spohn approached the salon, satisfied with the report she would make to Chase. Events were starting to come together, and it looked like both of them would have what they wanted. At least for a while.

She stepped into the salon. Chase sat over in his usual corner. Looked like he was drinking coffee again. He drank more than he used to, and the result was that he frequently became nervous and irritable. Almost everyone had started avoiding him much of the time. So unlike past missions. It was more than just the coffee, of course. Losing Lyona must have affected him more than it had first appeared.

Well, the news she had should cheer him up some. She

approached the table, knowing that although he didn't look at her directly, he was aware of every step she took. When she stopped before the table, he looked up. She shuddered inwardly. The look in his eyes was so unlike the Chase she knew. This Chase was dangerous, and not just to his enemies. God help those on the *Starbourne*.

"The captain says we're less than a day from Miga," she said. "The *Starbourne* has landed."

"Has Egan agreed to delay them?" Chase asked, referring to the port commander.

"Yes, he has. And so has Kerio, the head of the trade guild. We should get there before they even sell the lifeweave. Their ship will be disabled immediately, of course."

"Nothing better go wrong."

"It won't. Migan officials can be bought but, once bought, they hold to the bargain, even if a higher price is offered."

Chase raised an eyebrow.

"That's their reputation." She answered the unspoken question. "I've known traders who dealt there. One or two who knew Egan. He controls the trading post completely. Even Kerio wouldn't dare go against him."

Most guilds, and their leaders, were relatively independent of local authority. Egan must be quite an official.

Chase opened his right hand and, for the first time, revealed a wadded piece of lifeweave fabric. Released from the pressure, it slowly opened up to lie across his hand, the edges hanging over. About four inches square, it shimmered in the light, predominantly purples and reds.

Chase looked up, noticed her attention.

"From her gown," he said. "The one she died in. I cut it off before anyone else came to her room that last day. I knew she was dying."

"That stuff's addictive, you know," Spohn said. "Even that small a piece."

He looked down at his treasure. Probably the only thing he had of hers, the woman he loved. No, he had more than loved her; he had worshipped her. Why, one couldn't even guess. Perhaps because of her helplessness. The seeress was already grey-haired and nearly blind when Chase returned to the post in her household. Being sent back to her service had even been a punishment for some infraction in the field. Months later he was offered a new and better position in the military, a chance to return to the work he had loved. He had refused. By then, Lyona had become the most important thing in his world.

"Do you really intend taking Jessa back to Glory?" she asked. It was quite possible that he had other plans for Jessa.

His head jerked up, and the anger in his eyes was almost maniacal.

"She must take her mother's place," he said in a hard tone. "She abandoned her mother, never came back when Lyona needed her most. Jessa owes her."

"I was afraid . . ."

The words stuck in her throat. He had loved the mother; would that devotion possibly be transferred to the daughter? Or would his anger bring death to the daughter? Chase irrationally blamed Jessa for Lyona's death. The princess could have done nothing, had she stayed on Glory, except endanger herself.

"Nothing is written in stone," he said with a cold smile.

It was all taking too long. Nearly two full days had passed since they had landed on Miga. They hadn't even taken rooms in a local hotel because everyone was so sure that selling the lifeweave would take no more than a day, but the tradesmen were dragging their feet for some reason. Also, the only way they had to pay for rooms for them all was with the credit disc in Leesan Knohr's name, and they decided not to take the chance of its being traced.

Neither crews nor passengers were allowed to stay on board ship in Miga's port which was totally enclosed against the lethal elements of the planet's atmosphere. The policy helped prevent disagreements from happening in the first place, and kept them from spreading throughout the port in the second. An exception had been made for Vida, whose hip still gave her problems.

Or so the port commander said. Rafe told her that the rule was not new, but Arden couldn't help feeling uneasy at being kept off the ship, and at Turner's almost morbid attention to her every move. In spite of Rafe's new protective stance, the investigator hovered closely as they moved endlessly around the promenade, waiting for word, growing more and more tired and restless.

The Newton Cafe was busy as usual. The brandy hadn't helped relax her nerves. She held up the empty glass, and another soon appeared on the table. Across from her, Jessa frowned. Let her disapprove all she wanted to. Brandy at least satisfied the need for something tasty as well as for an anesthetic.

The captain had gone off with Liel for another meeting. Tahr mumbled to himself on her right. Turner sat on the left except when he jumped to his feet and circled the table. Once, he had even stood behind her chair when a crewman from another ship approached. The man's drunken purpose had been to talk to Jessa, but Turner's forbidding figure discouraged the man's romantic intentions. Jessa grinned slightly, as if in appreciation of the stranger's efforts. Or did she appreciate Turner's discouraging him?

The princess must have warded off dozens of men in dozens of ports. Her black hair, dark eyes, and slender figure gave her an exotic beauty that must be rare in the spacing game. However, she only had eyes for Turner.

No one had even thought to approach Arden. Turner had made it clear from the first moment that she was under his protection. He had taken on an attitude of wariness that made him look dangerous. He scared her as much as he scared the other men.

Frequently she had stolen a quick look at him, as he sat stony-faced beside her. He did not seem to notice the princess's attention. Was she still attracted to him, or had Rafe or Liel told the princess their suspicions, too?

Arden adjusted the sword resting across her back and bent over to rest her forehead on her arms crossed on the table. A headache was starting behind her eyes, and shutting out the light helped. Cutting out the noises in the cafe would help, too, if she could just do that. Sometimes the surrounding voices, clinking of glasses, banging of doors and drawers, actually drowned out Tahr's muttering. Amazing that the rest of the crew could put up with him on a continual basis.

The entry door banged open, and someone hit the tabletop. Arden raised up, squinting against sudden light and pain. Once her vision cleared, Rafe could be seen approaching, alone. He looked grim and very tired. He grabbed a chair from another table and sat down between her and Turner.

"It's done," he said. "We got a good price for the lifeweave and they are offloading it now. We can't leave for a couple of hours, though."

"Why not?" Arden asked.

"They can't deliver the scrip for another hour or so, and the commander says there are five ships cleared for departure ahead of us. We can get on board in an hour. Liel has gone ahead to wait for them."

"What is bothering you?" Arden asked.

He reached over and squeezed her hand on the tabletop. Turner's jaw muscle twitched, but he said nothing. His gaze returned to checking out the room.

"We've been here too long," Semmes answered. "I'd hoped we could get in and out more quickly."

She nodded.

"We're all going to be killed over this whole thing," Tahr said. "You wait and see."

The captain scowled at him. Clearly, he was in no mood to hear doom and gloom. He ignored his pilot and laced his fingers through Arden's. The small intimacies still amazed her. They had come about gradually, without either of them saying a word about how they felt. Under the circumstances, it was as if they wanted to take advantage of the moments they had. It was difficult to imagine how their feelings would develop if things worked out in the end. For the moment, they were content with what they had.

Everyone at the table sat silently, the others thinking negatively about their chances at getting away, judging by the looks on their faces. Turner's expression was less readable. If only they could trust him again. No longer trusting him, could they afford to take him on the *Starbourne* when they lifted from Miga?

"We can start back toward the docking bays," Rafe said later, after a quick look at his watch. Nearly an hour had passed. He stood. "By the time we get there, we should be able to board."

She rose to stand beside him. Jessa and Tahr took the lead. Behind them was Owen. Turner came last, maintaining a constant distance behind the two of them, too close for her to ask Rafe the question that had come to mind.

No guards waited at the ship to keep them from boarding. Her breath caught in her throat. An emptiness churned in the pit of her stomach. Arden called to the two in the lead. Everyone stopped, looking at her. Danger lay ahead, but she did not know what it was. How could they understand if she couldn't tell what she felt? All of them stood for the space of several heartbeats, waiting.

"Something is wrong," she said at last.

"What?" Rafe asked.

"I don't know. Maybe nothing. It's just a feeling."

Rafe nodded to Tahr and looked to Turner. The investigator said nothing, nor did he move from his position. The captain turned from him to look at the ramp of the ship. He drew his sword with his good hand and started forward, his eyes searching for anything out of place. Arden drew her sword and took a step to follow, but he turned and shook his head. She stopped. He turned again, flanked by Tahr and Owen, and the three started into the ship.

She followed at a discreet distance. The katana felt good in her hands. Jessa picked up a hammer of some sort from an assortment of tools and parts lying nearby. Without a word, they followed up the ramp. The two men had disappeared. She looked back to see Turner following.

Once inside, she considered the direction. The men probably went toward the bridge. Arden started in that direction, Jessa behind. The feeling of danger still lay in the pit of her stomach. *Better catch up.* She quickened her steps, fear for Rafe pushing her on.

He and Tahr were on the bridge when she got there. Nothing else, no one else. She expected Rafe to at least give her a look of impatience, but he just looked grim and moved toward the crew's quarters. A burnt smell filled the corridor. The captain and Tahr looked at each other knowingly.

The first cabin, Liel's, was empty. In the second, they found Vida on her bunk, a charred wound in the middle of her forehead, her eyes staring at the ceiling. Rafe checked her pulse, but it was clear the woman was dead. The two men squeezed out of the cabin, started toward the next one. Arden slipped inside, gently closed Vida's eyes, then hurried to catch up. The rest of the cabins were empty.

"The salon," Rafe said in a low voice.

He led the way, checking around every blind turn before allowing the rest to follow. They stood back while he glanced around the edge of the door from one side. She saw him stiffen but could not see what had startled him. He stepped through the doorway, and she caught a glimpse of Liel lying on the floor.

A figure stepped from the right, behind Rafe. Arden shouted a warning, then pushed past Tahr, raising her sword. People appeared from all sides and the room exploded into combat. She had pushed an opponent away and was trying to fight her way to Rafe's side when someone grabbed her from behind. Her arms were pinned to her sides. The sword clattered to the floor.

A very large man came up to her and looked her full in the face. It was Colin Chase, the man she had hoped never to meet again. His expression was triumphant. His immense frame was poised for action, but there was nowhere to vent that need. He turned toward the captain, who lay face down on the deck, seemingly unconscious. He kicked Rafe in the side.

"Stop it!" she shouted.

The arms holding her tightened until she could hardly breathe. Chase turned back to her and slapped her. Her head jerked to one side, and she could taste blood where her teeth had torn the inside of her mouth.

"Tahr!" she cried.

Where was he? Why didn't he help Rafe? Chase blocked her view of the salon.

The captain arched his back, trying to get to his feet. The attacker turned his back on her and hit Rafe on the back of the neck with the butt of the rifle he had been holding. The captain grunted and collapsed.

Arden stomped on the foot of the person holding her and wrenched free. She ran at Chase and kicked him in the back of his knee and his leg collapsed under him. He rolled instead of falling straight down. Other hands clutched at her, but she pushed them away and moved to get between Rafe and this man. That was the important thing. Don't let him hurt Rafe again.

She straddled the still figure and turned to face the whole company. Chase was rising to his feet, his expression like thunder. Turner stood closest, and she realized that he must have been the one who held her!

Jessa, Owen, and Tahr stood with their backs against the wall. Pinning them there with the point of a rifle was another familiar figure.

"Spohn," Arden called.

The woman grinned over her shoulder, then motioned to

someone off to one side. A stranger took Spohn's place. The blonde woman came to stand in front of Arden. What the hell was her connection to Chase?

"Hello, Captain Grenfell," Spohn said, and slapped her, hard.

"I guess you two have met before," Colin Chase said, glancing from Arden to Spohn.

He had just finished introducing himself and his friends, during which Liel had sat up, rubbing the back of his neck. He took in the scene without a change of expression until his eyes lit on Semmes. Then his jaw muscles twitched and his gaze hardened.

"Yes, we've met," Spohn said.

Arden held a hand to her burning cheek, looking from Spohn to the gun in Chase's hands. Slowly, she brought both feet in front of Rafe's still form.

Lower the gun only a moment, she thought. *That's all I need.*

Chase absentmindedly motioned with the weapon for Spohn to move away, out of immediate reach. His attention turned to Jessa, who was pressed against the bulkhead.

"We've come for the Princess Jessa," Chase announced to no one's surprise. "The rest of you will be taken care of here."

"What about the warrant against us?" Liel asked.

"That's up to Don Vey," Chase said.

"We are taking all of them to Glory," Spohn said. Her hands had tightened into fists and her face had reddened.

"My commission is only for the princess and her bodyguard," Chase said.

"Not so," Spohn argued. "Vey and the emperor will want all of them. The rest helped her and the princess to escape Caldera, and they will certainly want to punish her former bodyguard."

Chase looked around at the people surrounding him and Spohn. His expression had hardened. Clearly, he was not accustomed to being challenged, least of all in front of others.

Spohn was right: Vey would definitely want Arden brought before him, and the others must be dealt with also. Having that done quietly and away from other officials would be to his liking, since the charges were trumped up and even included the princess. Arden was surprised that Chase was not concerned with getting them all to Glory, and worried about what he might have planned for them. Once she got to Glory, she hoped to convince Vey that she had been left with little choice in leaving Caldera the way she did and that the crew of the *Starbourne* had acted with the best of motives.

Spohn turned sideways to Chase and crouched slightly. Why did it matter to her so much? The rest of Chase's people stood stock still, faces frozen in surprise. They were a hard-looking bunch, probably mercenaries. Jessa stayed with her back against the wall, looking nearly catatonic. For once, Tahr wasn't muttering anything.

Rafe moaned from where he lay behind Arden's feet. Keeping her hands in plain sight, she knelt down and brushed the hair back from his forehead.

"It's all right," she said when he opened his eyes.

A bigger lie she had never told, and his expression said he knew. He let her help him to a sitting position. For a moment he held one hand on the back of his neck and the other on his side. Shaking his head slightly, he started to stand. Liel came to his other side, oblivious of the jitters his sudden movement gave those who held weapons.

The captain stood unsteadily, accepting support from both sides. Even Tahr looked relieved that his captain was able to get up. Jessa's expression had not changed throughout.

Chase turned from watching Rafe back to Spohn. She had not taken her eyes off her leader the whole time.

"You're right, Spohn," Chase said. "We'll take them all with us."

"Please," Rafe rasped. "Leave one of my crew behind to take care of the ship."

"Don't worry about it," Chase said. "It's not your ship anymore."

"I'll give you the scrip we got for the lifeweave if you leave Tahr behind. Give him a chance at the ship."

Chase looked at the pilot, then at Rafe.

"No deal," he said. "I doubt that any of you will have any use for either the money or the ship in the future." He set the butt of the gun on the floor and leaned on it like a cane. "Where is the money, anyway?"

"It's supposed to be delivered soon."

"Oh, that's right," Chase said, and grinned.

He knew the schedule all along. Had probably been behind the delay in the negotiations, operating behind Miga's officials and pushing them into cooperating.

Chase nodded to Spohn and disappeared.

"Let's get them bound up," she said to her companions.

Arden was familiar with the type of bonds, opened only by a magnetic key. All of them had their hands bound behind their backs by the time Chase returned. He carried a security case in place of the rifle he had before. He caught Liel looking at the case and patted it.

"Not the money you were hoping for," he said. "We've decided to keep the lifeweave and take it and your ship back to Glory. It belonged to us in the first place, after all." He turned to Spohn. "Get them aboard our ship. Part of the crew is going to take over the *Starbourne* and get it back to Glory. We'll have to take over some of their duties."

She nodded and signaled the others to move the prisoners out. Rafe shuffled slightly as he made his way through the door and out of sight. The warmth of his arm clung to Arden's hands. She looked over at Liel, and he gave her a slow wink. Was there some unspoken plan evolving between him and the captain, perhaps something they had rehearsed many times in the loneliness of space? "What if . . ." planning. They sure had had no opportunity to plan since this all started.

The last to leave the ship, Arden watched the others walking in single file ahead of her. She also had an opportunity to look over their captors once more. She was still sure that they were mercenaries, maybe even bounty hunters. However, they clearly had worked with Chase before and, except for the short confrontation between him and Spohn, they totally accepted his leadership. It was clear now that Spohn was also "regular army." However, she had an agenda of her own.

That could prove even more dangerous to her and the *Starbourne*'s crew. Chase held to a singleness of purpose, linked to the way he kept looking at Jessa and his initial insistence that they take only her back to Glory. Scary, that.

It had not seemed to bother Jessa. She might not even have heard anything Chase had said for all the reaction she gave.

Then there was Spohn, strolling around, taking everything in, keeping a close eye on her former acquaintance. Arden rubbed her cheek again, remembering. The anger behind that blow was a surprise.

More of a surprise was Turner, in spite of the suspicion that had settled about him. What was his real role in all of this? She was still not sure whose side he was on.

Too many machinations in all this. It could make one's head spin. And there was more than enough confusion without trying to figure out everyone's motives.

Motives.

Where was Turner?

No sign of him. He had slipped away without her seeing.

Remember, you dunce, a familiar voice said inside her head. *He held you when Chase was beating on Semmes. The tracer. He's one of them.* As if things were not bad enough, she was beginning to hear Pac Terhn's voice without using the lifeweave.

Can't tell the players without a scorecard, she thought. Abbot Grayson would be so proud of her for remembering that one.

They were herded aboard a small, sleek ship. Their footsteps in the corridor sounded empty and forlorn. Everyone gathered in the salon waiting for Chase to join them to sort out the arrangements for the journey to Glory. When he appeared, Rafe did not take his eyes off him. Only Arden and Liel could see the look in his eyes. It was the first time she knew she could be afraid of him.

Chase showed up first; then Turner walked through the door.

"Eli," Chase said. "It's about time you showed up again."

"Just checking some things out," the erstwhile investigator said. "Where do we go from here?"

"Home," Chase said, casting his eyes toward Jessa. "It seems a long time since..."

He stood motionless, lost in thoughts no one guessed at, or at any rate, interrupted. Least of all Jessa.

It appeared that the princess had hardly moved since the scene began unfolding. She had walked the whole way moving nothing but her legs. She had made no sound or movement when her arms were bound behind her. She watched Chase like a womba hare watching an eagle. No, watching a cat. A cat teased, made the prey think it would jump at any moment, yet held off. All the while the hare watched and died slowly of fright.

Arden had seen such scenes many times in Lower Forest on her walks around the monastery. She now felt fear much like all of those hares herself, only instead of a cat the predator was Colin Chase, who hated her and Jessa for reasons she could not quite fathom. He watched and waited, for what she could not even guess.

13

Tahr even mumbled in his sleep. Rafe could have gone the rest of his life without knowing that and been very happy. He liked his pilot. He really did. But in smaller doses. Being confined with him for nearly a week was more than a person should have to take.

At least he was alive, irritating or not. Unlike Vida, who had never been irritating. Chase or one of his mercenaries had shot the mechanic seemingly without remorse, possibly without any thought at all. The brutality of the murder weighed him down with a feeling of impotence.

How little he had known her, even though she had been part of the crew for at least three years. Liel he had known longer than any other member—fifteen years probably. Tahr—could it be ten years since he first came aboard the *Starbourne*? Vida and Jessa joined the crew within a month or two of each other, Owen just shortly before them.

Although there had been rough times, they had melded into a damn good crew. They worked together smoothly, each knowing their task and when to perform it. They lived together amicably in the relatively small space of a salvage ship, where room for cargo was more important than room for people.

Yet, with all that, they knew so little about each other.

And, for one of their number, it was too late.

The rest of their fates were coming to a head, too. For the past couple of hours, the Glorian ship had been decelerating. That meant they must be coming up on Glory itself. Home for Chase and his team, or as much home as they had ever known probably. Mercenaries to the core, except Chase, who was clearly Glory-born. Military through and through. Spohn was more difficult to read. She had shown a certain amount of deference to Jessa, making him believe she might also be from Glory. Her hatred for Arden was the clearest emotion she had displayed, and it had surprised Arden a little.

She and Chase were the ones with personal stakes in this little expedition. The others simply followed orders, with a certain amount of loyalty to Chase.

Well, he could guess all day and night and never figure out what Chase was all about. Anyway, that was the least of his worries. What did concern him was the immediate fate of Arden and Jessa. Damnedest thing about those two. This whole thing was about them after all.

Not that he blamed them. Well, maybe Arden, a little. She had acted like an innocent, from her agreement with Don Vey to her involvement with Turner, and so foolishly believing them. One did have to wonder if, in the end, she had changed her mind about getting Jessa back.

Now that they were nearing Glory, their peril was even more immediate. What did the emperor and Don Vey have in store for them? From all that had been said, Jessa would be chained to a loom until the need for lifeweave controlled her existence and she was able to weave pretty pictures for the war effort. It might be better to call it deathweave under the circumstances. Arden's future was not so clear.

Rafe stood up, flexed both legs, and bent forward from the waist to stretch the muscles in the backs of his legs. He managed to take four small steps from the head of the bunks to the door. He paced back, swung both arms over his head, then around himself. He sat back down, leaning toward the opposite cheek; the left was still numb.

Tahr mumbled unintelligibly and turned over on the bunk. At least he was getting some sleep. He wondered how Liel and Owen were faring in the other cabin. Ever since being shoved into the cabin, Rafe had slept little. Not just because the bunk was hard and the blanket rough, but also because he found himself in a situation he could neither control nor predict.

He didn't even know where the two women were being held. He'd tried pounding on the walls on either side, but one side elicited muffled shouting and the other only silence. Farrell, who brought their food, could not be cajoled into telling them anything more than his name.

The one person he had not wondered about so far was Jackson Turner. Just thinking the name made him clench his fists. He had fooled all of them so thoroughly. What was it Chase had called him? Eli. That was it. Rafe was willing to bet they had not yet come to know all the names the man was known by.

He folded his arms across his chest and settled back against the wall. Whatever was going to happen, it wouldn't be much longer. Half a day at most.

"You'd better eat something," Arden told Jessa for the hundredth time.

At least it felt like the hundredth, anyway. Cooped up in this cabin for days with the princess for company had been no picnic. Jessa spoke only in monosyllables, sometimes words not even pertinent to what Arden had said. This time Jessa said nothing at all.

It looked like she had gone over the edge, starting with their capture and ending with her being told that her mother had, indeed, died. Chase had verbally bludgeoned Jessa with the news on his first visit to their prison. She had been in one of her aware states, but that had not lasted even a minute after Chase finished.

Of course, she could be putting on an act, but what would

that buy her in the end? Did she think her father wouldn't set her at the loom if she was insensible?

And if the princess didn't work out, would they find out about Arden working with lifeweave and put her to work? She had made Rafe promise not to let that happen, knowing that Turner's promise was no good. Yeah, and Don Vey would give the captain free rein so he could keep that promise. And Spohn knew about the existence of the squares. Had she guessed their possible significance? Turner certainly knew.

She fingered the netsuke absentmindedly. There had to be a way out. She just could not believe that this was how it was all going to end. Then, she had not believed that Turner was anything other than what he had told her.

She couldn't even conjure up a memory of the passion he had aroused within her during their first meeting and subsequent days. It was easy to remember wishing they were in love, but the emotions that drove that wish were gone, destroyed by his betrayal. No, the destruction began earlier, when Rafe entered her life.

Feelings for the captain she remembered all too well. Now all she could do was worry about how he was surviving their confinement. And worry about what would happen to him when they reached Glory.

What would happen to them all? She had speculated for hours. What else was there to do? Zierah would say nothing when she brought their food. Under orders, no doubt.

Colin Chase would take no chances of any kind. A very careful man. And spooky.

He had looked in twice more. Just that, no words spoken. He hadn't even stepped into the cabin. The only pleasure she could derive from his visits was that he looked unhappy.

Had he made Spohn look unhappy, too, after their little confrontation? She had not looked in at all. One could only hope she had been punished. But, if there was any justice, Turner and Spohn would go down together.

Jessa stirred in her bunk, and Arden looked toward her.

"Where are you, Jessa?" Arden asked softly. "Do you know who Colin Chase is?"

"My mother's bodyguard."

Arden started. It spoke, it made sense. Therefore, it lived.

"Are you all right?" she asked.

"No, I am afraid."

"Why have you been so uncommunicative? I thought you had gone crazy."

"The thought of going back . . ." Jessa stopped, remained silent for a short while. "I could not face it easily. When I was a child, my mother taught me how to go into a trance. It was her way of shutting out the world when it became too painful. Until lifeweave took over her life, that is. Then, lifeweave became her refuge.

"You have no idea how life can be for a concubine. All the palace intrigue. The wife making her life miserable when she can. My father loved my mother. I think he might have made her his empress if he could have. They stayed together until I was about fifteen."

Jessa sat up on her bunk and began unbraiding her hair. Let loose, it fell to her waist in greasy strands.

Arden picked up a can of dry shampoo from the table between bunks.

"Here," she said, and tossed it over.

"Thanks."

Maybe when they got to Glory they could at least get a bath. Their captors acted like they might escape if they were let out of the cabins. And go where?

"I didn't realize your hair was so long," Arden said.

"My one vanity."

"But you always keep it put up."

"With it down, I look too much like my mother," Jessa explained. "I figured that anyone who came looking for me wouldn't know what I looked like anymore. Not exactly, anyway. If I looked like my mother, it would be easier to find me."

She brushed the shampoo through her hair.

"How did you know me?"

Arden could not bring herself to admit that she had not recognized her at first. Nor did she want to admit that it was the lifeweave, as if using it in that way had become a sin.

"Was it the lifeweave? I saw the square you did on board the *Starbourne*. I guess Turner told you."

"Yes, he told me." Of course she knew. "It was the lifeweave." Arden turned to let her legs dangle off the edge of the bunk. "Does nothing like that happen to you? No telling the future—nothing?"

"Nothing. At least not with lifeweave. I can sometimes read other people's emotions. But they have to be pretty close to me. And the emotions have to be very strong."

"Then you didn't inherit your mother's talent at all?"

"No. Lifeweave has little effect on me. I guess I'm not susceptible."

"Maybe because you grew up with it? I'm not addicted to it, either, although I do use it to see things I can't otherwise see. Things I can't know. Most of the time I have to be seeking something. Sometimes—like the time you saw the square—things come unbidden, although rarely. Those are the times that scare me."

"Who was the woman in the square I saw?" Jessa asked. "I never really saw it clearly."

She had finished brushing her hair and put the brush down. While they spoke, she braided it and coiled the braid at the back of her head.

"It was Spohn."

"The woman with Colin?"

"Yes."

"You never met her before?"

"Oh, yes. I'd met her before. A little bit of treachery when I first met Turner in Vega City."

She stopped. How could she have been so wrong about Turner? The question would not go away. And her own feelings: so strong, so physical. Although she had liked him as a person, it was the physical attraction that had betrayed her.

She had never been so betrayed by a man in her whole life.

He was the one she should hate—more even than Spohn. At least *she* had shown her true colors early on. Turner waited to manufacture a greater betrayal.

"You aren't the first woman to be betrayed by a man," Jessa said.

"Very few women drag their friends down with them."

"We trusted him, too."

"Did you? I don't believe you ever trusted me, much less him. You just had no choice. You needed our help to release the ship."

Arden lay down and stared at the ceiling. She laced her fingers behind her head.

"What I don't understand," she continued, "is why he helped us on Caldera. He was the one who released the stasis field to free the ship. Chase and his gang could have taken us there with much less trouble."

"Maybe because there was danger of one of us getting killed. We were being shot at."

Arden rubbed her side. The wound still felt tender under her fingertips since it had reopened during the fight in the hangar.

"That was at the end of the fight, though," Arden said aloud. "He was afraid you might be hurt. But orders must have been passed on to make sure you weren't."

The whole thing just did not make any sense.

"No," Arden continued. "Turner could have delayed us at any stage. It's almost as if he wanted to hang on to the charade as long as possible. Keep playing the friend."

She snapped her fingers.

"That's it! He is employed by the Wilson Agency. He has to play the role he was hired for. Make it look good."

She turned onto her side and looked at Jessa. The princess frowned, then shook her head.

"That sounds awfully lame," she said. "Somehow I don't think the job with Wilson is very important to him. Without being self-centered, I would think the idea of not wanting me injured would be more plausible. If his job was to get me back to Glory in one piece, he may have felt that he could not accomplish the task on Caldera, under those circumstances."

"Well, it's all we have at the moment," Arden said. "Whatever his motives are, I think we need to figure it out. He may be the one weak link in their chain."

Arden hesitated to ask the next question. It wasn't meant to frighten Jessa, but to warn her. Of course, her fear might be groundless. Still, it would be better not to ignore it. Just in case.

"Have you noticed the way Chase looks at you?"

"What do you mean?"

"There's a combination of . . . of . . . hate and . . . something. Jessa, I think he might be more dangerous to you than we think."

She could not quite bring herself to say aloud what she actually felt. Yet she could not shake it off.

"He looked in on you twice while you were in your trance. Not me. Not us. You. I'd tell you to be careful, but I don't think we have many choices. However, if you have any tricks up your sleeve, keep them in mind."

"He would not dare threaten a princess . . ."

Arden jumped as the cabin door flew open, banging against the wall and bouncing back. Colin Chase stood at the threshold. Again, he did not enter. His gaze brushed past Arden, rested on Jessa. Her quick intake of air was the only sound in the sudden silence.

Threat emanated from his large body, poised as if to pounce. Arden's muscles tensed, readying to spring in defense. However, he made no move to enter the cabin. After another moment, he rubbed his hands together once, grabbed the door handle, and slammed it shut. Vibrations shook the air. Arden finally exhaled. Her hands and arms started shaking, and she slid from the bunk to stretch.

"What you saw in Colin Chase?" Jessa said.

"Yes?"

"It was hard old-fashioned lust."

Good man, Colin Chase. Jessa is coming back, and everything will be like it was. I will be in charge again.

Granid Parcq sank back into his favorite chair. The ship was approaching Glory and would be docked by evening. The shipment of lifeweave was close behind. As soon as word came, he wanted to order the loom prepared, lifeweave spools checked, everything made ready for Lyona's daughter to begin. In the end, he decided that could wait. There were other things to be seen to.

Those fool military men! And his own son. Thinking they could win the war with their own talents, without the aid of a seeress. How did they think they had gained victory so many times? Not with their limited skills. Until Lyona gave them the edge, those men had hardly won a battle.

What made them think things were different now? Of course, they had learned from the battles won while Lyona was alive. But they were not omnipotent yet.

They had learned. Some things. Damn them!

Yet, they had learned nothing. Most generals and admirals would welcome such advance knowledge: where enemy ships were dispersed; what formations would be used; how many ships and men the enemy deployed.

No, he could not wait. The loom must be ready when she arrived. She must begin immediately.

What does she look like? He had asked Chase that question when the erstwhile bodyguard reported directly as ordered. The man's voice had become strained—was that the right word? Yes, strained. He would not answer directly, saying only that the princess was pretty as her parentage demanded.

What a strange way to put it.

Maybe it would be best if he did not see her. Not at first.

Does she look like her mother?

They would show everyone, he and his...Lyona's daughter. Jessa, princess of Glory. Soon to be seeress to her emperor. A true daughter, following in her mother's image.

No, not image. She must not look like Lyona. Lyona was dead. Long live the seeress.

The hatch opened. Fresh air chased away conditioned air. It smelled and tasted sweet, unmetallic.

"Oh, I had forgotten the evening air," Jessa said. She closed her eyes and took a deep breath.

The six prisoners were herded down the ramp to the ground, walking a little clumsily with their hands bound behind them. A few feet from the ship, Arden looked back. They had set down in an open field, not very far from a hangar. Chase or someone must have decided there was less danger of escape out in the open. Helpless as they were and with armed men and women around them, at that moment, escape was the farthest thing from her mind.

Yellow and white wildflowers grew all around. That was the source of the sweetness in the air. Glory did not have many trees, but wildflowers were abundant most of the year.

"It's beautiful," Arden said. "I missed the flowers when I was locked away."

A large truck with military markings roared up to the hangar, and a squad of armed men in uniforms jumped to the ground. The newcomers formed up, then marched toward them. Chase waved them off when they were within a few feet. Apparently he did not intend relinquishing control of the prisoners.

The extra guards were certainly unnecessary. The squad leader, a sergeant, called a halt with an expression of confusion. Chase started to lead the group around them to the left. A second truck pulled up to the hangar, but no one got out.

"Commander Chase," the squad leader called out. "We were ordered to take charge of your prisoners."

Chase whirled, gun in hand by the time he stopped. Only a few feet separated the two men.

"No, thank you, soldier. We will escort my prisoners to the palace."

Spohn and the others rested their hands on their holstered guns. The sergeant turned red; his eyes concentrated on the pistol. Young though he appeared to be, it was clear he was more angry than afraid.

"Very well, Commander," he said.

He started to turn toward his men but stopped. His gaze rested for an instant on the gun, then rose to Chase's face.

"By the way, Commander," he said. "Circumstances at the palace are not as you left them."

He turned to his men quickly and ordered an about-face. Without another word, he marched them back the way they had come. Chase stood as if thinking about what he had just heard. When the squad had disappeared into the truck and it had driven off, he signaled for everyone to move again.

The driver of the second truck remained in the cab. The truck was old and out of date, but sturdy beyond its years. Inside, a long bench on each side provided seating. Everyone piled into the back except Chase, who joined the driver in the cab. Spohn and Marat stood in the front, keeping a wary eye on the prisoners, while Farrell and Zierah sat at the back. Thoms had remained with the ship. Turner had not appeared.

The road was bumpy at first, making the wound in Arden's side ache slightly as she clung to a strap attached to the metal bench. After a short time they turned sharply left and the road was smoother. The rattling decreased to almost nothing.

"Okay?" Rafe asked, leaning toward her from the other side.

"Yes," she answered. "Still a little tender." She released the strap.

He nodded.

"No talking," Spohn ordered.

Rafe leaned back and gave a quick smile. If that was to impart confidence, it did not work. Especially with her lifeweave squares in Chase's custody. She had caught a glimpse of them inside the bag that Chase had thrown into the truck. His having possession of them could only mean danger for her. Spohn had held them when she delivered a bag of personal items to Arden. The blonde showed them with a triumphant grin that would have been slapped off her face if things had been different. There had been no trace of her sword, a greater personal loss.

If only, she started to think, wanting to list all of the wrong moves she had made. Then something Grayson had made her memorize came to mind.

The moving finger writes; and, having writ, moves on: nor all thy piety nor wit shall lure it back to cancel half a line, nor all thy tears wash out a word of it.

Old Khayyam had been right. Nothing could change what had occurred. And no one could predict what was to happen. However, she feared that predicting was just what she would be made to do.

A servant fussed about, arranging the hem of the velvet robe around the throne. *Go away, little man*, the emperor thought as he waved him away impatiently.

Maybe it wasn't such a good idea to receive the prisoners here in the throne room. Such a reception might give them an inflated opinion of their importance. However, he had chosen here rather than in his receiving room as a means of overpowering their senses. Give them some idea of the power they had chosen to disobey.

Yes, that was the right thing to do. Particularly Lyona's

daughter. She must be received here as fitting to her station. Of course, she had forfeited any rights when she fled from Glory. Still, the attorneys had not finished debating the legalities involved in that.

Let them debate. Soon she would be performing her duties, serving Glory, as a . . . as a consort's daughter should do.

How much longer? They were reported at the gate fifteen minutes ago.

The massive doors at the opposite end of the hall opened silently. The herald stood in the center of the opening.

"My lord," he said in his full, baritone voice. "The Princess Jessa, Commander Chase, and party."

Damn, he had told them not to use "Princess Jessa." Someone would lose his position for that.

No time to think of that. Here they come. Where is she? Is she . . .

My god! No, she is not supposed to . . . Lyona. So much like Lyona.

Huge doors opened and they were herded through. Arden looked behind to see Chase's people stop just inside the threshold. Chase led the way inside, and they all approached the center of the room, their footsteps echoing. The great hall sounded empty, but it was far from that. Guards stood along both sides, armed with swords and rifles. Several more flanked the throne at the other end. And, of course, with Spohn and company behind them, they were once more surrounded.

This was getting tiresome.

Arden stole a sideways glance at Jessa next to her. What must she be feeling inside, seeing her father for the first time in years, but as a prisoner rather than as a beloved daughter?

Jessa flinched; her eyes widened, but her jaws tightened. She looked so different with her long hair hanging loose like that. Arden looked from her to the emperor. His eyes were wide, his jaw slack. He could not believe what he was seeing.

The princess had said that she resembled her mother, especially when she wore her hair down. She had taken it down during the ride in the truck. Deliberately! Whatever the outcome, she had decided to play this last card.

One could only hope it was a trump card.

"But, your majesty," Chase said.

Granid Parcq held up his hand, demanding silence. After the prisoners were removed to the cells in the basement, they had moved to his private sitting room, where the argument had been going on for nearly an hour. Everyone had an opinion on what he should do. Chase had voiced the strong opinion that Jessa should be set at the loom immediately to take her mother's place. The problem was the amount of time it might take to find out if the princess had any abilities. Then there were the generals, who had sent a message reiterating their position. All of the complications.

But Jessa was his daughter. There: he had said it, if only to himself. *She is my daughter*. She was a royal, second in line to Waran. And, gods, she looked so much like her mother. Except her eyes still saw, her hair was still black. Sadly, those things would change after a time at the loom.

"Your majesty," the young woman standing by the door spoke for the first time.

Everyone turned to look at her. She was tall, strongly built, and as blonde as Jessa was dark.

"You are . . . ?"

"Spohn, your majesty. I was with Commander Chase when we found your . . . the princess."

"Ah, yes. I remember you in the throne room. Do you have something to add?"

He dropped into the chair that fit so well and picked up the glass from the table.

"Yes, your majesty, if I may."

Chase gave the woman an angry look, then turned to lean

on the mantle over the fireplace. Ignoring him, she approached. She licked her lips before continuing.

"It could be a very long time before the princess proves or disproves her abilities at the loom, is that right?"

He nodded.

"There may be a shortcut."

"There is no alternative," Chase broke in.

"Let her speak," the emperor commanded. "Go on."

She glanced at Chase, then back. Don Vey watched with intense interest.

"The woman, Arden Grenfell, has some ability in foretelling with lifeweave."

"Arden Grenfell?" Vey snorted. "She is a pain in the ass and will be executed."

"Not unless I command it," the emperor said. He turned back to the woman. "How do you know this?"

"I saw some squares she wove with lifeweave. I am sure that is how she found Jessa. The princess."

"You saw some squares of lifeweave?" Chase almost shouted. "So she weaves lifeweave. That is no proof."

"How else could she have found the princess in so short a time? She wasn't even sure what Jessa looked like after six years. She could not have known for sure if she was on a ship at the time."

"She checked with the spacer's guild. They would know what ship and where it was."

"Salvagers are independent. They don't hire through the guild."

"There are a hundred ways Grenfell could have found out where the princess was," Chase nearly shouted.

Spohn stood silent, looking at her commander. Reading her expression was impossible, except to know that the outcome of this conversation was important to her. Just as important as it was to the commander.

Granid Parcq took a long drink from the glass, allowing the silence to stretch out. He set the glass down and steepled his fingers in front of him.

"Well?" he said at last, looking at Spohn.

"The princess wasn't expected in Vega City, your majesty. Even if anyone knew the *Starbourne* was anywhere near Caldera, they weren't scheduled for a visit to the city. They did so only because the ship was damaged. Yet Arden Grenfell waited there for her to appear. She could not have known any other way except through some kind of foretelling."

"Spohn," the commander said. "Wait for me outside."

"No," she replied quietly.

"I am your commander, and you will do as ordered. Otherwise, I will have you arrested."

Interesting, Granid thought. In spite of the earnestness of her argument, Spohn hesitated. Ingrained obedience. And, if he remembered the records correctly, they had served together more than once in the past, which might reinforce Chase's authority.

She straightened without looking at Chase. Her eyes pleaded with her emperor just before she turned on her heel and left the room.

Too easy. She had a plan, something Chase was not aware of. The commander looked pleased that his authority had at last been recognized and obeyed.

"Now, your majesty," Chase said. "We can discuss this situation more rationally. The Princess Jessa owes you and the people of Glory for abandoning her duties in this time of war and deprivation. She pursued her own pleasures without a thought for her responsibilities."

"Why are you so sure she can replace her mother?" the emperor asked.

"Who else? She must have inherited some of Lyona's skill. If so, it would take less time to acclimate her to the loom than it would someone else, and you would soon have your battle plans and maps again."

"Why don't we try both women?" Don Vey said from the corner where he had been observing. "Whichever is better at the task will remain. Perhaps both of them, in tandem, so to speak, will provide the information, the insight, we are seeking."

"A contest, perhaps," the emperor said. "If we promised each a reward, something strongly desired, they might be induced to show what they can do."

Chase stood with hands on hips, looking from one to the other. Did he feel betrayed at that moment? Why, exactly?

His attachment for the seeress had been no secret. Some might have called it love. More of an obsession, especially given the inability of Lyona to ever return any affection by the time Chase took the post as bodyguard. Some sort of punishment, wasn't it? The commander had turned punishment into devotion. His kind usually did. Devotion to a cause, a person, to something outside themselves, drove men like him. Often to death.

Then there was Waran. Although he never said it outright, he had never wanted Jessa to return. Even though his position as heir was assured by law, he feared his half sister and her misguided following.

Where was that son and heir? There had been no word since he disappeared several months ago. No one seemed to know—or would tell—where. Spohn had put him in mind of the prince, with her blonde hair and good looks. As like his mother as Jessa was like hers.

He sighed. He was repeating himself, to himself.

"We will test them," he said at last. "Perhaps solving more than one problem in the process."

He stood, stepped up to the fireplace, and held his hands out. They were still so cold.

"You may leave now," he told both men. "Oh, and I want to see those squares that young woman spoke of."

Don Vey bowed and started out. Chase looked at his emperor in disbelief. He started toward the door, remembered to bow, then disappeared into the hall as the prime minister held the door open.

"It looks like you may have your weaver after all," Granid Parcq said.

"It will benefit us," Vey said. "All of us."

Word of the contest came to Spohn from the usual source. She had friends throughout Glory watching and waiting. This new plan, set to start within the next two days, made matters more difficult. Once set to the loom, Jessa might never be freed, no matter how determined the group was. They would have to move very fast.

The princess must be freed before that happened. Distracting the emperor and Don Vey with Arden was only partially successful. At least they saw her as a potential alternative and might not be so eager to find Jessa after she disappeared.

The main question now was, how could Jessa be alerted and approached? Thank goodness Chase's team had been given temporary lodging within the palace. But that would last only a few days. The rescue must be initiated at once.

However, another question nagged at her: what was Chase's real reason for getting Jessa back to Glory? His stated reason that he wanted her to replace Lyona as seeress was a means to an end, a justification for his actions. Could his feelings for Lyona color his perception of the daughter in ways no one had yet considered? He had said more than once that Jessa had abandoned her mother.

She recalled the look on Granid Parcq's face when the princess entered the throne room. As if he had seen a ghost. So, she looked like her mother at a younger age. Before Chase had known her. Maybe he had known the seeress before his last stint as her bodyguard, and that devotion was formed long before anyone suspected. No reason to assume he still wasn't devoted. That kind of man could conceivably love all the way to the grave. And beyond.

To the daughter?

My God!

An unconsummated love. The loved one returned, this

time young and able to see again, with coal-black hair and, he hoped, at his mercy.

Spohn slammed out of the cell-like room and headed for the real cells in the basement. She must find Jessa quickly.

The room was comfortable enough, and lunch had been brought a few hours earlier. What was surprising was that they had left her and Jessa together. After all, one was a princess of the ruling family while she was . . . well, Arden Grenfell, warrior and erstwhile captain of the imperial guard. However, under current circumstances, their differences seemed to mean little to those in power.

Was there any chance that Abbot Grayson knew where she was? He always had his own ways of knowing things, but even the monastery was under suspicion these days. He would have to be very careful in taking any action, even if it was only to keep up with what was happening.

She could not help worrying as much about Rafe. Overshadowing it all was a strong desire to find and kill Turner.

Something about the former investigator had been hovering at the edge of her mind ever since they had landed on Glory. He had disappeared, that was a mystery, of course. But that wasn't it. Her mind worried over it like a cat with a mouse, yet she could not quite focus on it.

Arden turned from pacing to ask Jessa for help, but the princess either was asleep or had gone into another trance. Dammit, it was spooky the way she kept doing that.

A key rattled in the lock of the door at the far end of the room. It slammed open. Arden jumped, her heart skipping a beat. Colin Chase stood silhouetted against the brighter light of the hallway. This time he stepped inside.

Only a few steps at first. He ignored Arden, looking only at the reclining princess. It was like some fairy tale from old Earth: the sleeping princess and Prince Charming. Except this was neither a prince, nor was he charming.

Chase moved to stand beside the bed and reached down as if to take Jessa in his arms. No, he had to be stopped.

A scream rose in her throat, a warrior's kiai. Before he could turn around, Arden hit him hard in the back with both hands, a kidney punch that nearly brought him to his knees.

Her expertise lay in kendo—sword fighting—not hand-to-hand. His grunt said the wind had been knocked out of him. But before she recovered to deliver a second blow, he whirled to face her. Off balance, he swung his right fist at her jaw. She dodged, feeling the wind of the miss against her cheek.

She crouched. Find an opening. Damn, he was recovering too fast. He was too big. If only there was a shinai, at least. That she knew how to handle, and it was long enough to keep him at bay.

Wasn't there supposed to be a guard outside the door? She tried to look around Chase, but he cut her off, probably thinking she wanted to run away. Not a bad idea.

He rushed her, arms wide to grab her. She sidestepped, but his fingernails scraped her arm. Effects from the kidney punch still slowed him a little. And somehow he had managed to keep himself between her and the door. He also had her closer to the corner.

When he came at her again, she stepped aside just enough to lift her right leg, catching him in the stomach with her knee. He grunted, more in surprise than pain. One arm caught her across the breasts, throwing her against the wall. The world turned red, then nearly black.

Stars flashed in the blackness as something hit the side of her head. She tumbled through pain into emptiness.

14

The first thing that returned was light. Too bright. No sound reached her ears, and she feared she was deaf. What could have caused that?

Slowly, Arden sat up, resting her back against a wall. She closed her eyes to block out spinning light. A moan sounded. She heard that. It came from her. Opening her eyes once more, she saw a familiar room—although through haze and from a lower angle than before. The pain in her head matched the roaring in her ears.

Next question: how did she get on the floor?

Pushing away from the wall, she moaned again. God, her head hurt. Hardest trick was going to be getting to her feet.

A memory flashed through her mind: the expression on Chase's face when he looked at Jessa. She pushed to her knees, paused to recover her balance. Slowly, she got to her feet, swaying slightly, her vision gone blurry again.

Her eyes cleared. No one else in the room. Chase had taken Jessa, and she hadn't the slightest idea how long ago. Being familiar with only one part of the palace, she also had no idea where.

She stumbled to the door. On the hall floor, a guard lay spread-eagled, eyes closed, his holster empty. She knelt down to examine him. He was breathing in spite of the bloody gash on the side of his head.

Footsteps, running, approached from the left. Arden backed through the doorway and peeked around to see who the new arrival might be. Mixed emotions flooded through her when Spohn came into view.

The blonde stopped at the sight of the guard, then approached cautiously to check him out. She knelt down, back toward Arden. Spohn might have some idea where Chase had taken Jessa. She might even be in on the abduction.

Arden stepped silently into the hall, crept up behind her, and quickly locked her arms around Spohn's neck. With a slight twist, she could break her neck. Hold on too long, and unconsciousness would result.

Spohn grunted, tried to rise, but the pressure on her neck kept her on her knees.

"Where is Jessa?" Arden asked.

"What?"

The voice came choked, and Arden loosened her hold slightly.

"Where has Chase taken Jessa?"

"He's got her? When?"

"A few minutes ago." Hopefully it had been only that long.

"We've got to stop him."

"Why?"

"He'll harm her. I don't know exactly how. When the emperor . . ."

"Again, why?"

"He was in love with Lyona. He holds Jessa responsible for the seeress's death."

"Why not the emperor?"

"We don't have time for this! We must stop him." Spohn twisted her head, then went still when Arden applied a little more pressure.

"Tell me where he might have taken her."

"I'll show you."

"I don't trust you, Spohn."

Muscles tightened under Arden's grip, as if her prisoner had tried to shrug.

"I don't blame you. But unless you release me, I will tell you nothing."

Spohn was right about one thing: there was no time. Another thing was true: even if Spohn told her where Chase might have gone, there was no way she could find it in the palace complex. Chances were even worse if he had left the palace.

"All right," she said, loosening her hold. "We'll settle our differences later."

She let go altogether. Spohn slumped, gasping for breath. She wavered to her feet, gave Arden a dirty look, then started down the hall.

"This way," she said, while rubbing her throat with one hand.

Arden followed, feeling like she had just stepped into a pit of vipers. The way led through many halls, around many turns, up some stairs, always keeping to little-used areas, until they moved into a part of the palace that had not been used for some time. The lights were dimmed, some turned off. Dust stirred around their feet. Cobwebs quivered in corners. And a set of footprints, larger than theirs, led the way across the deep red carpet.

Spohn slowed, then stopped, her eyes concentrating on the big footprints that trailed around another corner ahead.

"We're in Lyona's apartments," she said in a whisper when Arden came up beside her. She would never have guessed that so many signs of misuse could occur in so short a time.

"I wasn't sure which room, but Chase's footprints are easy enough to follow," Spohn commented. "He's alone, but he is one of the strongest men I've ever known. I'm not sure the two of us can take him."

"We have to get Jessa free," Arden said. "Maybe we can use our wits instead of trying to match strength with him. One thing, Spohn." The woman finally looked up from the floor. "Jessa may still be in a trance. She's spent most of her time like that since you and Chase caught up with us. If she is, she won't be of any help to us; we may even have to carry her."

Spohn looked down at the carpet, then back at Arden, and the significance of the single set of footprints furrowed her brow. "Yeah" was all she said.

Arden nodded to Spohn, whose expression had not changed. Without another word they moved on, still single file, Arden checking behind them periodically. For some time, she had felt the prickling feeling that meant someone was watching. There was no sound or glimpse of anyone to verify the feeling, and she put it down to imagination.

A voice suddenly sounded ahead, not loud enough for her to hear the words. Almost a rumbling. Had to be Chase. They pressed their backs against opposite walls and continued on. The voice grew louder.

"Damn you, wake up!" were the first words that came clearly.

Jessa must still be in the trance, unless he had done something to her.

They reached the doorway through which the voice sounded. Spohn peeked in quickly and jerked back. Arden moved beside her.

"The bedroom," Spohn whispered.

Arden nodded. Now what? They had made no plan, discussed no strategy. They would have to play this as it developed.

"Where is Jessa?" she whispered back.

"On the bed," came the answer. "Chase is standing beside her."

"What is he going to do to Jessa? He . . . You don't think . . ."

The man meant to punish the daughter for abandoning the mother. If she wasn't going to be forced to replace Lyona at the loom, Jessa must be punished in another way.

"You knew that Chase was in love with Lyona?" she asked.

"More like obsessed," Spohn answered.

"Then he could... We *will* have to make this quick, then. For a moment, I thought we might have time to get help."

"And pray that he hasn't heard us."

If he had heard, they were in deep trouble. They were in trouble even if they still had the element of surprise.

The door remained open. Spohn peeked in, stayed longer this time.

"He isn't there," she whispered.

"Where . . . ?"

"I don't know. There are rooms on either side. Let's just get in there and grab Jessa."

"I'm not sure . . ."

"Then stay here."

Spohn slipped around the edge of the door and out of sight. Taking a deep breath, Arden followed. She dropped to the floor and rolled to the left. Rising to a crouch, she swept the room with a quick glance.

Spohn rushed to the side of the bed.

"My god," she said, a little too loudly.

"What is it?"

Arden took one more look around the room. A door stood closed on the opposite side. Another stood ajar behind her. No sign of Chase.

She stood and moved to the bed. Jessa lay there, eyes closed, her clothes half ripped from her body. A bruise was already forming on her left shoulder.

"She knew what he would do," Arden whispered. "She must have. The trance was her only escape."

Spohn looked at her a moment in disbelief. "Let's get out of here before he has a chance to fulfill his fantasy," she said. "You carry her and I'll keep watch."

Arden nodded and reached to pull Jessa's arms together.

"Stop right there," a rough voice commanded.

Arden spun around. Spohn stood with a poker raised over her head, poised to bring it down on something. The closest target was Arden's head.

Colin Chase stood in the doorway where the door had been ajar when they entered. He held a gun, the barrel seemingly pointing right at her breast. He walked to Spohn and hit her on the side of the head with the weapon. The poker fell to the floor.

"You betrayed me," he said quietly. "No one is going to spoil this for me. Not you." He turned to point the gun at Arden. "Not you."

"Why do you want to harm Jessa?" Arden asked.

Chase scowled at her, at first seeming angry at the question, but when he next spoke the anger was aimed at Jessa.

"I loved Lyona. I'm sure someone has told you that by now. Because of Jessa and the emperor, Lyona died much too soon. I accepted that she was too good for me. I was, after all, only her bodyguard. She was seeress to the emperor, his former consort.

"They can put *you* to the loom if they want to. If Jessa doesn't replace her mother there, then she is no longer princess. That makes her mine. I will have what was denied me."

He looked down at the white face framed by long black hair.

"She looks so much like her mother," he continued. "Even the emperor saw that in her. Because of that, he couldn't punish her as she deserves. He once loved her, too."

Did the last statement refer to Lyona or Jessa? They were getting mixed up in his mind, interchangeable so that he could exact the payment—no, the satisfaction—he had been so long denied.

The princess moaned, and he started toward her. Arden dropped to one knee and grabbed the poker from the floor where Spohn had dropped it. She swung up and sideways, the quickest move. The metal tip caught him behind the knee.

Chase dropped to all fours. Arden brought the poker down on his back. He crumpled. She swung at his head, easing up at the last minute. The blow was enough to keep him out for quite a while, but it was plain from the movement of his sides that he still breathed.

"Kill him," Spohn said. She had grabbed up his gun and was pointing it at him.

"He's your friend," Arden reminded her. "You kill him."

"If we don't kill him, none of us will ever get away from the palace."

"He'll be out long enough for us to get away."

Arden moved to Jessa's side. She was still unconscious, but was starting to come to.

"Put that gun away and do something useful," she said over her shoulder to Spohn.

Arden instructed her to lift the princess's feet onto a pillow. She rubbed the unconscious woman's hands, not knowing the best way to bring her around.

"I'll do it," Spohn said, taking over as if she knew what she was doing.

"What's in this for you?" Arden asked, backing away. She replaced the heavy poker in the stand beside the fireplace. "Why are you helping her?"

Jessa coughed.

"I belong to a group here on Glory that feels that this war must end. It's been going on for ten—almost eleven—years. The emperor and that stupid son of his believe in it. It's become a way of life for them."

Spohn helped Jessa sit up. The princess moaned and laid back, closing her eyes again.

"We want Jessa to take over as empress."

"Have you asked her what she believes in?" Arden asked. "What if she believes in the war, too?"

"She must believe in peace, or she wouldn't have left Glory when she did."

"She left because of what Granid Parcq and Don Vey were doing to her mother. She was powerless to help her, and afraid they might turn to her when Lyona was no longer able to perform. Which is exactly what they did."

"She cares about stopping the war!"

"Maybe. I don't know."

"If she doesn't, we will use her as our symbol anyway. A figurehead"

"I am against the war," Jessa said softly, startling both of them. "But I do not want to be empress. I have other plans. Palace politics are poison to me." Her voice had the quality of a child's, pleading for understanding.

She struggled to sit up straight, shaking off Spohn's helping hand.

"Everyone wants something from me," she continued, her voice stronger. "They always have. I have my own desires."

"We are wasting time," Spohn interrupted. "We have to get out of the palace now."

She stood up and pointed the gun at Arden.

"You're staying here," she said.

Arden stood slowly, keeping her hands in sight.

"Why?"

"You're taking Jessa's place at the loom. I know you have the power. I saw the squares in your room back in Vega City."

"I know you did. But it's not the same."

"You can't do this," Jessa said.

"Be quiet," Spohn ordered. She waved the gun, motioning for Arden to move toward the chair. To Jessa she said, "Take off your belt, highness, and tie her hands with it. Then her feet with her belt."

Jessa did as she was told. Arden kept thinking there were two against one, and they could rush her. However, one of them would more than likely get hurt, and she'd had enough pain for one day.

The princess tried to bind her gently, but the belt around her wrists was faux leather, and the edges bit into her flesh. Once Jessa had finished, Spohn checked the knots, tightening them. Arden winced at each pull and twist but said nothing. Spohn pushed Jessa toward the door. "Happy dreams," she said over her shoulder; then the two of them disappeared into the hall. The sound of their footsteps was muffled in the carpet, and silence fell.

Arden looked over at Chase. How long before he woke up? There would be no doubt in his mind about who hit him. She wished then that she had killed him as Spohn urged.

Chase stirred slightly but settled back into silence. The air in the room also stirred, cooling her wet skin so that Arden shivered. Between fear and the pain in her wrists, she had worked up quite a sweat. Shouting for help had produced little result—only slight echoes of the kind that occur when a room is furnished but not lived in.

Rest for the moment. And pray. Pray to be found before Chase wakes up. Pray that Jessa can be found. In spite of Spohn's revolutionary protestations, she and her followers might hurt the princess if she did not cooperate.

Empress! Women did do things like that. Inherit empires. Inherit businesses and land. And sometimes they did damn good jobs. Just not on Glory.

Their world might be better off with Jessa leading them, but only if she wanted to rule. Of course, her half brother, expecting to inherit the throne, would probably object pretty strongly.

Chase stirred again, his eyelids fluttering slightly this time. Right then, almost anyone who walked through the door would be a welcome sight. Even an enemy would be protection against Chase. The man was crazy or sick.

Time for more philosophical musings? What else could she do? Contemplate the ways in which Chase might do away with her. Contemplate the possibilities that might come after being saved by various would-be rescuers. Contemplate her navel.

The soft tread of someone in the hall came through the open doorway, followed soon by a person. At first glance she recognized the sergeant who had met them at the landing field. He looked first at her, then at Chase. Not a man to mess with, since he probably still held a grudge from Chase's treatment of him in front of his squad. He checked the rest of the room, including opening the other two doors that Spohn had unwisely ignored.

Satisfied that no one else was in the apartment, he moved against the far wall, from where he could see all three doors. He keyed his wrist comm and spoke quietly to someone.

"Khamran in the east wing, closed apartments. I've found Commander Chase and the Grenfell woman."

The other party said something unintelligible to her ears.

"No, the princess is not here. The commander is unconscious and the woman is bound."

Another buzz of voice from the other side.

"Yes, sir, I'll wait."

He repositioned his hand to help support his rifle, looking once from Arden to Chase. His eyes moved constantly, observing everything. Nothing else moved, and she was sure even the chairs and drapes were too afraid of his eagerness to kill something.

She cleared her throat, and he tensed. If she had not been watching him intently, she would not even have noticed.

"Could you at least untie me?" she said, careful to keep any pleading out of her voice. "My hands have gone numb, and I'm sure that my wrists are bleeding."

His gaze met hers. The look in his eyes was cold and impersonal, and he clearly did not care if her whole arm went numb and fell off. She shifted, broadly, moving every part that would move without too much pain. Khamran leveled the rifle at her.

"If you don't do something, I just might lose the use of an arm or hand," she said. "Then how will I weave for the emperor? Neither he nor Don Vey will be very happy with you if that happens. All the effort of finding me, bringing me here . . ."

He appeared to consider that, then reached for a knife at his belt and pulled it from its sheath. He came up beside the chair, and she leaned forward. He sawed at the wide belt, all the time holding the rifle with one hand. Arden gasped as the point caught her left wrist.

Her shoulders had already stiffened, and pulling her hands in front took longer than she would have believed. Dried and fresh blood smeared both wrists. She dabbed at them with the hem of her tunic, licked the wounds, the salty taste of blood on her tongue, and wiped again with the cloth.

Circulation returned slowly as she rubbed each wrist in turn, careful not to chafe the cuts. Then she rubbed each shoulder, rotated her arms, managing only to work out a little of the stiffness. When she reached to untie her ankles, the rifle poked her shoulder.

"You don't need your feet for weaving," he said in a monotone.

She leaned back in the chair, and he raised the point of the rifle. He was a careful man, and she had probably accomplished everything that was possible with him for the moment.

Chase moaned, brought both hands to his head, and moaned again. He rolled over on his left side, pushed himself to a sitting position, and rubbed the back of his head. As he rolled his head from side to side, his gaze fell on Arden. His eyes squinted to slits.

"Bitch!" he roared.

He tried to jump to his feet but fell back on his backside. He tried again, but Khamran stepped in front of the nearly helpless prey.

"Commander," he said. "Sit still. Prime Minister Vey is on his way."

"Vey can go to hell. I'm going to kill that bitch."

"No, sir, you are not."

Khamran bent at the knees, balanced on the balls of his feet.

Chase looked up at the younger man for the first time. His eyes took in the rifle, but there was no sign of recognition. He sneered and shakily got to his feet.

"Who's going to stop me?"

"I am, sir. If I have to."

Chase lunged. Khamran snapped the butt of the rifle up, catching Chase on the chin. He staggered back, regained his balance, and lunged again. This time the rifle butt caught him in the stomach. He doubled over, paused a moment, then butted Khamran in the stomach. The motion slammed the sergeant into the wall. He grunted, his eyes rolled in his head, but his grip on the rifle did not loosen. He brought the butt down on the back of Chase's neck. The commander crumpled to the floor, moved once, then lay still. Thank goodness the commander had been still suffering the effects of getting hit earlier. Otherwise, he might have won that little battle.

Arden had her ankles free. She tried to stand, but her feet were numb and would not support her. Perhaps she could crawl out of the room. Just then Khamran's eyes focused on her. She spread her hands wide and relaxed. At least circulation was coming back to her feet.

The three of them stayed still for some moments, the quiet broken only by both men's labored breathing. No one had moved when another guard burst through the doorway, this one an officer. His eyes took in the situation in the room while he held his rifle at the ready.

"All clear," he shouted.

A third guard entered.

"Are you all right?" the officer asked Khamran. The sergeant nodded.

Don Vey followed, then two more guards who took up positions on either side of the door.

"Where is she?" Vey asked, looking at Arden.

"How the hell should I know?"

"You had better."

"All I know is that Spohn took her."

"Spohn? Why would she do that?"

"Oh, something about making her empress. Ending the war. Getting rid of you and the emperor. Things like that."

He turned his attention to Chase, who lay quietly, reacting to nothing.

"What happened to the commander?"

"A lot of things."

He turned on her, coming close, put one hand on her neck, and squeezed a little.

"Smart-ass remarks will be the death of you," he said.

A muscle twitched in his lower left eyelid. She watched it, saying nothing, resisting the temptation to knee him in the groin, or just slap him upside the head. Calmly, now, look him straight in the eye. Don't flinch. The trump card had switched hands.

"Where did Spohn take the princess?"

His hand released its hold. His expression, although angry, had grown less sure. He stood straight.

"Help me up," she said, holding out a hand.

He took it and supported her as she stood.

"Thanks," she said, and freed her hand.

She took several steps in a circle. It hurt. It felt good. Each step got a little stronger.

"Mr. Vey," she said after a moment, "I have no idea where Spohn took Jessa. It could take you and your men hours, maybe even days, to find her, depending on how well you know Spohn and how lucky you get."

She stretched her arms over her head, then winced as a muscle cramped a little in her shoulder. It felt as if she was getting old—at least too old for adventures like this. Vey waited quietly for her to continue.

"I am relatively sure I can find her for you," she said.

"How?"

"The same way I found her the first time."

"And the price?"

He didn't ask the method used the first time. Either he had guessed or someone had told him about the squares.

"Release my friends. Let them leave Glory peacefully. Cancel the warrant for our arrest."

"Done."

Surprise quickened her heartbeat. He should have at least argued a little. Such quick agreement meant that he probably had no intention of keeping the agreement.

"Also," she continued, "I want Jessa set free to do as she pleases. If she chooses to weave for you and the war effort, then so be it." Might as well go for it all.

"Don't you want us to consider placing her on the throne in place of her brother?"

Sarcasm curled the corner of his mouth upward.

"Why would I want to do that?"

"You are a woman."

"Yes, I'm a woman. However, the choice of who rules Glory is none of my business. I have no need or desire to meddle in your politics. Although you might give some thought yourself to women ruling."

No need telling him that Jessa did not seem to have any interest in being empress. Just in case.

"All right," Vey said. "We've done well enough since Lyona's death."

Something in his expression, in his eyes ... His goal was something different. Having Jessa weave was not his highest priority, at least not personally. That he would pursue any project or policy for his emperor, his world, might be true. In spite of his methods in dealing with her, it was just possible that this was an honorable man, as honor in politics goes. And his emperor still wanted Jessa at the loom, as far as she knew.

"Shall we, then?" she asked.

He raised an eyebrow and smiled. "This way," he said.

He led her through the door and down the hall to the right. At the end were double doors, closed and sealed with an oversized, old-fashioned padlock. Vey motioned to one of the guards, who produced a large ring with equally old-fashioned keys. All modern locks used sonar, magnetic, or laser keys. If Abbot Grayson had not insisted on using antique terran locks in the monastery, she might not have recognized the keys for what they were. Not a bad idea, really, when so few lived who could pick one.

The guard stepped back, the padlock in his hand and the hasp on the door thrown aside. Vey pushed both doors inward. The same guard entered, and in a moment the pitch-black room was bathed in muted light. Clearly, he had been in there a few times before.

Arden stepped in beside Vey. The room was larger than the bedroom, but not much. In the center stood an enormous wooden loom. A few torn threads hung from it, gleaming even in the bad lighting.

"Lyona did not need much light," Vey said in a near whisper. "It was always kept like this."

Arden nodded, remembering her only visit here prior to Lyona's death. She stepped up to the loom and placed both hands on the back beam. She ran her hands along it, then down the rear post. Still kneeling, she touched the crossbeam, up the front post. Standing now, she touched the breastbeam, but there she felt Lyona's presence too strongly, and she backed away. She knew the parts; she even had a pretty good idea how such a loom worked. However, she had never actually used one like it, and she doubted that there was time to learn now.

"I need my hand loom," she said. Vey's expression started to turn stormy. "I don't know how to use this," she said, pointing at the antique machine. "I forgot how complicated a piece it is."

His expression softened into seeming patience.

"Where is your hand loom?" he asked.

"If all of my things weren't brought off Chase's ship, it will be there. He had all of my bags, clothes—everything—transferred from the *Starbourne*."

Vey snapped his fingers, and a guard started out.

"Does he know what to look for?" Arden asked.

The man stopped and looked at her and then at Vey.

"It's six inches square," she said, indicating the size with her hands. "The frame is made of acrylic, light blue, and has metal pins stuck into it so that when the frame is set down flat, the pins stick straight up." She turned to Vey. "I'll need some lifeweave. There should be some in the same bag."

With a nod of permission from Vey, the man sped away. The prime minister took a chair off to one side. The guards had assumed positions at the door and around the room. Three more chairs added to the feeling of desertion that pressed against her. Near the treadles sat the four-legged stool, its seat worn smooth.

Arden touched the seat with her fingertips, remembering when she had seen it before. A hint of the pain of its long-time user lingered, and of the pleasure. The extremes the seeress had felt. Hers was the only spirit that would be found in this room, maybe in the whole of the palace. She might be the one to show the way. She would still care that no harm came to her daughter. Wouldn't she? But would Pac Terhn protect Arden from the mother?

Focus on the question at hand. There can be no false starts. Hurry, please. Bring the loom, so this can be done and soon forgotten.

There were many reasons to fear this contact: Lyona so recently dead. Her life so full of extremes. Her blindness. Her death from despair.

The guard burst into the room.

"Chase had everything moved to his room here in the palace," he explained.

A little breathlessly, he held out the loom and the small

bag that held the lifeweave. It was the last of her supply of the fiber.

With the loom in hand, Arden felt even more reluctant to start. However, at the moment it was the only weapon she had.

She sat on the stool and held her hand out. Already her breathing had slowed and become more rhythmic. The guard placed both articles in her hands. She pulled the end of the thread loose and set the bag on the breastbeam of the larger machine and the smaller loom in her lap. She tied the thread around pins in the first loop.

She took one last look around the room. Everyone watched her, even the guards who pretended not to. This could not work. Too many people watching. Too much self-consciousness. Too much fear of what it would mean if this worked. Try! Once her eyes closed, the people would disappear. Once the spirit comes, it will fill the consciousness. Her hands worked the thread around the pins.

Turn inward, settle the demands of the body to minimal amounts. Everything in tune. You have done it before, many times. No need to search this time. Wait.

Weak spirits appeared: people long dead, who had passed through; weaker spirits of beings who had lived on this world before humankind arrived. They knew nothing.

Where was she? Where was Pac Terhn?

"Lyona," she called. "Your daughter may be in trouble. We have to find her."

The spirits scattered, disappearing. Still, Lyona did not appear.

"Jessa needs you. Don't abandon her again."

"How dare you!" came the answer from behind. "How dare you accuse me of abandoning my daughter."

Arden whirled, nearly toppling from the stool. Lyona! It could be no one else. Her hair totally grey. Her eyes totally blank. Older than Jessa, but with new life in her face and body that was strongly reminiscent of the daughter. Even the voice was hauntingly familiar.

"She looks like you," Arden said.

"Don't patronize me."

"It's true," Arden continued. "As long as she lives, you will never die. But the kind of life she has hangs in the balance right now. She has been kidnapped."

"I know."

"Will you help me find her?"

"Yes. But remember, there is always a price."

"What price could you want from me? I don't understand."

"You will."

"You frighten me."

"Clear your mind, and the information you seek will be yours."

So many misgivings about this, so many fears. Yet, to try to save Rafe and the others, she had no choice. She took a moment to look for Pac Terhn, but there was still no sign of him. Arden tried to clear her mind, but fear and doubt got in the way. Hurry, time is running out. She tried again. Think nothing. Go to sleep. Awake in a short while, and it will all be over.

Energy jolted her. Lyona had given of herself, but it was too soon.

"I'm not ready," Arden cried.

"I am."

The flow of energy overwhelmed her, then ceased as suddenly as it had begun. Time to wake up. Arden opened her eyes, but someone had turned the lights out again.

"Please turn the lights on," she said, fingering the square still in the loom. "I can't see the picture."

Silence. Where was everyone? Then, soft footsteps approaching. Must be Don Vey. None of the guards would come near without his permission.

"The lights are on, Arden," he said. A breath of air caressed her face. "You're blind."

15

Rafe stared at the ceiling, wishing that he had never heard of Glory or its emperor. For him, Owen, Tahr, and Liel, coming dirtside had meant trading one cell for another. Almost two whole days cooped up together—after nearly two weeks on the ship—and not a word about their fate. Especially no word about Arden.

He sat up on the bunk and dangled his legs off the side. In the truck on the way to the palace, he had promised to keep the Glorians from chaining Arden to the loom. How in the hell could he keep that promise? Even when it might have been possible to take some action, killing her would not have been top priority, only a last resort. She had made it clear that, for her, death was preferable.

The decision was taken out of their hands, at least for the moment. And for the foreseeable future. Escape was of primary importance, but none of the men had been able to come up with much of a plan, or even a hope. They knew no one on Glory. They had lost everything with which they might bribe a guard or an official. He chafed at being cooped up, not knowing if he would live to see tomorrow—everything that made up his life at the moment was listed on the negative side.

The lock in the door buzzed. Rafe jumped to his feet just

as Tahr pressed himself against the wall beside the door. Owen and Liel kept to their cots, watching. Exactly what they had discussed. First step in a plan with only one step.

The door slid into the wall, seating with a thump. The guard who had been their only outside companion stepped inside. Something was wrong. His arms were out to his sides, his eyes narrow and cautious. Tahr must have seen it too, because he hesitated.

Another figure stepped inside, holding a pistol in his hand.

"Well, gentlemen, I understand you are in need of rescuing," an unfamiliar voice said.

Rafe got to his feet and studied the stranger, partly hidden behind the guard. He wore loose brown trousers, a matching tunic, and two swords slipped under a tie belt.

"Who are you?" Liel asked. Tahr remained behind both men.

"I am Brother Bryan from the Lower Forest Monastery." He prodded the guard forward, then turned toward Tahr. "Would you close the door?" He held the key card out. "We shouldn't attract any attention just yet."

"By brother, do you mean a monk or something?" Rafe asked as he took the card and complied with the man's request.

His clothes appeared rather ordinary. The only items out of place were the swords, one of which looked very much like Arden's.

"I am a priest, sir, and a warrior. More important, I am a friend of Arden Grenfell. We heard that she had returned but was unable to visit us."

He handed Liel a pair of bonds and shackles. Owen ripped a strip from his blanket to use as a gag. "You'll never get out of the palace," the guard said in a tight voice. Owen immediately gagged him while Liel pulled his hands behind his back.

"Captain," Bryan said. The two of them moved off a bit. "I didn't get here as quickly as I'd hoped. The monastery has been under surveillance ever since Arden left Glory."

"What is your connection to her?" Rafe asked.

"She grew up with us after her father died."

The captain nodded, realizing again how little he knew about her. He realized also that this was not the time to ask questions, although he was very curious how this monk knew who he was.

"Are you alone?" he asked instead.

"Yes. Getting one of us out of the monastery without being seen was difficult enough. I'm sorry, Captain, but there is no plan to speak of. Except that I was going to release Arden and spirit her away to a hiding place, against her will if necessary. Oh, I did locate your ship at the port."

"Have you located Arden yet?"

The guard was secured and had been laid out on Tahr's bunk. Everyone was trying to listen to his conversation with the monk, but looking like they were not. Liel had placed himself near the door, clearly dividing his attention between it and them.

"Neither she nor the princess was in their cell when I got there," Bryan answered. "There was a trace of blood on the floor. I don't think they left easily, nor do I think they were taken officially."

"Any idea where they were taken?"

"None. I felt that I needed help in locating her, so I came looking for you."

Liel left his post at the door and approached them.

"I'd suggest that we get some weapons and get the hell out of here," he said. "If we stay much longer, his absence is going to be discovered." He nodded toward their prisoner.

Rafe looked over at the guard. "I don't imagine he has any idea where they might be."

"I can find out," Tahr volunteered.

The prisoner's eyes widened, but he did not try to protest. Rafe's instinct was to believe Bryan's assessment that the women had been taken unofficially. If that was so, the guard might not have any helpful information. They needed to get to the computer at the guards' station if possible. If there was an order to move anyone, or if prisoners had turned up missing, there should be something in there. He told the others this.

"It must be the middle of the night," he said, looking to Bryan for confirmation. "Liel and I'll see if we can get into the computer and check it out. The rest of you stay here. Keep alert. If there's any sign that we've been found, get the hell out of the palace." Tahr looked dubious. "Understand?" Rafe said to him, then checked with the others. They all nodded.

He and Liel slipped out the door. The corridor was dimly lighted and empty, as was the guards' station. Their prisoner must have been the only guard on duty. They probably rarely kept dangerous prisoners in these cells below the palace, especially since Glory was at war. Come to think of it, there had been few signs of war in what little they had seen since landing. The Glorians must have managed to keep the war concentrated on the other worlds.

Liel went to the computer and turned on the monitor.

"Looks like they leave the security program on all the time," he said.

He keyed in a few commands, frowned a couple of times, and worked a little more. Rafe kept an eye on the monitors, but few people were moving around.

"Something happened, that's for sure," Liel said. After another moment: "Here it is. A squad was ordered into the east wing, third floor. That's why only one guard was here. The rest went up there. It looks like . . . yeah. They were ordered to search for the princess and Arden."

"Did they escape, or were they taken?"

"Can't tell. This only carries the alert and the orders that are given."

"Let's get the others and get up there. Maybe this is the break we needed."

They returned to the cell and quickly informed everyone of what they had learned. Brother Bryan was the only one who had the slightest notion of the layout of the palace, so he led the way. The bulk of his knowledge was the location of the stairways and elevators, which was where they needed to start.

Tahr rechecked the guard's bonds, then joined the others at the door.

"This is going to be like trying to find two needles in a haystack."

"At least we know exactly what these two needles look like," Rafe said tightly. "If the emperor plans to make Jessa or Arden do the weaving, the most logical place to find the two of them will be in those apartments."

"I don't see why we have to risk our lives to save either one of them," Tahr said. "Jessa—"

Rafe grabbed the front of his shirt and pushed him against the nearest wall.

"Jessa is one of us," he growled. "If you don't want—"

A hand on his shoulder stopped him. Without turning, he knew it was Liel, but he continued to press against Tahr. His insides shook and, damn, he wanted to hit something.

"He knows," Liel said.

Rafe released Tahr's shirt and stepped back. This was not the first time his crew had seen his temper flare, but it was the first time it had been aimed at one of them.

"I'm sorry," he managed to say.

"It's okay, Captain," Tahr said, straightening his shirt. "I know I get on people's nerves sometimes."

Their eyes met. Tahr's devotion to Jessa was real; it was the words that had been false, mouthed out of habit. This incident would never be forgotten, but it was forgiven. In months or a year, they would joke about it in some bar on some world they might not even have heard of yet. If they ever got off Glory.

"We don't want to draw any more attention to ourselves than we can help," Rafe said, echoing Bryan's words. "Get his ID," he said, pointing to the guard. "It probably won't get us in everywhere, but maybe enough places."

Tahr pulled the card from the uniform blouse. The man grunted, but he was too securely tied to move. Tahr handed the card to Rafe.

He slapped Tahr on the shoulder. "Let's go."

Liel peeked out, left and right, again, then waved everyone forward. They stepped out and Bryan took the lead.

The first barrier was the door into the basement itself. The card worked fine. The way led into a common room for guards: tables and chairs, lockers.

"I guess this late at night, they don't get much action around here," Liel commented.

Rafe had to keep reminding himself that it was night. Strange, losing track of time like that, in just two days.

"There might be uniforms in these lockers," Tahr said. "Wouldn't we better off changing clothes?"

"What if gaol guards aren't allowed in the rest of the palace?" Rafe argued.

"We could always be taking prisoners for interrogation to Vey or someone," Owen said. "A couple of us wear uniforms and the rest don't."

"It might work," Liel said. "Except they're all locked."

"Break them open," Tahr said.

"No time," Rafe said. "The more time we spend fooling around with things like that, the more likely we are to be found."

Rafe studied their clothes a moment. Their blue ship's uniforms sure didn't look anywhere near as elegant as what most of the people in the palace wore. Maybe this late at night they could be cleanup staff, or repairmen sent in to fix something. Maybe those people all had uniforms, too.

Hell. Either way they all stood out from the norm. And time was running out.

They moved on, stopping to check around corners before proceeding. The main corridors were easy to find—they were the widest, and Bryan had already found his way through them. After a time, they found an elevator.

"Is this the way you came in?" Rafe asked.

"No. I took one from the loading dock. It's down the hall a ways. Don't see why this one won't do as well."

He inserted the key card and pressed a button, and the doors opened in a matter of seconds. The elevator was empty. When they checked the control panel, they found that it went to the upper floors, apparently without restrictions. The only way to know for sure was to try it.

"This will take us to the third floor. I just wish we knew for sure if that's where Lyona's apartments are located," Rafe said.

It took the key card to get the elevator moving. The indicator above the doors flickered, then lit steadily as they moved upward. Was the ease of their escape thus far something he should worry about? A moot point. He *was* worried. Rafe shrugged mentally. Chalk the lack of interest up to late night. But keep an eye open.

The light showed "1," and the doors slid aside. The group jumped to either side of the car. A man stepped inside and looked around at them. Just as his eyes widened in surprise, Liel hit him on the back of the head from behind. The man slumped into Liel's arms and was pulled out of sight. Luckily, the car was quite a bit larger than the one in the hotel back on Caldera.

Rafe reached for the "door close" button on the control panel and hesitated. A group of people were crossing the immense foyer, headed for the outer doors. The group passed along the opposite wall, quite a distance away, but he was sure that the woman surrounded by seven or eight men was Arden. In the moment she was in sight, he could have sworn that two men were leading her by the arms. Something about her posture was all wrong.

"Let's go," he said, and stepped out of the elevator.

"What about . . ." Liel began.

"It's Arden!"

This time he checked outside very quickly. The other group had passed through the doors, where a guard stood on either side. In order to follow, they would have to bluff their way past. The guard on the right watched them carefully, then signaled to his mate. They raised their rifles simultaneously.

"You fellows don't belong here," the left guard said.

The one on the right moved to the doors, key card in hand. So much for finessing their way out. Without a word, they rushed the guards. The left guard thumbed off the safety of his rifle. He raised the gun and fired just as Tahr hit him. The shot went wild, and the man went down with Tahr on top. It took the pilot only a moment to knock him unconscious.

The remaining guard had dropped the key card and thumbed off the safety of his rifle. Liel hit him before he had a chance to fire.

Rafe pushed through the doors and ran onto the portico. Ahead, Arden and her escorts had made it through the garden and neared the gates. He shivered in the cool darkness. Liel stooped down to pick up one of the rifles. Tahr got the other.

"Hurry, or we'll lose them," Rafe said, and rushed down the steps.

The quarry disappeared through the gate, to the left. Hurry, or they would get too far ahead! Outside the gate and no sign of them. They had turned a corner, but which way?

He ran to the end of the block. No one in sight to the left. Down the street to the right, dark shadows bobbed up and down. For a brief moment he wondered why they were walking instead of using a vehicle of some kind. He shook off the question. Best to be thankful for small favors.

He whistled and waved the others to join him. Not waiting, he took off running, determined not to lose sight of them again. But they were too far ahead, the late night was too dark, and there were too few streetlights. He lost sight of them around two more turns. As he stood cursing his luck and wondering which way to go, Tahr and Bryan caught up then Owen appeared.

"Which way?" Tahr asked.

"Dammit, I don't know. They were just too far ahead."

Liel caught up and bent over with his hands on his thighs, trying to catch his breath. Rafe turned in a circle. Three choices: straight ahead, right, or left.

He had to find her. Which way?

"Let's split up," Bryan said. "Meet back here in half an hour either way."

"All right," Rafe said. "I'll go right again. Liel, you go left. Tahr, take the street straight ahead. Owen, you wait here and watch for us. Bryan, stay with me."

They dispersed, their running footsteps lost in the emptiness of the night. Rafe and Bryan came to the first crossroads, stopped, and looked both ways. Nothing. They ran to the next and stopped again.

A woman screamed in the distance. It didn't sound like Arden, but it could not be a coincidence.

Arden let herself be pulled and pushed down concrete stairs and into the night coolness. No use trying to resist. She was blind. Blind? How could she be blind? What did Lyona do to her?

"I recognize this place," Don Vey had said back in the seeress's room, after taking the lifeweave square from her.

He had said no more about her being blind and she felt unable to ask anything.

"Let's go," he had said.

Two men—probably guards—had grabbed her arms, lifted her from the chair, and tried to pull her along. She dug in her heels, bringing the men to an unexpected stop.

"Wait!" she cried. "Help me. I can't see."

Tears soaked her cheeks and she couldn't even wipe them away. She had tried to pull free. She must go back! Lyona had to undo it.

Someone slapped her. Her head jerked to the right. Her cheek stung.

"We don't have time for this," Vey had said. "We must get to the house before Jessa disappears again."

"You don't need me," she cried. "What can I do for you?"

"If they move her before we get to her, you will have to locate her again."

"I need to go back in there now. If I wait, I may never see again. Please."

"You will do as I tell you."

Dammit, they couldn't do this. Pull harder. Make them let go. She kicked out, first one side, then the other. The first time she caught someone's leg, but the hold on her arm didn't loosen.

Someone had grabbed her by the hair and pulled her head back. His breath warmed the dampness on her cheeks. Heat from his body pressed against her.

"It would give me great pleasure to kill you here and now," Vey said. "You have caused me a lot of trouble." He released her head and moved away. "Now let's go."

Other footsteps had surrounded her, bodies crowded around. They moved too fast. She might have stepped on something or tripped. If she held back, though, Vey might really hurt her. She had to depend on those leading her to make sure she didn't fall down a flight of stairs or some such thing.

They stepped into an elevator, and bodies crowded closer. For the first time in her life, she had felt the car's descent. Usually, they moved so smoothly that the sensation never happened. She listened intently. The sound of people's breathing surrounded her.

Senses didn't become that acute so quickly. Maybe it was the lifeweave; maybe it had made her more sensitive or more adaptive than she had realized.

No matter how adaptive she might have become, the last thing she wanted was for the blindness to last. It would be better to concentrate on what happened to cause it. How could Lyona manage it? Had she done it at all? Why hadn't Pac Terhn protected her?

The fact that Lyona lost her sight—and to the effects of lifeweave . . .

If only she could remember what happened, what the seeress had said while they were in contact.

Think! Rarely did memories linger of those contacts, just a vague sense of the spirit or spirits. Often, nothing at all. But Lyona's personality was so strong. She remembered that. And anger, but at whom was it directed?

The elevator had stopped, the doors slid open, and she was pulled out. Footsteps now echoed as in a cavern. The foyer of the palace. One of the few places she had seen without plush carpet. They had hurried across it. Suddenly she was outside, going down those concrete steps. The air was cool, chilling, and she realized that she had been sweating.

Where was this place that appeared in the lifeweave square? Not far, please. The fear of falling still plagued her. She tripped over something on the walkway, but the guards tightened their grips and proceeded as if nothing had happened. She fought to keep her feet under her.

The air smelled sweet and clear. Might be very early morning. No sunrise yet. Would she ever see a sunrise again? Or the shimmer of lifeweave?

Waiting to confront Lyona wasn't a good idea. It had to be done soon. What if Vey did not allow her the time, until it was too late?

They turned a corner a little too fast and she lost her balance again. Everyone paused a moment. She got the impression they were deciding on which direction rather than showing concern for her discomfort. In the new silence, distant footsteps touched the darkness. Someone was following.

"This way," Vey said, and they started off again.

Apparently her companions did not hear the other footsteps. If only it were Rafe who followed. More wishful thinking.

After more twists and turns, they finally came to a stop. Some of the men broke away, as if at a silent command. She waited with the rest. A bird called in the distance. A night bird, or would sunrise come soon?

A crash, and she guessed that a door had been broken down. Her personal escort held back, keeping her from the melee that seemed to engulf whatever building she stood in front of. Furniture crashed, doors gave way, people shouted, and, as she was moved forward, a woman screamed. Arden strained to see. Could it have been Jessa? She didn't think so. It hadn't sounded like her. More like Spohn.

More yelling and cursing as she moved deeper into the building, up a flight of stairs and down a hall into a small room. The door closed behind her. Below, people were led from the building, their voices disturbing the silence.

"You did this, you witch," Spohn shouted. People scuffled and someone gasped. "Another few minutes and we would have been gone where no one could find us," Spohn said, her voice tight with anger.

"Well, Mr. Vey," Jessa said. "You have me again."

"Yes, your highness. For keeps this time. But perhaps for another reason."

"What . . ."

"We must be leaving now," he said. "We will have a busy day tomorrow."

"No," Arden said. "I will never weave for you unless you let me try to get my sight back right now."

"Arden," Jessa gasped.

Sometime in the past hour, Arden had accepted the fact that once Vey had seen her weave a square that gave him the information he wanted, he would put her to work at the loom. Not Jessa. What the princess's fate might be she could not say. Equally unpleasant if he had his way.

"You will just lose it again," Vey said. "Just like Lyona did."

"Perhaps. But it doesn't matter if I don't weave. I . . ."

"Don't forget your people in the monastery," he interrupted.

"They may be at your mercy no matter what I do."

"I promise . . ."

"Please forgive me, Mr. Vey, but I put no trust in your promises."

"Why does it have to be here?"

"It's the time, not the place."

The door opened and closed. Someone walked in but said nothing.

Arden wrenched free from the hands that held her arms. They didn't grab her again, and she assumed Vey must have signaled them. She stretched out both hands and took small, tentative steps. There must be a chair or something to sit on.

Her foot found a chair first, and the pain in her big toe caught her up short. She reached down. A straight-backed chair. Carefully, she turned and backed up to it, catching the edge of the seat just above her knee. She sat, feeling for the edges with both hands. No need to look silly by falling off the chair.

She held both hands straight in front of her with palms up until the hand loom was placed in them. She set it in her lap then held out her hands for the lifeweave. It shimmered in her hands as if it were alive and, in a way, she could see it as she started the square.

That was what had driven Lyona to keep weaving. Even when she could no longer see the wonder of the colors, she could feel them. The effect was subtle, something no one with sight would notice because the senses were overwhelmed by what the eyes saw. The temptation to linger over this discovery was squelched by fear. She relaxed, controlled her breathing.

It was done in a moment. Lyona waited, expecting her return. And Arden could see her.

"Why did you take my sight?" Arden asked without preamble.

"I had to be sure you would return. Finding Jessa was the first thing. However, I need to tell her things. About her future."

"You are..."

"Lucid. Logical. There is no lifeweave here to cloud my mind."

"I wondered before. That means the effects on the mind aren't permanent?"

"Of course they are permanent," Lyona said with a short, bitter laugh. "Until one dies, apparently."

"But you're still blind."

"Yes, I am still blind. Why that is different, I can't pretend to know. There is no one to explain."

"How did you make me blind?"

"I simply suggested that it would happen when you first visited. It worked a little like a posthypnotic suggestion. That is one of the dangers of your approach to telling the future. You go into some sort of meditative trance in which you hand over control to other beings. Do you remember everything that happens while you are weaving?"

"Not all. I remember the information and where it comes from very gradually. Except when I talked to you. Anyway, you wanted me back for some reason."

"Yes. I did. Tell Jessa that I am sorry. For deserting her. For making possible all of the bad things that have been happening. Tell her that I love her very much."

"Anything for the emperor?"

Lyona's face twisted in very real pain. She still loved him, whether or not she blamed him for her own early death or for hunting down their daughter. For a fleeting moment, Arden wondered whether anyone would ever feel such pain over her own death.

"No, nothing," the seeress interrupted. "He needs nothing, now."

Arden looked away from those eyes. Even in their blindness, the pain was all too potent.

"Will I be able to see when I get back?" she asked, still keeping her gaze turned downward. "And will I remember what you have said?"

"Yes, to both. You must go soon. Don Vey grows impatient, and he is difficult enough to deal with under the best circumstances.

"Tell my daughter two more things. The first is for you to remember, too. Don't trust Vey. He will do anything to get his way. He is loyal to Glory and himself. He enriches both by carrying on the war. The reason for everything he does."

She paused, as if deep in thought. Arden waited a moment, then asked about the second thing.

"Oh, tell her that the man she loves will return. They can be married if she stays on Glory, even if that means becoming empress."

"Jessa is in love?"

Lyona nodded. "She was afraid that if she returned to Glory, they would have to give each other up."

"I'll tell her," Arden promised. She started to ask who the man was, but Lyona interrupted.

"Thank you. Now go."

Lyona turned and moved away, fading from sight as if she had walked into a fog.

A moment's panic struck. How did she get back? Arden had come out of the trance only once by herself. Where was Pac Terhn? Was he playing the trickster once more?

Dammit! Wake up!

The room took gradual shape, the people in their places. She could see again. There was Don Vey lounging on a sofa, seemingly at ease, yet watching her intently. Jessa sat at the other end of the sofa, also watching. He must have told the princess who Arden was seeing in her lifeweave-induced trance.

Several guards—more than she had realized had accompanied them—stood around the room: guarding the door, flanking the windows, flanking her, and the princess seated on the sofa. Noises downstairs probably meant there were more guards down there. Where was Spohn? Had she been taken away to some prison?

"Well, Arden Grenfell," Vey said as he sat up straighter. "You are back. Did you get what you wanted?"

"Yes, Mr. Vey, I did." She turned to Jessa. "Your mother asked me to deliver a message to you. I think you might appreciate hearing it in private."

"Your highness," Vey said abruptly. "Are you satisfied?"

Thinking he was speaking to Jessa, Arden looked to her to answer. Instead, another familiar voice replied from near the door.

"I think so. We can't have my future wife blinded, can we?"

Jackson Turner walked to the center of the room and smiled at her.

16

Jessa and Arden looked from Vey to Turner. The prime minister had just called the private investigator and spy "your highness." He even bowed his head in slight obeisance.

Turner nodded to Vey, then looked at the two women, gauging their reactions.

"You . . . You are . . ." Jessa stammered.

"Your brother, Waran," he said smoothly. "Or, rather, half brother."

"I didn't realize that you had grown so tall."

"How could you? You left when I was so young. And helpless."

"You were never helpless, as I recall. Nor were you so young."

"Inexperienced, then."

"Maybe that."

He turned to Arden, then went to sit down beside her. He took her hand in both of his and looked into her eyes.

"And you. I had such plans for you and me." He kissed her hand. "If only Semmes and his crew hadn't found the second tracking device. I think everything still might work out, though, don't you, Vey?"

"Of course, your highness. We did discuss more than one possible plan."

"Which one seems the most logical to you at this moment?"

"The first scenario works whether or not Miss Grenfell is willing," Vey said.

How dare they talk about her and Jessa as if they were not even in the same room?

"Shall we let them in on the plan?"

"If you wish, your highness."

"You see, ladies," Waran said, regarding each of them in turn, "our original plan was to bring Jessa home where we could control her. To eliminate her as a threat to my gaining the throne. In the meantime, I met you, Arden, and won your heart. You could have become my concubine."

"You mean all that courting was for real?"

"Oh, yes, I never misled you in that regard," Waran said. "I've always been attracted to strong women. The second plan was to take over Weaver. The excuse was to be the lost shipment of lifeweave. Your friends finding the ship and salvaging that treasure messed things up a bit."

"You have miscalculated," Jessa said. "According to the agreements between Weaver and all of the worlds they deal with, only a member of the Belle family can own that world. Only their children can inherit. Every world that deals with Weaver agreed to that and, as far as I know, is committed to keeping them independent."

"Is this true, Vey?"

Cold anger hardened his voice. His face flushed, and veins stood out on his forehead. A strange look passed over Jessa's features but was quickly gone.

"No, it is not," Vey said. "I researched the laws thoroughly and found none regarding inheritance."

"It's in the corporate bylaws," Jessa said. "Remember, they are a business, not a government. The charter has been ratified by all of the governments with which they do business, including Glory. A copy is filed with every one of them. It is one of the things that has prevented an invasion of Weaver for many generations. It will keep you from getting control now or in the future."

"And if the current owners should die without children?"

"They have two children," she said. "Didn't you check into their background? It should show that the current matriarch has been pregnant more than once."

"Yes, but . . ." Vey sputtered.

"How do you know this?" Waran asked.

"I researched the family some time ago," she answered.

Waran looked at Vey, who shrugged his shoulders.

From what Lyona had said, Arden was beginning to suspect who Jessa's love interest might be.

"I'm sure you found birth records for only two of them. The other embryos are frozen, preserved, for the day they might need them."

Jessa watched all of them, eyes wide, probably wondering where all this put her future. In Waran's mind, the only two choices for her must be weave or die. Either way, he could block his half sister from the throne.

"What about your father, the emperor, in all this?" Arden asked. "What do you plan for him?"

He dropped her hand, stood up, and began pacing.

"The old man is senile, or whatever the fashionable term for old is these days. He wants his Lyona back, and he sees her in Jessa. He used to sit and watch that witch weave for hours. All the time my mother sat in her rooms and cried from loneliness."

"And you?" Arden asked softly. "Were you lonely too?"

He turned on her, and it seemed sure that he would strike her. Somehow he kept his hands, his fists that shook in her face, from striking out.

"I hated my mother for her weakness," he said through clenched teeth. He resumed pacing. "My only companion was my half sister. Weren't you, Jessa? Do you remember? I was very young, but I remember. You dried my tears.

You played with me and protected me when father was angry."

He sat in another chair, calmer now, cold.

She had pushed too far. The real reasons for his anger and fear were too tightly connected to Jessa, and that placed them both in great danger. He might thrust aside political and romantic considerations for cleansing this old wound.

"Suddenly, one day, I was sent away to school. When I returned, you were gone. I searched the palace. I even went to your mother's apartments, even though I despised her. When I was old enough, I tried to find you, but as an independent spacer, you weren't registered. I became a private investigator, created a new persona, learned all the tricks of the trade, but settled space is very big, and you moved among the worlds and ships frequently.

"About a year ago, with Vey's help, I hit on the idea that led to your discovery. I stole spools of lifeweave—one or two at a time—sold most of them, burnt a few, until suddenly they were all gone. No one had a clue, since I had placed my own servants in charge of the lifeweave. The shock killed your mother. She depended on it so.

"My father was determined to get you back, with a little nudging from Vey," he said, pointing at Jessa. "We had already planned on taking over Weaver. It seemed so logical to send you after Jessa." Now he pointed at Arden. "We would have you both, and Weaver."

"What will you do now, Waran?" Arden asked.

He looked at her long and hard. "I want you to become my concubine," he said at last. "You cannot be my wife, of course, but I want you to share my life."

"No."

"Because of Captain Semmes?" His voice was hard.

"In part. But I just don't love you."

Were the guards close enough to hear any of this? Was it to her advantage to have witnesses? They stood around the room like statues, clearly personal guards who were trusted, probably devoted to their charge. They had no reason to care what happened to a former captain of the guard or a princess, neither of whom they knew.

Vey would not gainsay his leader. After all, he was in this plot up to his eyeballs. His future was irrevocably tied to that of the prince.

What would become of Rafe and the crew? Or Abbot Grayson and the monastery?

Waran stood up and looked around the room as if seeing it for the first time.

"This is the house of conspirators," he said. "It would seem fitting to burn it. Maybe that will warm my father at last."

"Yes, your highness," Vey said.

Waran turned toward Arden. "I'm saving you from the loom, you know. My father ordered that the two of you be put to the loom in tandem."

He turned on his heel and walked out. The prime minister bowed as his prince strode from the room, followed by three of the guards.

"Get fuel," Vey said to the corporal of the guards. "Ethylene, oil, something that will burn fast and hot."

"Vey, you can't," Arden said. "Too many people know the princess is here."

"That may be; however, they will not know who lit the fires."

"All of the troops here will know. Spohn's people will know."

"None of the guards will say anything. And no one will believe traitors like Spohn. People who conspire against their emperor are never considered trustworthy. She's probably dead already anyway. The Parcq dynasty is much admired. All sympathy would be ours."

He thought a moment, then smiled.

"We could even state that the traitors kidnapped you. Anyway, there was a warrant for your arrest. For kidnapping, no less. No. When we are finished with our communique on this terrible tragedy, the Parcq dynasty will not be blamed."

The corporal returned with another guard. Between them they carried four five-gallon jugs. At least one of them wasn't full—the liquid in it sloshed noisily—but there was enough to take care of a house and two women.

"Shall we tie them up?" the corporal asked.

"No. The bonds might not burn completely. We need to leave ourselves free to create any cover story that fits all circumstances."

The corporal handed his two jugs to two other guards. A third took a jug from his companion. The four started splashing the strong-smelling liquid on drapes and furniture. The corporal stopped one of them.

"Take that one downstairs," he said. The man disappeared through the door.

Vey took a look around. "Light it," he ordered.

"You won't get Weaver out of this," Arden told him as he passed her.

"We will. Some way. Lawyers have devious minds." He gave a mock salute. "Farewell, Captain Grenfell."

She kicked him on the shin as hard as she could with the toe of her boot. He cried out and bent over to grab the injured limb, raising the leg at the same time. She caught him on the side of the head with the other foot.

One of the guards whirled, lighter in hand. She grabbed a lamp from the nearest table and threw it. The lighter went out as he dropped it but sparks from the lamp shorting out set the flammable fluid alight. With a roar, one side of the room was engulfed in a wall of flames.

"Let's get out of here," the corporal yelled.

Jessa was on her feet. She started to follow the guards.

"Wait!" Arden cried. "We have to get Vey out."

"Why?" Jessa shouted.

"We may need him to clear the warrant and all."

"Dammit."

Jessa turned back and helped lift the unconscious prime

minister from the floor. He hung between them, totally limp, a dead weight to be dragged.

"What about the guards?" Jessa yelled. Smoke was filling the room. "Will they let us get out of the house?"

"If we have to, we can use Vey as a shield."

They moved to the door, which was standing open after the flight of the guards.

"If he gets shot, he can't clear us."

"We'll just have to take that chance," Arden said.

Smoke billowed up the stairs from fires set on the first floor. Arden's eyes stung, and her throat burned. Vey grew heavier with each step. He rocked against her, and she balanced precariously a moment on the edge of the staircase.

"Wait a minute," she yelled.

Jessa looked up. Her eyes were watering, and her face looked strained.

"There's an easier way," Arden yelled again.

She pulled his left arm around her shoulders, taking hold of it with her left hand. With her right hand she reached as if to pick up his left leg, all the while glancing over at Jessa. The princess nodded understanding, then draped Vey's right arm around her shoulders. Together, each grabbed a leg and hoisted. The staircase was just wide enough for them to descend in tandem.

Another step and Jessa began coughing. Halfway down Arden began coughing. They should get down on hands and knees and crawl out, but they couldn't move Vey that way. If things got any worse, they would have to abandon him.

Jessa missed a step, stumbled onto the next one. She threw out her arm to catch herself, releasing her hold on Vey. With the extra weight thrown against her, Arden tumbled headfirst to the floor below, landing almost on top of Vey. She had to grab Jessa and get the hell out.

She raced back up to where Jessa lay sprawled on the stairs and pulled on her arm. It seemed almost as limp as Vey's had.

"I can't," Jessa croaked.

Okay, they should stay low anyway. Arden sat down hard, bruising her tailbone. Her side ached. She looked back up the stairs a moment. Flames pierced the doorway of the room they had just left.

"We crawl," she yelled in Jessa's ear.

"I can't."

"You will. Now!"

Taking a strong hold on Jessa's wrist, she pulled her forward. With the downward momentum begun, Jessa had no choice but to move. They could not go side by side because they could not go straight down. Slip a little sideways. Thank goodness for carpet. Easier on the knees.

Jessa slowed, and Arden gave her a little nudge. Both of them coughed continuously. The stairway acted like a chimney, drafting most of the smoke to the second floor. They had to get all the way down.

Which way was the front door, left or right?

Something crashed behind them. The stairs shook. Risking a look backward, Arden saw that the ceiling had fallen in, catching the top of the stairs on fire. Flames licked the top of the rail, then crept downward. *Fire doesn't burn downhill. Does it?*

Only a few more steps to the bottom. Jessa's arms collapsed, and she slid. Her head and shoulders rested on the floor, her torso and legs stretched up the last few steps. The bend was all wrong. She would hurt her back that way.

The carpet was getting hotter under her palms. Another crash, somewhere, above or behind. Bits of debris rained down. Arden threw her arms over her head. Little needles stung her forearms. Her right hand slipped on the next step. She slid the last few steps. Her head pushed up against Jessa's hip. Fire roared overhead, blazed around the left corner. She tried to rise.

The arms just would not hold her weight.

I'll just lie here a moment. Get my breath. What's that noise? So far away.

17

The house across the street was well lit and full of activity. Rafe was sure the scream had come from there but, so far, they had been unable to investigate closely because of the soldiers that surrounded it. He was convinced that Arden was inside, and his companions were willing to follow his lead.

A dozen or more guards surrounded the house, most of whom must have come from another direction. Not long ago, Jackson Turner had suddenly appeared. The guards had stood aside with a little bow as he went inside. Who was this man, really?

Rafe stopped wondering, drawn to renewed activity. Turner emerged from the house, and guards ran around again. Two of them returned inside, each carrying what looked like five-gallon jerry cans.

"How are we going to get them out?" Tahr asked for the third time.

"I don't know," Rafe answered sharply.

He stooped lower behind the rock wall that hid them all and took a deep breath. God, he only wished he *did* know.

All hell broke loose. The windows were brighter than before. Men ran from the house, panicked, eager to get as much distance behind them as they could. Rafe waited a moment. Vey had not appeared. Nor had Arden.

"Let's go," he shouted, knowing his voice might be drowned out by the pandemonium across the street. Most of the guards were nearly out of sight. As the remaining members of the *Starbourne*'s crew followed up to the door, a guard stumbled into Rafe's arms. The captain grabbed the man's lapels and brought his face up close. Smoke swirled against the brightness inside.

"What's going on?" Rafe shouted.

The man was dumbfounded. Rafe handed him to Liel behind him, then slammed the door wide open to reveal a small entryway. Doorways stood open on either side. More smoke swirled outside.

The house was nearly engulfed by fire.

"Liel, you and Owen go that way." Rafe pointed to the hall on the left.

Again, he was taking the right. Or had it been the left before? Where the hell was Arden? Rounding a corner, he tripped over something in the smoky twilight. He rolled off whatever it was and got to his knees. Tears blurred his vision even more, and he swiped at his eyes with a sleeve. Then he took hold of the obstacle, pulling it closer so that he could see what it was.

Don Vey, unconscious but alive.

"Captain," Tahr cried out. "Over here. I think it might be Arden."

"Liel, here, take Vey."

He crawled in the direction of Tahr's voice. A darker shadow moved, low to the floor.

"Arden?" he called, his voice slightly husky.

The form kept moving. He called her name again, and this time the form stopped. It slumped, as if all the air had been let out. He crawled faster. Closer now, it became clear that there were two of them. One lay prone, with Tahr bent over it, the other slightly raised. On her elbows. Arden.

She coughed weakly and held out a hand to him. He took it, pulled her to him.

"We have to get Jessa out of here," she whispered close to his ear.

"Jessa?"

He let go of Arden and helped Tahr turn the other form over. The princess's face was too white. No sign of breathing.

"You're going the wrong way," he said. "Stay low, back that way." He pointed toward the door, and she turned around.

"Jessa?" she said.

"We'll bring her. You keep moving."

Arden crawled away slowly. He grabbed hold of Jessa's arm and, with Tahr's help, draped her limp form across his shoulder. Her skin felt cold and clammy. They had better hurry if she was to have a chance.

In spite of the extra weight, he caught up with Arden quickly. She seemed barely able to put one hand in front of the other. Both knees dragged across the carpet. Several times he pushed against her rear when she seemed to freeze in place.

It was taking too long. He needed the others, but they had their hands full with Vey. Nor could they hear him call out over the roar of the flames. If they got out with the prime minister, they would come back for the rest. Meanwhile, keep moving.

Sure enough, a form appeared a moment later. It was Bryan. He knelt beside Arden, prepared to lift her in his arms.

"Vey and the others?" Rafe asked.

"Outside."

Bryan lifted Arden and started off without crawling. He had stayed outside in the fresh air to back up the others. Rafe no longer felt sure that he could stand.

"Captain," Liel said from behind him.

The weight was lifted from his back. He was helped to his feet. Liel smiled as he led the way.

• • •

Arden lay on her back in the wet grass, trying to look up at the stars, but her vision was still too cloudy. Her eyes watered, her nose ran, and she couldn't stop coughing for very long. The coolness of the dew against her skin felt soothing, and it was good to be alive.

Everyone was alive. Even Don Vey, although he was still unconscious. The fall must have been worse than it looked, although Tahr said there were no broken bones. Concussion, probably, but only a real doctor could tell for sure.

She rolled onto her right side and looked down the neighborhood. Houses were all built right on the street, some with adjoining walls, some freestanding with large side yards—like the one she had just escaped from. The roof had fallen in. Smoke rolled out the open door even more heavily than before. Flames brightened the windows, but the house lights must have finally gone off. No one fought the fire. It didn't even look like anyone had called for a fire squad. Waran had just walked away, taking his guards with him, and now the street was deserted.

The windows in all the other houses were dark. It looked like no one on Glory watches what the palace guards are up to, something she had never noticed when she was one of them.

Rafe finished checking with the others and came to sit beside her. His face was blackened by the smoke, and his eyes looked weary.

"Everyone's pretty much okay," he said as Tahr and Liel coughed behind him. "Jessa's come around and doesn't seem much the worse for wear." He brushed a strand of hair off her forehead. "How are you feeling?"

"My throat hurts. My eyes won't stop watering. My nose won't quit running. And my tailbone aches. Otherwise, it's a beautiful autumn night."

"Autumn?"

"Doesn't it feel like autumn to you? Crisp and cool but not quite cold."

He shrugged and pulled her close to him.

"We don't have seasons where I come from. Oh, I've seen them often enough, but I don't have the feel for them. Not like that, anyway."

They sat in silence, and Arden realized how little she knew this man. So much to learn. So little time. But not at this moment.

"What now?" she asked. At that moment she spotted Brother Bryan kneeling beside Jessa. Rafe saw the direction of her gaze.

"Yes. He's the one who got us out of the cell in the palace."

"Then the abbot knows I'm here," she mused. "Not that they can help us a lot. We had better get moving," she said.

"What was Turner doing here? I saw the guards show him a great deal of respect."

He stood and gave her a lift to her feet. It took every bit of willpower she had not to fall into his arms right there.

"Uh, Turner is not his real name. It's Prince Waran Parcq to us commoners."

"The heir apparent?" She nodded. "Well, I'll be damned."

They moved to squat in the grass near the others.

"We need to get out of here before anyone comes to check this out," Rafe said.

"Where do we go?" Tahr asked, but stopped short of complaining.

"Your ship is in the port," Bryan said. "If we could make it there, perhaps you could lift off. Oh," he said, and removed one of the swords from his belt. "I found this in one of the hangars at the port. Where Captain Semmes's ship is." He handed it to Arden, and she took it with great thanks.

"Anyone else have a better idea?" Rafe asked, referring to the *Starbourne*. No one said a word. He turned to Bryan. "Can you lead us to the port?"

"I can," Bryan said.

Rafe nodded, then helped Arden get to her feet. Owen carried Vey over one shoulder. Bryan led the way down the street. He promised that the shuttle was not far. Liel brought up the rear.

There was a crash and Arden looked back. The house had caved in, the still burning rubble the only lighting on the entire street. Movement caught her eye, and she turned her head. It could have been the curtain in the second-floor window of a neighboring house but it was gone.

As they walked, Arden related her adventures since she and Rafe had been separated two days ago. It felt like it had been much longer ago than that. She talked as long as they walked. The sound of her voice in her own ears drowned out the echo of their footsteps.

The lights were low, but that did not matter. He had sent for her quite some time ago, but the emperor was patient. She would be able to see to work with her hands and fingers. She would come and sit on her stool, and the sound of the loom would fill the room.

It would have to be cleaned. Damn those servants for letting everything get so dusty. Cobwebs literally vibrated in the corners.

This was a great day. Lyona was returning to the loom, and his son had returned from some mysterious trip off-world. He should have ordered a banquet to celebrate.

Maybe tomorrow or next week.

Where was that woman? Probably brushing out that lovely long hair. Was it still black, or had it turned grey? Funny, the things that were hard to remember.

For instance, he could have sworn he had a daughter.

"Aren't we headed toward the spaceport?" Tahr asked.

"That's it just ahead," the monk said.

Bryan's "not far" had turned into a twenty-five-minute walk. Exhaustion slowed everyone's pace, although none of them looked quite as tired as Arden felt. If she could look at herself as she looked at the others, would she be putting on as brave a front? It wasn't worth the effort.

They stood on the edge of a flat field. The lights on the other side must be the port.

"I think we could use a rest," Arden said.

Owen grunted in agreement. Vey must be getting awfully heavy for him. Tahr supported Jessa, whose strength had not quite returned after the fall down the stairs. A chorus of further agreement rose weakly.

"All right," Bryan said, with only a hint of relief. He was probably in better shape than any of them.

They collapsed where they stood, Tahr a little more gently as he eased Jessa to the ground. Rafe helped Owen set Vey down. He sat behind Arden and started massaging her shoulders. She would love him forever for that. The night's work had been hard on all of them. The revelation of the true identity of Jackson Turner had sort of caught them off guard, too.

Odd that making love to a prince had seemed no different than making love to most other men. She had grown fond of him for a time, and being in love with Jackson Turner might have been fun. Being in love with the crown prince of Glory, though, had no appeal at all. Particularly not after that scene in the house. She had met ruthless men before, but nothing to compare to him.

Or Vey, for that matter. Whether the prime minister was ruthless for his own gains or for Glory's benefit was still unclear, in spite of what Lyona had said. Mostly because both could be served by the same actions.

Rafe stopped massaging her shoulders, reached an arm around her, and pulled her against him. His warmth accentuated the chill of the night, and she shivered.

"Cold?" he asked.

"Not especially. Although I will be glad to get aboard the ship, if we can. I only hope there's a sweater there."

"Time to move," Bryan said.

"He seems to think he's in charge," the captain said.

She looked up at him. He was smiling as she had suspected he would be. His sense of humor was revealed on rare occasions and was one of the things she found endearing about him.

They all got to their feet with a lot of moaning and complaining and started off toward the lights again.

"You haven't told me how Bryan got here," Arden said.

She had taken Jessa's other arm when the princess demonstrated obvious difficulty resuming their march, but refused Tahr's offer to carry her.

"When we have more time," Rafe replied.

She couldn't hold back a chuckle. "You never did know how to keep a story short."

"You haven't known me that long."

"I have," Jessa broke in.

The three of them laughed quietly, then moved on in silence. The field was uneven, and it took a lot of concentration to keep from tripping over holes or clumps of grass. They walked a good while before the lights drew closer and darker shadows of buildings could be discerned. Owen dropped behind, Vey slowing him down. Liel should have taken over after the rest break. Arden could call out to the exec, but he was several feet ahead now, and voices carry in the night.

"Should we wait for Owen?" she asked Rafe. He had a better idea of the man's strength.

They stopped and he looked back.

"He'll catch up. We're getting pretty spread out, which may not be a bad idea."

Bryan in the lead had marched up close to the first building in their path and was starting to veer right. They must try to be very quiet if their escape was to be successful.

Suddenly, lights blinded her. She threw up her right arm to shield her eyes, then dropped to the ground, pulling Jessa with her.

"Halt!" a voice ordered.

Liel fired, hitting the light. Another light came on.

"Stay down," Rafe whispered.

"They must have seen us," Arden said. "They probably have night scopes."

"Look at the lights," Rafe said. "They're concentrated on Bryan and Liel in the lead."

Someone fired at the monk, making him keep his head down while the searchlights swung straight behind him, trying to trace the trail back to the others. Finding no one in that direction, the lights began panning back and forth in a wide arc toward the way they had come. Arden pressed forward against her forearm so that neither her face nor her eyes would shine. They were clearly depending on the spotlights, so they might not have scopes after all.

"Get your head down," Rafe said.

Arden looked to the side and saw him push Jessa's head toward the ground. The three of them lay as still as they could. Grass glowed under her arm, and Arden held her breath. The light moved on.

Someone groaned behind them. Damn, Vey must be waking up. The groans grew in volume until a voice shouted. Vey was fighting off Owen's restraint.

"Let me go. What do you think you're doing?"

"Halt!" the voice said again.

A gun fired. No one cried out. Warning shots.

"It's me, Don Vey. Over here."

Grass rustled as if a struggle ensued; then footsteps pounded against the ground.

"Here!" Vey shouted.

Arden looked up to see the prime minister running clumsily toward the lights. If he had come just a little closer, she could have reached out and tripped him. But when she looked to that side, the light had picked up Vey's running figure.

"Don't shoot!" someone behind the lights ordered.

Sounded like Waran. How had he found them?

"Could Vey have been wearing a tracker?" she whispered under her right arm to Rafe.

"Might even have one implanted," he answered. "Government officials often do."

"Why didn't we think of that before?"

"Grab that man," Waran shouted.

"I give up," Owen said.

He stood transfixed in the beam of light that had already found him. He walked at an angle to their position, drawing attention away. To no avail. In a moment another searchlight had found them.

"Drop the rifle, Liel," Waran said. "Come along, Captain Semmes. You too, Arden. You certainly are difficult to get rid of."

They stood, shielding their eyes with their arms, and started forward.

"Leave the guns, please. And don't forget my lovely half sister."

He had seen her after all. Since he had not called her name, Arden had assumed . . .

Tahr reached down and helped Jessa to her feet.

"Everyone into the hangar."

Guards appeared behind them; how many it was difficult to tell. Blinded by the lights as they were, the uneven terrain became even more treacherous. Jessa tripped twice, nearly bringing Tahr to his knees. At last, they made it inside the hangar, where the overhead lighting seemed dim.

By the time everyone was assembled, her eyes had adjusted. The guards surrounded the smaller band, their rifles pointing, menacing. Twelve of them, including the prince and Vey, who now stood beside his master. Waran held a sword in his right hand. Several of the guards were similarly armed, although at least four held guns. Nearly two-to-one odds. Not that it mattered, considering that the larger number also had the weapons.

Waran turned to Vey.

"You are unharmed, Prime Minister?" he asked.

Vey nodded.

"How did you know we would be here?" Rafe asked.

"We didn't," Waran replied. "I was just here to check out the shipment."

He took six steps, half the distance between him and them. He stood with feet wide and hands on hips. A cocky stance. The distance was still too great for her to rush him without getting shot to hell. To divert her attention, she looked around the hangar, which was more of a warehouse. She recognized lifeweave containers from the *Starbourne*.

"I assume that you rescued your women?" Waran asked.

"They were doing fine without me," Rafe said with a quick grin in her direction. "I hope you don't plan your wars as poorly as you plan your murders."

"We do well enough." Waran turned toward Arden. "Since you were clever enough not to die in the fire, I will give you one last chance to join me."

"Is that what this is all about?" Rafe growled.

"He seems to think it's a match made in heaven," she said.

Waran frowned and gave the order for the two guns and swords to be taken.

"Your majesty," a voice cried from outside. "Your majesty."

A guard ran into the hangar, waving something in his right hand. Everyone's attention went to him. Arden drew her sword and rushed toward Waran.

The prince raised his own weapon and met her charge. Shots were fired around them as the two fought in the center of a general melee. Arden did not know what her friends used for weapons; her entire attention was concentrated on Waran and their swords. They jockeyed for position, tested each other's strength. He was good, better than she had expected.

After a rapid exchange of blows, they pressed against each other. His breath was warm and smelled of alcohol.

"You would be a worthy mate," he said with a grin, then pushed her away.

Arden stumbled slightly. Boxes, barrels, and crates lay

everywhere, scattered by the battle that now filled the hangar. They were in the middle of the next exchange of blows when total darkness smothered the hangar. Shouts filled the darkness; then silence fell, so that all Arden heard was the pulsing of her own blood in her ears.

She moved several steps to her left and dropped to one knee. Her tension increased with each moment of silence. Slowly, quietly, she moved away from the center of the fight with Waran to keep him from guessing where she might be. As she concentrated, she began to hear others breathing, shifting. She could almost smell the fear that spread throughout. Her senses, heightened by the moments of blindness she had experienced, reached out, detecting the slightest of sounds, the barest of smells. Even her eyes could detect shadows and forms.

Strangest of all, she could sense lifeweave nearby. A spool must be lying open, unshielded by a crate, its colors and addictive properties projecting for those who were sensitive to it. A noise behind her made her turn her head slightly. The body of a man lay there, sprawled facedown. On the other side of him lay a spool of the fiber. Within its glow, Pac Terhn appeared. He grinned, spread his hands widely, and she knew that he had saved her from accidental discovery by whoever the fallen man was.

She nodded to the trickster, unsure how he had managed it, then moved around the circle formed by the stored goods. Just as suddenly as the lights went out, emergency lights flickered on. Waran stood almost with his back toward her. She rushed forward, ready to press her advantage.

He spun around at the last minute, barely met her sword with his own. The blow pushed him off balance. She swung her blade rapidly, as hard as she could. He took a wild swing at the first opening. She dropped to one knee, under his blade, and thrust upward. The tip caught him right under the rib cage. His own momentum forced the blade upward.

Waran thrust the point of his own sword against the floor, leaned against it to stay on his feet. He looked down at the katana protruding from his abdomen. His head raised, and he looked at her. Pain twisted his face; sweat covered it.

"I loved you," he said through clenched teeth.

She pulled the katana free and sat back on her heels. He stumbled and swayed, but continued to face her. Blood soaked his white linen shirt, and she swallowed hard.

"I know," she said. "As much as you could love anyone."

A questioning look passed over his face, and he looked as if he wanted to say something, but he collapsed without another word. She sat without moving for a moment, watching him, feeling as though she could see his life essence float away. Incredible sadness overwhelmed her and she bent over, letting warm tears flow. Eventually, the sounds of continued fighting pressed against her mind.

She screamed. If only he had not made her kill him. There must be no more killing. The fighting had stopped.

"Prince Waran is dead," she shouted when she got her breath. "The prince is dead," she repeated when another shot was fired.

Everyone fell silent this time.

"Your highness," Vey cried out. He waited for an answer. When none came, he shouted, "Arden Grenfell, I will have you killed very slowly for this."

"Come do it yourself," she replied.

Him she would gladly cut down. She needed someone to blame, and he fit the bill nicely. She was damned tired of being hunted and shot at and blinded.

"Wait!"

The guard who had rushed in just moments earlier rose from the floor and sat up, rubbing his head.

"Is Prince Waran truly dead?" he asked.

Arden looked over at the body. He lay on his side, still and quiet. The eyes stared without seeing.

"Yes, he's dead," she said quietly. The words echoed back at her. Or was it her imagination? Maybe even the effects of the lifeweave?

"The emperor is also dead," the guard said. "I was sent to tell the prince that he is now emperor. I mean..."

"Think we could call a halt to this?" Rafe asked. "Your new empress is over here."

No one replied. An empress. They must be reeling with that bit of news.

"Put down your weapons," Jessa said. "I am Jessa Parcq, daughter of Granid Parcq, last of my dynasty and heir to the throne."

"No!" Vey screamed.

He came running into the open, grabbed a rifle from one of the soldiers, and started toward Arden. Jessa stepped out.

"Don Vey," she called. "Prime Minister Vey."

He skidded to a halt.

"It's over," she said.

He looked at Jessa a long moment. Arden's vision blurred with tears—whether of pain or emotion or both, it was difficult to tell. She raised the sword, but it was too heavy to hold for long.

Vey let the rifle slide to the floor. Still looking at Jessa, he slipped to one knee.

"Your majesty," he said in a low voice.

EPILOGUE

Arden rolled the goblet between her hands, then took a drink of the sweet red wine. This was probably one of the last times she would sit in the presence of Jessa, soon to be crowned empress of Glory. Arden had just accepted the princess's offer to assume the position of captain of her personal guard, but not without reservations.

"What about Captain Semmes?" Jessa asked. "I thought the two of you had come to care for each other."

"We have, but I have my duty and he has his ship."

"Does he know?"

"Yes."

They sat in silence for a moment; then Arden asked, "Are you sure that you want to be empress? You seemed so against it before."

"I'm still not comfortable with the reality of it," Jessa said. "However, your message from Lyona made all the difference."

"Which part?"

"The second part."

"About your lover?" Jessa nodded her assent. "Who is he, anyway?"

"Jonas Belle."

"Belle? Heir to lifeweave?"

"Yes. I can tell you because you're sworn to me, and because he's on his way here. He will attend my coronation, and we will be married soon after. My father will get what he wanted at last, at least in part."

"And knowing that you could marry him made it possible for you to accept the throne?"

"Yes. There were some things about his inheritance and, frankly, I never expected to become empress. I would not conspire against my father or my brother, but now that they are both dead, I really don't have much choice."

Very much like my own circumstances, Arden thought. She did not have much choice either, although her own duty took her away from what she wanted most.

A guard knocked on the door, then entered. "Captain Semmes has arrived, your highness," he announced.

"I'll wait outside," Arden said.

"Thank you," Jessa said.

They met at the door and smiled at each other. The rest of the crew of the *Starbourne* waited to say their own goodbyes. Arden was not sure, but she would have bet that Tahr had shed a tear or two.

Rafe reappeared, and the others were escorted inside. Arden knew that he, the crew, and Jessa had had several long talks earlier, and was not surprised that Rafe had not stayed long.

They wandered away, arm in arm.

"Are you sure you have to stay?" he asked.

"As sure as you are that you have to leave."

He nodded. They had talked several times, too often at night as they lay in bed. In the end they agreed that for various reasons, both had to return to their ways of life. At least for a time.

"I'll be back," he said. "We salvagers get all over."

"I know."

He shook his head, but said nothing. She shared his frustration, but could not help wondering: if she had not made the promise to stay with Jessa, would she leave even then?

"Jessa gave us half of the lifeweave," Rafe said suddenly. "In payment for our help, she said. At least we didn't do this for nothing."

He grinned, and her heart sank even more. His sense of humor still surprised her sometimes.

She led the way into her own sitting room. They stood close, but side by side, awkwardly, as if they had no idea what to do next. She turned to face him, placed a hand on his chest, and leaned her forehead against him.

"I'll miss you," she said.

"Same here. I swear to you I'll be back."

"I know."

"I can't give up my way of life, just like that." He snapped his fingers. "I don't expect you to do that either. We need to come to terms with our feelings and..." He let the statement trail off.

She stretched up and kissed him lightly. They drew apart. A long, deep look passed between them, and he put his arms around her. This kiss was longer, more stirring, and as poignant as the first.

Voices rose in the hall, and they knew that the rest of the crew members were coming. The time had come for the last goodbye to be said, but neither could say the words.

"I'll go with you to the port," she said.

"No. No, please. Don't. I don't want you waiting there for us to lift off. Stay here."

She swallowed and turned away. Through the window on the other side of the room, the sunset was coloring a few clouds on the horizon. If she went to the window and looked down, the garden below would be full of autumn flowers.

Rafe put his arms around her one last time and kissed the top of her head. He released her, and a moment later the door opened and closed, accenting the new emptiness of the room.

She stood still, looking out the window, until the sun was fully set and darkness hid the horizon. Autumn was a wonderful time to be in the country, she thought. Maybe after the coronation, she would visit the monastery for a short while.

STEVE PERRY

__THE FOREVER DRUG   0-441-00142-4/$5.50
When Venture Silk's lover was murdered on Earth, the only thing Silk escaped with was his life. A master at deception, he must now keep enemy agents from the vital secret contained in her blood.

__THE TRINITY VECTOR   0-441-00350-8/$5.99
There were three of them...strange silver boxes, mysterious devices which individually could give you tomorrow's weather, or tomorrow's winning lottery number. Three people, each with a piece of the puzzle. Three people with nothing to lose. And everything to gain...

__THE DIGITAL EFFECT   0-441-00439-3/$5.99
Gil Sivart is helping a young lady whose boyfriend put his head in a stamping press. The Corporation calls it suicide. His lady friend calls it murder. And now Gil has to flush it out, level by level—before his discreet inquiries get him permanently spaced without a suit...

THE MATADOR SERIES

__THE ALBINO KNIFE   0-441-01391-0/$4.99
__BROTHER DEATH   0-441-54476-2/$4.99

Payable in U.S. funds. No cash accepted. Postage & handling: $1.75 for one book, 75¢ for each additional. Maximum postage $5.50. Prices, postage and handling charges may change without notice. Visa, Amex, MasterCard call 1-800-788-6262, ext. 1, or fax 1-201-933-2316; refer to ad #536b

Or, check above books	Bill my: ☐ Visa ☐ MasterCard ☐ Amex _____ (expires)
and send this order form to:	
The Berkley Publishing Group	Card#_____
P.O. Box 12289, Dept. B	Daytime Phone #_____ ($10 minimum)
Newark, NJ 07101-5289	Signature_____

Please allow 4-6 weeks for delivery.   Or enclosed is my: ☐ check ☐ money order
Foreign and Canadian delivery 8-12 weeks.

Ship to:

Name_____	Book Total	$_____
Address_____	Applicable Sales Tax (NY, NJ, PA, CA, GST Can.)	$_____
City_____	Postage & Handling	$_____
State/ZIP_____	Total Amount Due	$_____

Bill to: Name_____
Address_____ City_____
State/ZIP_____

PUTNAM ⓟ BERKLEY
online

Your Internet gateway to a virtual environment with hundreds of entertaining and enlightening books from the Putnam Berkley Group.

While you're there visit the PB Café and order-up the latest buzz on the best authors and books around—Tom Clancy, Patricia Cornwell, W.E.B. Griffin, Nora Roberts, William Gibson, Robin Cook, Brian Jacques, Jan Brett, Catherine Coulter and many more!

Putnam Berkley Online is located at
http://www.putnam.com

PB PLUG

Once a month we serve up the dish on the latest science fiction, fantasy, and horror titles currently on sale. Plus you'll get interviews of your favorite authors, trivia, a top ten list, and so much more fun it's shameless.

Check out PB Plug at http://www.pbplug.com